∼ THE SON OF LAUGHTER

Other Books by Frederick Buechner

The

SON *of*

LAUGHTER

~

Frederick Buechner

HarperSanFrancisco
A Division of HarperCollins*Publishers*

THE SON OF LAUGHTER. Copyright © 1993 by Frederick Buechner. All rights reserved. Printed in the United States of America. No part of this book may be used or reproduced in any manner whatsoever without written permission except in the case of brief quotations embodied in critical articles and reviews. For information address HarperCollins Publishers, 10 East 53rd Street, New York, NY 10022.

Library of Congress Cataloging-in-Publication Data

Buechner, Frederick
    The son of laughter / Frederick Buechner. — 1st ed.
            p.   cm.
    I. Title.
    PS3552.U35S67   1993
    813'.54 — dc20
    ISBN 0-06-250116-x
                                92-53899
                                CIP

For

THOMAS S. BUECHNER *and* NANCY B. LEWIS,

who were there from the beginning

Contents

ONE
THE PROMISING

1

THE BURIED GODS

THEY ALL HAD NAMES, but I have forgotten them. One name sounded like a man hocking up a bone. Another went *lu lu* like a man with a woman under him. Another rattled like the god of a tree. One name was so tiny and dry you hardly dared speak it for fear it would crumble to dust on your lips. They were no taller than from my wrist to the tip of my middle finger. They lived on a shelf in my uncle's cellar. My uncle was Laban. The cellar walls were of earth. It was always black down there even when the sun was high.

One of them was a bearded child in a high peaked cap. Another wore a skirt of fish scales with plump toes and a round, full belly. Another was bald and beardless. He held his member out before him in both hands. He had no eyes and only a crack in the stone for his mouth. They told my uncle many things that he lusted to know. They told him where to look for the missing goat or the strayed lamb. They told him when to plant and where in the city of Haran to buy for least and sell for most. They told him about rain. I have seen him come lurching up the ladder so drunk on their secrets that his eyes were rolling around in his head and his jaw hanging.

He kept a lamp burning down there for them at all hours. He fed them on barley cakes, honey cakes, radishes, beer. He rubbed them with oil—their beards and bellies, their fat toes. He burned things for them. Every day he talked to them. You could hear him at it. He wheedled and bullied and teased the way he traded oxen. My uncle was an ox himself. His neck was as thick as his head was wide. He said it would come in handy if they ever tried hanging him. His face was the color of brick. He always put his arm around your shoulder when he was talking to you or patted your cheek with his hand. "As long as we love each other, darling," he would say. "That's all that matters." His other hand was probably in your pocket.

After twenty years, we finally left him. I waited till he was off at a shearing so he wouldn't know. There were enough of us by then to stretch as far as the eye could see—my wives and the children, the servants, beasts, baggage, tenting, everything we could carry with us. We also carried with us my uncle's gods with their large members and fish-scale skirts though I didn't know it at the time. It was of all people my timid-hearted wife, Rachel, his daughter, who thought of taking them. She dreaded what might happen to us on our long journey, and she was afraid of what my brother might do when the two of us came face to face again after so many years. She was afraid he might kill me. He had good cause. She believed the gods would keep us safe. So she stole the whole pack of them and had them stowed in a sack which she kept close by her both waking and sleeping.

We had been traveling some days when my uncle returned from his flocks to find us gone. He overtook us just as we were making camp among high, wooded hills. His face was streaming with tears.

How could I leave him without so much as saying good-bye? How could I cheat him of the chance to throw one last great feast in my honor with music and dancing? How could I rob him of his daughters and his grandchildren, the only comfort he had now that old age was upon him? He wailed and thumped his chest. His small eyes were pink with grief and fierce reproach.

Worst of all, he said, how could I steal his gods? I did not know yet that Rachel had stolen them.

I said if he could find them, he was welcome to them. I swore I would have whoever took them killed on the spot. So he rushed like a madman from tent to tent searching till he came to Rachel's tent. She had just time to sit down on the sack and spread her skirts over it before he entered. She asked his pardon for not rising to greet him, that gentle, courteous woman. It was her time for bleeding, she said. She meant him to believe it was the unclean blood a woman sheds by being a woman, and so he believed. The truth was otherwise. She bled indeed, but it was the stone gods she sat on in their sack that bloodied her with their pointed caps and sharp edges. Her flesh was white and soft as cheese where they wounded her. Her father leaned over and kissed her brow for the pain he saw in it, little guessing what it was that pained her. You could tell he was full of shame at having suspected her of thieving. Even the gods must have been moved by the tenderness of the scene.

It wasn't long afterward, when Laban had gone, that I got rid of them. It was for the Fear's sake I did it. The Fear came to me in the night and whispered words of hope into my ear. He told me that he loved me as he had loved Laughter, my father, before me and Abraham, my grandfather, before that. He repeated the ancient promises that never fail to frighten me with their beauty just as the Fear himself never fails to frighten me. So when the time was ripe, I did it. We were in Shechem, where two of my sons had brought terrible shame upon us.

I had a pit dug under an oak tree that stood so tall and reached out so far with its crooked arms that no other tree dared grow near it. I told my people to place their gods in the pit. They thought I had lost my wits, but they didn't dare defy me so far from home. I stood by the raw grave and watched as one by one each father among them came up and threw into it the gods he had fed and worshiped all his life and his father before him.

Some of the gods were stone like my uncle's. Others were painted wood, or bone, or baked clay. Some were stuck all over with feathers. Some were shriveled and black as carrion. When the men were finished, I added my uncle's gods to the heap. I added the silver god that was mine. Then I told every last man and woman of them to throw their earrings in on top of them. I threw my own earrings in on top of them. I hoped the gods might find all that treasure some consolation for being treated so shabbily.

They are there in the earth to this day as far as I know. They and the earrings are all tumbled together in the dark. The earth stops their eyes and fills their mouths. The god of the oak fetters them with roots stronger even than they are strong.

When I say that I have forgotten their names, I mean that I cannot remember their names without trying. There are also times when I cannot forget their names without trying.

Maybe they also remember me. Who knows about gods? Maybe they have seen every step I have taken ever since. Maybe they are still waiting for me to call once again on their queer and terrible names.

2

The Ram in the Thicket

The water in the bottom of a well looks far away and black. Sometimes there is a star in it. My father's eyes were like that—black, liquid, faraway eyes. My father's name was Isaac, which means Laughter. Abraham named him Laughter because on the day that the strangers told him that his wife Sarah was going to bear him a son when she was an old woman, he fell on his face laughing, and in the door of the tent Sarah almost laughed herself into a fit as well.

Sometimes there was a star in Laughter's eyes. He was a slow-moving, heavy-set man, heavy on his feet and heavy-limbed. He had no hair on his head, and his mottled scalp was shiny as polished stone. When he talked to you, he tilted his head to one side as if he admired you so much that he couldn't bear to look at you straight on. He gave you a sad little smile. He made you feel he was holding great strength in check out of deference to you.

There was never a more deferential man than Laughter when things were going well with him, which they rarely did. He could suit even his shape to your whim. If he felt that his presence was becoming distasteful to you for some reason, he could hunch, shrug, shrivel himself to a size no bigger than a child's. If he wanted to be warm and welcoming, he could make it so that you had to flatten yourself against the wall to leave room for him.

When he spoke to his friends, of which he did not have many, it was less like speaking than crooning. He tuned his voice to be so easy on your ears that you might not hear it at all if you happened to be thinking of something else. Even when you did hear it, he said what he said in such a sidelong way, took such pains never to press his point home, that you often didn't have any idea what he has talking about.

When I was a boy, he sometimes talked to me about his father—Abraham, the father of fathers, the Fear's friend. Abraham was a barrel-chested old man with a beard dyed crimson and the hooded eyes of the desert. He had a habit, when he spoke, of putting his hands on your shoulders and of drawing you gradually closer and closer as the words flowed until at the end his great nostrils were almost in your face like twin entrances to a cave. He was rich in herds and flocks, not to mention also in silver and gold, in tents and in women. He was the bane of many small kings and in many ways was more of a king than any of them. It is said that Abraham talked with the Fear the way a man talks to his friend. He would argue with him. They say that sometimes he would even nag him into changing his mind. Perhaps that was why my grandfather was the one whom the Fear chose out of all men on earth to breed a lucky people who would someday bring luck to the whole world.

All that and more was my grandfather Abraham, yet sadness always rose in me when my father talked about him. I pictured him laboring under his wealth and his honors like an ass under three hundred weight of millet. I pictured his eyes red and bleary from years of whipping sand. I pictured him breaking wind, groaning, as he heaved himself out of the pit of sleep at sundown to lead his precious train of kin, beasts, baggage, mile after moonlit mile in search of pasturage and whatever else he spent his days in search of. I saw him as a homesick, sore-footed man. A wanderer. A broken heart.

I remember Laughter lying on his back once on a pile of rugs with one arm over his head and the hand spread out on his naked scalp like a crab. You could hear the wind whistling through the tent ropes outside. The flap was open so the thin smoke of the burning dung could escape. He was speaking slowly and to no particular end as far as I could see. I was only half listening. Then little by little it began to dawn on me that for once he was telling me a story about Abraham that I had never heard before.

"You know what killed my mother, don't you?" Laughter said. His mother was my grandmother Sarah. "Of course you don't know what killed her. How could you know when I have never told you? I will not tell you now either. I will leave it to you to decide for yourself what killed her. You are old enough to figure it out. Figuring out will make you older still. My mother was herself very old by then. Something else would have killed her soon enough if this thing hadn't, but it was this thing that killed her. You will understand it for yourself if you have any sense at all."

He was not crooning now. His words fell heavy and dense like cow dung. First a heap, then another heap.

"Your grandfather told two of his men to saddle one of the best she-asses," Laughter said. "The beast was white as milk. She was doe-eyed and gentle. Her belly was soft as a girl's. There was no need to bridle her. You could tell her with your knees whatever you wanted her to do. She was so light on her feet they called her Swallow. He had them girth her up with the saddle he had used at his wedding. It was of braided hides, fringed, with a pommel of goat's horn and teak. He said the two men were to come with him. He said I was to come with him. He told me he was going into the hills to make a gift to the Fear. The Fear had told him he would welcome a gift. He had me help the men cut the sticks, three large bundles of them, one for each of our backs. He said we were to find green sticks as well as dry ones because he would need much smoke to float his gift to the sky. He said he would ride Swallow with provisions enough for a three-day journey, and the men and I would walk behind. It was summer, but over his tunic he wore a mantle of henna wool that my mother had embroidered for him with vine leaves. Around his neck he wore the collar of jasper and topaz that I had never seen him wear before except when he was meeting in full council with the fathers or palavering with kings. He daubed holy signs on his cheeks and forehead with wood ash so that he would be acceptable in the Fear's sight when he approached him. He wrapped his face in the folds of his headcloth so the holiness would not be soiled by the eyes of strangers."

Laughter groaned and rolled over on his back. He placed his hands side by side on his face to cover his eyes. The tip of his nose jutted up between them. For a while he breathed so slowly and heavily I thought he had fallen asleep.

He said, "We reached the place on the third day. It was high in the hills. There was an outcropping of rock overlooking the valley. He told the men to stay below with Swallow. He made me carry all three bundles of sticks behind him. He carried a live coal in a cup. I had to stop several times as we climbed. He could hear it when I stopped and would wait for me. He never looked around at me. He never spoke."

Rebekah, my mother, came in about then and interrupted Laughter. She was a short woman with a large mane of curly hair. She did not dress or bind it then like other women, and her little face was almost lost in the midst of it. She had puffy cheeks and large front teeth that made her look like a coney peering out of a bush. Laughter raised one hand from his eyes to see who it was. He replaced it when he saw.

"Please go away," he said. "I am talking to my son."

"It is high time," she said. "It is your other son you are usually talking to."

"They are twins," he said. "It makes no difference which one I talk to."

"It makes a difference to them," she said. "It makes a difference to the one you never talk to."

She said to me, "Why don't you speak up for yourself? Tell him how it feels to have a father who never talks to you."

"I am talking to him now," Laughter said. "Would you please go away?"

"You are talking to him now because you are ashamed of the way you have always treated him. You have good reason to feel shame. Just because he is quiet and stays at home doing what he is supposed to do, you treat him like dung under your feet. His brother is your heart's treasure because he is always off killing things for you to eat. You will know who to thank for it when you eat yourself into an early grave."

Laughter remained silent a long time after my mother left. He stared up at the lamp hanging over him. There were bats shuffling and creaking in the tamarisk outside. They were getting ready to fly out for the evening's forage. Finally he rolled over on one elbow to face me. He rested his cheek on the palm of his hand. It pushed his mouth crooked. He continued his story.

"My father, Abraham, carried the live coal in the cup," he said. "He also carried his knife. But he did not carry any gift as far as I could see. It seemed a queer thing to be going to the Fear empty-handed, and I think I asked him about it. I don't remember how he answered me. It has been many years. I was only a boy. I thought no more about it. I thought only that my father must know what he was doing. I was right. He knew what he was doing."

Laughter said, "Heels."

He sometimes called me Heels, which is the meaning of Jacob, because I was born on the heels of my twin. They say I tried to beat him out of the womb by grabbing his heels from behind, but I failed. He was the first of us to come out of the womb. Our father called him Esau, which means hairy. He was hairy all over. I was as bare as an egg.

Laughter said, "Heels, I am telling this to you, not to your brother." It was one of the times there was a star in his black, faraway eyes. "I know which of you is good at which things and which of you is good at other things, whatever your mother says. I praise the Fear day and night for both of my sons."

"Thank you," I said.

"Now I will finish my story," Laughter said. He started to weep.

It was the worst moment of my life up till then. I was so ashamed of Laughter's weeping that I thought I was going to be sick. I wanted to run out of the tent so I would not have to see his tears. Instead I stayed in the tent to punish him by seeing them. I stayed in the tent to punish myself by seeing them. It was slovenly, shameful weeping. Dribble ran out of Laughter's nose. His mouth ran spittle. He bared his gums in an ugly, comic way. He blubbered like a woman. His whole thick frame shook. I squatted by the smoking dung staring at him.

Sometimes he would pause in the middle of his story to utter broken bits of prayer to the Fear. Sometimes his words stopped altogether, and he waved his hands and made terrible faces instead. Once or twice he tried to rise from the pile of rugs where he was lying only to fall back on them again in a fit of tears. At one point he took hold of his linen shirt and ripped it as far down as the navel. At the end he crawled on all fours as far as the fire where he scattered ashes over his bald head. Then he lay down with his face buried in his arms like a dead man. That is when I left him.

His story ended like this. Abraham told Laughter to pile sticks on the outcropping of rock overlooking the valley, the dry sticks at the bottom and the green ones on the top. Laughter did as he was told the way he always did. There was never a son who more honored his father. He would wash Abraham's feet when he came in and when he went out. He would comb and oil his beard. When the white hairs began to show, he crushed bugs for dye to make it crimson. It is true that Abraham also honored him. My father was altogether lacking in beauty and a manly bearing, it is true, but he was the son the Fear had promised. It was from Laughter's heavy, unpromising loins that the lucky people would spring. In time they would cover the whole earth like a carpet of lilies. That was reason enough to honor him.

Laughter said that Abraham told him to clasp his hands behind his back. Then he tied his wrists together. Laughter's jaws shook so as he told me about it that he could hardly shape his words. Abraham tied his wrists with one of the cords that had bound the sticks. With the other two cords he tied his legs together at the ankles and at the knees. He needed Laughter's help to do this, and Laughter helped. He let himself go limp and as helpless as a lamb. When it was done, Abraham hoisted him up in his arms and staggered to the pile of sticks with him. Then he dropped him on top of the sticks. It was heavy work for an old man in a wool mantle. The holy signs on his forehead and cheeks were smeared and sooty. There was sweat on his collar of jasper and topaz. His nostrils swelled even wider than usual with the labor of his breathing.

Abraham did not tell him what he was doing. Laughter did not ask him to tell. He just lay on his back with the sticks poking into him and the blinding sun in his eyes while the sweaty old man stood gasping for breath over him. His hands were trembling so violently that he needed both of them to raise his knife into the air.

When I picture Laughter lying there on the sticks, I picture him not as the boy he was but as the man who was my father.

I picture him bald and shapeless. I picture the way his eyes glisten. He is looking up at the knife with his small, sad smile. He is asking for mercy so softly that Abraham doesn't even hear him. Abraham has wet himself in his passion, but he doesn't know he has wet himself. He is shaking the way a tree shakes each time you strike it with an axe. He does not hear Laughter speaking to him, but he hears something.

Perhaps it is the day he was first told that he was going to have a son that Abraham hears. He was sitting just inside the door of his tent staring at nothing. He had been sitting there for some time because it was high noon and too hot to do anything else. Abraham thought he was staring at nothing. Then little by little he began to see that it was not nothing after all. It was three strangers he was staring at. They were standing in the shade of the oak trees that he had pitched his tents to be near for luck. He had seen stone creatures like them in the city of his birth. They wore crowns on their heads and fierce bird faces and kept their wings folded flat to their sides. At first they said nothing.

Abraham quickly rose to his feet to bow his greeting, all bent over double like a man pulling weeds. He sent a serving woman to fetch water freshened with balsam. With his own hands he took off the strangers' sandals and washed their splayed, yellow feet. He dried their feet with the skirt of his cloak. He knew it would be unseemly to ask them too soon why they had come, so he offered them food and drink first. They answered with soft clucking noises and small darting movements of their heads. Their eyes were like beads. Abraham left them resting in the shade.

He had a calf slaughtered and spitted and ordered it served to the strangers with dried figs and curds. He told Sarah to make sesame cakes, and she had to scamper like a green girl instead of the old woman she was in order to knead, slap, bake them in time. She had already gone mostly bald on top where her hair was parted into a pair of cow tails. She had lost all the teeth in her head. She had never given suck, and her breasts hung flat as a hound's ears. Now that her beauty was long since gone, she never showed herself to strangers. She hid just inside the tent door. Unseen there, she could hear what the three strangers said when the feast was finally set before them.

It was the tallest of the three who said it. He squawked it out with his beak wide and his sharp, dry tongue wagging inside. He said that Sarah would conceive a child. *Skreek. Skrawk.* It would be a boy. She would hatch him in the spring.

No sooner were the words out than there was a wilder skreeking and skrawking yet. It was Sarah in the tent. Her gums were bared in a fit of laughter. She stuffed her fist between them. Under the oaks the strangers covered their ears with their wings. One of them spattered the earth with his droppings. There are tiny white flowers growing there to this day. With my own eyes I have seen them. Abraham's eyes were starting from their sockets like eggs. He also could not help but burst out with laughter at what the strangers had told him. He rocked from side to side. Some say he fell to the ground. It was why they named the boy Isaac, which means Laughter.

Who knows? Perhaps that was what Abraham thought about years later when he held the wobbling knife high in the air over the boy that the strangers had promised. He needed both of his hands to do it, one hand to hold the knife and the other to hold that hand steady. The fleshy boy lay belly up under it. Abraham's eyes started from their sockets like eggs again. He was seeing something.

Laughter told me he could not see it himself, trussed up as he was, but he saw his father see it. He himself saw it only in the sudden change that came over the old man's soot-streaked face the way you see water suddenly flatten when the wind drops. The rutted cheeks and hooded eyes, the beard flaming out under the great nose, his face went suddenly still.

What Abraham was seeing was the glint of a crown, the opening of a beak, a wing pointing. The wing pointed to a dense clump of thorns that grew just below where the rocks ended. The thorns were tossing and clattering. A sheep had gotten caught in them, a ram. He had tangled his horns among the cruel, unyielding stalks. He was hurling himself this way and that to butt his way free. His proud, dull-witted face was flecked with blood. His eyes were gold, his fleece better than a hand's breadth deep. He braced his hooves in the soil to tug himself backward. The more violently he wrenched his head, the faster it stuck.

Abraham used his knife to cut the cords that bound my father, and together the two of them overpowered the ram. It was too exhausted by then to be a match for them. Together they slaughtered it and prepared it as a gift for the Fear. When the time came, the dark smoke of the burning sticks was more than enough to float it into the sky. Together the two of them stood by watching,

It was not until Laughter reached the end of his story that he ripped his shirt and scattered ashes over his head.

He said, "When my mother heard what Abraham had nearly done to her son, she was dead within the year. What killed her? You tell me. And when you tell me what killed her, then you can tell me what killed me. Oh Heels, Heels!" he cried out. "My son, Jacob!"

He said, "I was not always the way you see me now."

It was then that Laughter fell down by the smoldering dung with his face buried in his arms and lay there as if he were dead.

3

THE RED BEANS

E SAU WAS OLDER THAN I by one grunt and a couple of squeals less from Rebekah as she squatted on the birthstones in the women's tent while Laughter swayed back and forth wringing his hands outside. They named him Esau, which is Hairy, because even at birth there was so much hair on him, red hair, that until I came along a few moments later without a trace of fuzz on me there were whispers among the women that Rebekah must have lain with a beast. There were others later on who whispered that they called him Esau because it sounded somewhere between Heehaw and Seesaw and was thus just the right name for that braying, simple-minded man who was up one moment and down the next. He was either weeping on your neck or threatening to wring it, either roaring with delight or looking as if he was about to hang himself. My mother agreed that he was simple-minded. Laughter loved him.

Hunting was my hairy brother's chief pleasure. He would lie hours behind a rock to catch a plump partridge and her chicks with a quick tug of the rope on his clap-net. For quail he set snares made of a springy twig stuck in the ground and bent double with a noose so lightly fixed to the free end that one misstep sprung it and my brother would leap out roaring with laughter at all the squawk and feathers. With his bow across his back and his sling in his hand, he went after larger game as well. I have seen him with his red beard flying bring down a gazelle that fled him faster than the wind. I have seen him lug two gazelles home at a time, one over each of his shoulders. I have seen their lovely eyes glazed in death and their tongues lolling out of their mouths. I have seen their curved, delicate horns knocking against his calves as he staggered along under the weight of them. They say he once wrestled to the ground single-handed a bear that had been ravaging Laughter's flocks, clubbing it to death, and many another he has caught in his mat-covered pits together with all manner of other thieving beasts such as jackals, foxes, wolves, and the like.

Almost as much as the sport of catching them, he loved the sport of eating them, and in this sport Laughter joined him. They would sit together long after Rebekah and I and the others had had our fill, their beards, their lips, their fingers glittering with fat. Bowls of cucumbers and curds, leeks, roasted onions, surround them. Stacks of ashcakes for scooping up stew. Baskets of figs and raisins. Honey. Ewers of date wine and milk. Little is left when Laughter and Esau finally finish. The roasted carcass of a sheep looks as though jackals have torn it. Laughter picks gristle out of his back teeth with his thumb and forefinger. My brother is asleep with his head sunk backward. His open mouth is a pit of shadows.

My brother ate because he was hungry. All his hunting emptied his belly, and he ate to fill it. When it was full, he was content. He went to sleep. Or he found a woman somewhere and then went to sleep. Laughter's emptiness was of another kind. He could no more fill it with food and drink than you can fill a tent with memories of the dead. No matter how much he ate, he was not content. He slept little afterward. As for women, I think he had forgotten by then that even Rebekah was a woman. No matter how much he stuffed, he was hungry still, but he loved Esau for trying to fill him anyway. Maybe he believed that someday his emptiness would be filled at last. He loved Esau also because he was the first born, if only by a grunt and a squeal. It was from Esau's seed that the lucky people would someday spring. You had only to look at that great bear of a man to see that from his shaggy loins seed would shoot forth in abundance.

One evening near sundown I was on a high moor with the flocks. The moor was blown almost bare by the wind, but there were still patches here and there for them to nibble on. I had just finished counting them as they trotted into the fold for the night, huddling together and skittish because of the cries of wild beasts from the hills. Below us in the valley the sands stretched silver and lonely. I called to one ewe with swelling dugs who was loath to leave her feeding, and she came along at a good clip finally with her gaunt face hanging in shame and two gentle-faced weanlings at her heels.

For dinner Rebekah had sent me off with a pot of red beans which she had boiled up thick with mutton fat and sesame. I had a fire going and was warming them over it when suddenly I found Esau looming over me. He had a black goatskin thrown over his shoulders. His game bag hung empty from his girdle. I was squatting on my heels by the fire. He was looking down at me with his brow furrowed.

"I'll give you anything you want for that," he said. He pointed at the beans. "That lovely, mushy stuff," he said. "I smelled it from the other side of the hill it smelled so good. I haven't had a bite since morning."

I said, "You'll give me what?"

You could see he was thinking it over. He stuck one finger in his ear and let his hand dangle from it.

Finally he said, "Oh well, I don't know. I said anything. I'd give you anything, probably."

His smile was a slow, wet baring of his teeth. He took a swipe at my head. We were both of us still unwed and at home then. Everybody was alive still. Rebekah was still pretty in her way. She wore earrings and tied her hair back with a fillet and painted around her eyes with black antimony.

"You want this?" he said.

He held it out. It was his best throwing-stick. It was forked at one end with a round stone routed out to fit in tight and lashed there with gut. He could wing it end over end in crazy x's farther than any of them. I have seen him knock a brick off a wall with it or brain a coney dozing on a rock a hundred paces off or more. But I shook my head at his stick.

He liked that because it made a game of it. You could see he was trying to think what move to make next. He could have bludgeoned me with his stick and taken what he wanted without giving me a thing for it, but that wasn't the game he felt like just then. Or else he just didn't happen to think of that game just then. He thought he would like to match wits with me, his wits against mine. That was the game he felt like. His wits were about half mine. His brawn was about twice mine and then some.

"Knife?" he said. He held it out to me on the flat of his hand. I gave his hand a slap from beneath which sent the knife spinning. That tickled him.

"How about if I give you little bow-legs?" he said. "The one with long braids? She'll do it whenever you want if I tell her."

I said, "She'll do it whenever I want if I tell her."

His eyes bugged out as he cocked his head to stare at me sideways. He was still smiling. I never once let my stare drop from his as I took a thumbful of what I had in my bowl and stuffed it into my mouth. The juice ran down my chin. My cheeks bulged.

"Ask anything. I'm starving to death," he said. "I'll let you piss in my beard."

He would have too. He would have squatted down and let me do it right then. He would have had a good laugh as I was soaking him. I started laughing myself at the thought. Then suddenly I felt my eyes puddling. I not only knew he would let me do it, but I also knew I would do it and would like doing it, such a sad and shameful thing. I wiped my eyes on the back of my hand and shook my head. He would have to think of something else.

What he thought of was all at once to pull me to my feet and hug me till I thought my bones would snap.

"Oh I'll love you forever, I'll love you to death, and for only what's left in your dear little bowl!" he said.

He covered me with kisses—my face, my neck, my shoulders. I could not help returning his embraces. Even in the womb we had hugged, battled. I slobbered his cheek with the beans in my mouth. Then I twisted out of his grip. I lifted my clothes and emptied all the piss there was in me onto the dry earth so that his beard would be safe from me.

He rolled his eyes at the beans. He groaned.

Laughter's black tents were an hour's tramp off. All about us the chalky downs crested and dipped like the sea. There was little enough for the flocks to feed on and nothing for graining a hunger like Esau's. I half hoped he would grab my bowl out of my hands and wolf it down then and there so we'd be done with it at last. I'd had my fill already and was sick of his begging, but the demon in me held me back from just handing it over and be welcome.

He wanted the beans so much. That is what held me back. He wanted them like life itself because life itself was what they were for him—a hot red mush to strengthen his hot red blood and thicken his seed for the fathering of sons once Laughter was gone to the land of the dead and Esau as firstborn would be father himself with the Fear's great promise to keep and the lucky people to plant.

He lowered himself to his shaggy knees, moaning. He placed his hands flat on the ground in front of my feet and thumped his brow against it. The reason he didn't just knock me flat and take what he wanted was this. He didn't want that bowl of beans taken. He wanted it from my hands. He wanted me with it.

I knew what I wanted.

I said, "You'll give me anything?"

"Anything. Everything," he said. The smile broadened till it cracked his face in two—the furrowed, bloodshot stare above, the big square teeth below.

"It's yours then. For everything," I said. "You know what everything means?" I wanted to be sure he knew.

"Tell me, tell me," he said.

This time it was his eyes that puddled. We were always doing it to each other for one reason or another.

"Everything means that when death comes to our father, I'll get twice what you get," I said. "Twice what anybody gets. Twice everything."

"Twice, that's nice," he said. He pulled himself up from the ground and squatted back on his heels.

"It means I will be first, not second but first. I will be father and first," I said.

"Not second," he said. "You will be father."

"You will swear it?" I said.

Esau got to his feet. He could have thrown me to the ground. He could have clamped one foot on the back of my neck to hold me. He could have shattered my skull like a pot with his other foot. Instead he threw back his head and brayed.

"Oh how I love you! You kill me!" he cried. "I'll swear."

"My seed, not your seed," I said. My mouth was dry. He nodded.

"Swear on my seed then," I said.

I set the bowl down on a flat rock by the fire. I stood before him with my feet planted wide apart. All the power of Esau's life was in Esau's face. It was as red as the sun, enormous. I could not look at it. I felt the heat of his face in my face like the sun.

"Swear on my seed then," I said.

He reached down between my legs and in the cup of one hand took hold of the sack a man keeps his seed in. He could have wrenched it off and hurled it into the fire. His big hand was gentle as a girl's.

"My seed, not your seed," I said.

"Your seed," he said.

"Father and first."

"Father."

"Twice everything."

"Twice," he said. "Everything. I swear it."

"So be it," I said. "Take and eat then."

He took it. He squatted by the fire with the bowl on his knees but did not immediately eat it.

A bird circled over us on ragged black wings. It gave a cry as harsh and dry as the name of a god. My brother's shoulders were hunched. His mat of hair was greased against the sun's burning. The sky was so big that even he looked small against it. I could feel where his hand had held me as if he was still holding me.

He raised the bowl to sniff it with his eyes shut. He scooped some beans on the flat of his thumb and touched them with the end of his tongue. Then he put them into his mouth and sucked his thumb, turning it this way and that way between his lips. Then a whole fistful, then another, each time sucking all five fingers like teats. He winked at me. When he was finished, he embraced me, kissed me.

That is how Heels got what Heels wanted and Hairy got what Hairy wanted. As to which of them got the better of the bargain, who can say?

4
THE TWO STONES

"YOUR FATHER MARRIED A BEAUTIFUL WOMAN," my mother said. "In Gerar I will be beautiful again. They will think more of your father there for having a beautiful wife. Certainly he has little else."

Her face looked smaller than ever peering out of her hair. She was sallow and hollow-cheeked. Like the rest of us she was starving.

"They will take us in at Gerar because that is the way of it," she said, "but in their hearts they will despise us for being so poor. Who can blame them? They will think your father has brought a curse on us all because of his foolishness, but at least they will see he has an eye for a beautiful woman."

There had been no rain for two winters. Every growing thing was dried up and black. There was not enough water left in the wells to get with a bucket. Children were let down on ropes to sop it up with rags. A few of the largest sand pools were left, but they were thick and foul-smelling, man-tled with green from the stale of the beasts who watered there. Even if you could get a swallow of it down, you only retched it up again. The shriveled dugs of goats and sheep gave less milk than dust. Some tried drinking their own urine. Some tried nicking the veins of beasts into cups and drinking that.

"No wonder he does these terrible things to us," my mother said.

She never spoke of the Fear by name. She had a way of making her eyes bulge out so you could see the whites of them above and below. It was her way to let you know it was the Fear she meant though "he" was all she said.

"Putting a beast's blood into your mouth is putting a beast's life into your life. Your father does nothing to stop it," she said. "They are always doing things like that. It makes him furious." She bulged her eyes to show which him. "We are lucky he hasn't long since swept us off the face of the earth." Again she bulged them.

It is not just strength that hunger saps. It works its way into the heart like lovesickness. The men lay about in the shade staring at nothing. The flocks that hadn't died went un-tended. The children gave up playing. They slept instead. You found clusters of them in odd places with their knees tucked under their chins. Their backs were bony, their little arms folded against their ribs like sticks. They had the leathery, shriveled look of bats. Everybody slept a lot. One moment you would be mending a tent. The next moment you would find yourself waking up with your eyes and lips caked with sand. The women no longer conceived children. They moved about slowly like women in a dream.

Only Laughter still looked fed. His round cheeks shone with health. Oil glistened on his beard. His paunch swelled and sweated like a water skin. He would pass among his people with his sad smile and liquid eyes trying to say things to them that would raise their spirits, but it didn't matter what he said to them. What raised their spirits was just the sight of him.

It was the child of the promise they saw. It was the seed of Abraham, who had talked with the Fear. It was the luck bearer. Women took food out of the mouths of their own children in order to feed him. Men laughed with pleasure when by crooking his elbow and clenching and unclenching his fist he made the fat on his upper arm bounce for them. When he let children reach up and touch the oily ringlets of his beard, their eyes sparkled as though he was giving them food. Everybody believed that as long as all was well with Laughter, all would be well with all of them. But toward the end of the second rainless winter it was plain that unless something was done in a hurry, nothing would be well with any of us because all of us, except perhaps for Laughter, would soon be dead.

"The Fear will save us. Does anyone have a bold enough tongue to argue with me?" Laughter said. "The Shield will not be angry forever. Do I know what I'm talking about, or do I not?"

The Shield was another of the Fear's names. According to Laughter, it means he shields the seed of Abraham the way a man starting a fire shields the flame. When Sarah was about to die childless, the Fear gave her a son. When Abraham was about to slaughter the son, the Fear gave him the ram. He is always shielding us like a guttering wick, Laughter said, because the fire he is trying to start with us is a fire that the whole world will live to warm its hands at. It is a fire in the dark that will light the whole world home.

"Maybe you are the only one who knows what you're talking about," my mother said.

She must have guessed what the Fear was going to tell us to do because already she was starting to work at making her face young again. She had chewed the end of a stick into a pulp and every morning cleaned her teeth with it. Even as she spoke, she was plucking her eyebrows and the hairs that grew between them.

"Maybe you talk too much," she said. "Maybe it is time for you to be something more than just a mouth. You are always either pouring food into your mouth or pouring words out of it. You have ears," she said. "Maybe you should try using your ears for a change. They will tell you what everybody is saying about you. You still have eyes such as they are. Maybe your eyes will help you see that if you don't do something to save your people from starving, you soon won't have any people."

"Is there a law that a man must always tell his wife what he is going to do before he does it?" Laughter said.

"Tell me or don't tell me. What difference does it make?" my mother said.

She had her mouth twisted sideways to pluck out several hairs she had spotted at the corners. She was kneeling near the door of the tent where the light was better. Laughter was sitting cross-legged by the fire behind her. We already had enough tent pegs to last for years, but he was whittling a tent-peg. He had a shawl wrapped around his thick shoulders. The tent ropes hummed outside. After a while he spoke.

"All right then, I will tell you," he said.

The polished bronze of the mirror my mother held in her hand caught the sun as she turned to look around at him. It shot a dart of light back into the smoky tent.

"Tomorrow at sunup I am going to cast the Two Stones if you want to know," Laughter said. "That way I will find out once and for all why the Fear is angry if he is angry at all. It is only you who says he is angry. If he is angry, I will find out why. Then I will do whatever he tells me to do to put things right again."

"Why bother to wait till tomorrow?" my mother said.

"Why bother me with your questions?" Laughter said. "These are matters that a woman knows nothing about."

"I don't know why I bother," my mother said.

At the mention of the Two Stones my heart turned to stone. I was sure that the Fear was angry, and I was sure I knew why. He was angry at me, and the stones would tell it. He was angry because I had duped my brother with a bowl of red mush boiled with mutton fat and sesame. He was angry because I had made him swear on my seed that I, not he, was to be father and first. I had made myself luck bearer in my brother's place. I had dared to meddle with the fire the Fear was trying to start with us and the plan he had for starting it.

Rebekah was the only one who knew I had gulled Esau with a bowl of beans. I had told her because I knew how it would make her heart rejoice. She had taken my face in her hands when I told her and looked so fiercely into my eyes that I had to close them.

"You are my son," she said, "You are the only son I have."

I had not told Laughter because Esau was the one in whom his heart rejoiced, and I knew he would never forgive me.

Esau had not told Laughter either probably because he had forgotten all about it while the mush was still warm in his stomach. My brother had made me a promise that could never be unmade any more than the words a man speaks can ever be unspoken, but it meant nothing to him. What difference to him whether he was first or second? It was nothing he could smell with his nose or stuff into his mouth. It was nothing he could couple with in the dung-smelling dark.

But the Fear knew what I had done without being told. There is nothing the Fear does not know either in heaven or on earth or in the dark kingdom of the dead under the earth. The next day at sunup he would surely tell Laughter through the Two Stones. Laughter would take me to some place high enough to catch the Fear's eye and then he would slit my throat there to make peace with the Fear the way Abraham had all but slit his. Then and only then would the Fear cause the rains to fall again and the grass to grow green again and milk to flow again, both the sweet milk of the goats and sheep and the thin, harsh milk of the camels that is first to sour and runs to hard curds in the stomachs of strangers and gives them cramps.

At sunup Laughter set off for the hill where the tent of meeting stood just as he had told my mother he would. I do not believe he had any intention of doing it until the moment he told her he would. I believe he was as afraid that the Fear was angry with him as I was afraid that the Fear was angry with me. By casting the Two Stones he would find out for sure, and he had put it off as long as he could, famine or not. But in the long run even the anger of the Fear was easier for him to face than my mother's badgering, so he went anyway taking my brother and me with him.

I with my stone heart walked beside Esau with his hairy arms swinging and his square teeth bared to the last star as though he and the star shared some witless joke between them. Laughter lumbered a pace or two in front of us with his bald scalp turning gold in the first light. He had daubed his cheeks and forehead with cedar ash. He had buckled the great goatskin pouch around his hips so his belly could hang free out over it. The flap of the pouch was held in place by the silver-tipped collarbone of a hare. He carried a brazier of live embers which he held out in front of him. Sometimes the smoke from it blew back into his eyes and made them water.

Some of the fathers were waiting outside the tent when we reached it. Their teeth were chattering. Their hands were tucked under their armpits. They had pulled their shawls up over their heads so all you could see of their faces were their sunken eyes and their bony noses puffing mist out into the chill air. Two of them bowed to Laughter and held the tent flaps open for him. Maybe to give them comfort, maybe to keep himself from falling to the ground in a faint, my father paused for a moment to place a hand on each of their heads before going in. Esau and I were the only ones he took in with him.

There were oil lamps burning from each of the poles. The flames bent at our entrance. Laughter took off his cloak and folded it carefully. His hands shook. Underneath the cloak his mantle was scarlet. The beauty of it made me feel sadness for him. There was sweat trickling down his cheeks and the thick folds of his neck. Sweat glistened on his upper lip.

"Esau," he said. He took my brother in his arms and kissed him on the mouth.

"Jacob," he said. "Jacob."

I do not know why he said my name twice. He took me in his arms and kissed me as well. His breath was sour. He showed Esau that he was to stand at his right hand because he was the firstborn. Esau made a feint at him with one fist as my father placed him there, but my father would not have noticed even if Esau had struck him. He placed me at his left hand. He did not know that now it was I who belonged at his right. He did not know that it was because of the Fear's anger at me that the flocks were dying, the children turning into bats. I thought he would know soon enough.

He got a fire going with his embers and scattered sweet gums on it and salt. The flames leapt blue and wild. The smell of the smoke made us all drunk. Laughter's eyes swam in their sockets. Esau could not keep a straight face. His shoulders shook like a girl's. I whispered my name over and over to myself for strength and comfort.

"Jacob, Jacob," I said. "Jacob."

Laughter also was whispering. He was on all fours in front of the fire. He was whispering and scrabbling at the carpets under him like a hound burying a bone. He peeled one carpet off and then the one underneath it. At the bottom was a straw mat. He rolled it back to uncover a patch of sand. Three times he touched his forehead to the patch, moaning and whispering. Then he picked up two handfuls of sand and washed his face and neck with it as if it was water. He rubbed his eyes, his lips, his ears with sand. The sweat made the sand stick to his flesh. Then he washed his hair and beard with it. When he finished, he was a man of sand. When he opened his eyes, sand clung to his brows and lashes. When he opened his mouth, sand fell from his lips as though they were crumbling. With hands of sand he scattered more gums and salt on the fire.

By now he had taken the Two Stones out of the pouch. He had had them from Abraham, his father, and Abraham from his father and father's fathers before him. They were six-sided stones. They had signs scratched into them. One stone was black for the night. It looked slippery and dangerous in my father's hand. It caught the firelight darkly. The other stone was white for the day. It was the gray white of bone.

Esau was weeping with excitement. His mouth was curled up at the corners. His nose was running into his mouth. I had my two hands shielding my seed as if for fear the Fear would kick me there for my treachery. Outside, the fathers were singing and stomping their feet to keep warm. I could feel their stomping shake the ground. Laughter was striking his bare chest with the Two Stones, one in each hand. They had broken his skin. There were bloody signs on his flesh now like the signs on the stones. I had never seen the blood of Laughter before. It was the power of his life snarled across his chest as frail as thread. It was the power of my life. He was breathing roughly through his teeth. Only the whites of his eyes were showing.

He was holding his hands out before him palm to palm, rocking them back and forth like a woman rocking a baby. The flesh on the underside of his arms jounced. The Two Stones cradled in his palms rattled. Laughter was silent now. The only sound in the tent was the stones' sound. I wondered if the fathers outside the tent could hear it. They had stopped singing and stomping.

There was a table of ramskin drawn tight as a drumhead behind the fire. Laughter reached out to it through the smoke. His scarlet mantle was dark with sweat around the neck. It was drawn tight across his buttocks the way he was leaning forward. In the quietest voice he had that wasn't a whisper he spoke what I knew must be the Fear's secret name. Only my father knew it and he never told me. My scalp ran cold with terror.

Laughter drew his hands apart and the stones fell onto the ramskin. The day stone bounced off and came to rest on the carpet. The night stone rolled over several times but remained on the ramskin. My father swooped forward through the smoke and fell on his knees to examine them. He had to hold them close to his eyes to see them because already his eyes had grown dim. He picked up first one and then the other. He traced with his finger the signs on the upward face of each. He placed them on the ramskin and studied them together. He placed the night stone on the left and the day stone on the right. Then he switched their positions and studied them again. Finally he turned away from them to look back through the smoke at Esau and me.

Some of the sand still clung to his face. There were traces there still of the ash marks. The threads of blood glistened on his chest. When his mouth shook, I thought he was going to curse me. Instead his whole face swelled with his smile.

"The Fear has forgotten his anger toward us," he said. "May the light of his face so shine that all men will behold it. Maybe it was only the sun who was angry. Maybe it was only the keepers of the rain. Who ever knows which gods are angry?"

Sand crumbled from his lips and nostrils. In his scarlet mantle, he rose from his knees like the dawn. He stretched out his arms. He filled the tent with the power of the stones that had filled him. There was no room to breathe. There was no room to move.

"The stones have named the name of Abimelech," he said.

"Esau," he said, "Jacob, we will go with all our people to Abimelech, who is king in Gerar. We will sow in his land and reap a hundredfold. Our flocks will become the envy of a hundred kings. All this the Fear will do for us out of love for Abraham, who was his friend. Your mother will live to regret her bitter words to me."

He picked up the day stone and wiped his blood from it with his sleeve.

"Never again will Rebekah, daughter of Bethuel, show scorn by plucking her eyebrows in her husband's presence," he said.

Even Esau looked no bigger than a child in his embrace.

"Darling," he said, kissing him.

Then he turned to me. He took me by the ear.

"Jacob, Jacob," he said.

I do not know why he so often spoke my name twice like that. Maybe he was trying to make himself remember it.

5

THE LIE OF LAUGHTER

WE DID WELL IN GERAR just as the Fear had promised. Our barley, lentils, flax grew thick outside the city wall. The flocks fattened. Esau and his brawny friends kept us in small game.

Rebekah's face filled out again. Every morning she combed out her mane of hair with camel stale to make it shine. No longer like the rest of our women did she wear only a bead of cloves in her nostril for everyday adornment but always the silver nose ring that she had from her mother and earrings big as bracelets. She painted her eyes with black antimony again, mixing it with oil to make it glisten. She stained her lips with cochineal. She wore a fillet around her brow with tufts of mewed ostrich feathers tucked into it and learned to narrow her eyes in a fetching way when she smiled. She also learned a proud way of holding her chin and a way of walking that was like crossing a stream on stepping-stones. The men of

Gerar bit their thumbs and fluttered their eyes when she passed. Sometimes in the evenings she would sing with the women as they wove goat hair into cloth for the black tents that we hoped one day to return to. The men would stand around in their filthy clothes and listen to her with foolish expressions on their faces.

"If I were you," she said to my father not long after we moved into the city, "I would tell them that I am not your wife. If they think that I am your wife, then the only way they can dream of taking me for themselves is to push you into a well." She narrowed her eyes at him in the new way she had. "Or stab you some night when you are sitting on the rooftop speaking to the moon."

"The Fear is the only one I speak to from the rooftop at night," Laughter said. "What makes you believe the men of Gerar find you so desirable that they would kill for you?"

"A woman knows such things," she said.

"Perhaps you know also then that Abimelech holds us sacred because he has given us shelter. He would not dream of letting anyone try to take you from me."

"Perhaps he dreams of taking me from you himself," my mother said. "A king has women the way a poor man has fleas."

"You are the one who dreams dreams," my father said.

Abimelech, the king, was a short, wily man. He wore his hair cropped short in the style of Gerar and shaved his cheeks so that his beard grew only out of the knob of his chin like the beard of a goat. His laughter was the stuttering bleat of a goat and came as often whether there was anything to laugh at or not.

It was true that he had six or seven wives who lived with him in his great house. The house was made of timber and brick with a bower on top which had a roof of brushwood and screens of willow so that you never knew when he was sitting up there keeping an eye on everything that happened in his city.

My father's house on the city walls was a poor thing, but at least it kept out the winter rains and had a cistern plastered with lime to catch them for water. The rest of our people lived in shacks like the people of Gerar. They were wretched dwellings patched up out of the rubble of older buildings. People lived in them in wintertime only and fled for the surrounding countryside as soon as the earth turned bright with wild anemones and cyclamen at the coming of spring. The city stank. Garbage and excrement littered streets too narrow for two to walk abreast. When winter came, we walked to our ankles in muck.

"You believe my life is in danger because of you?" Laughter said.

He was gazing out at the rain. It was dripping from the eaves of his house on the wall. The air was chill with it. Saddles and tent ropes lay heaped in a corner. It was if the tents had been a dream, and the ropes were all we had left of it. "You think somebody is going to push me into a well?" he said. "You think they would dare dishonor a son of Abraham?"

"You have seen how they honor the beasts they butcher," my mother said.

Laughter squeezed his cheeks between his palms so that his lips were pushed forward, twisted and wet. He groaned at the thought of what they did to their beasts. Knowing that dead flesh soon starts to stink and fester, the men of Gerar do not slaughter their beasts at once and drain the blood as we do because the blood is the life. Instead, to keep the meat fresh, they cut it off bit by bit while the beast is still alive and in torment. I have seen an old camel past labor trussed and shrilling in the dust as her owner carves what he wants from her flank and then sears the wound with iron to staunch the bleeding. I have seen their beasts so matted with flies you cannot tell what kind of beast they are.

"Listen," my mother said to Laughter, "it is very simple. Tell them I am not your wife. Tell them I am your sister. Then if one of them desires me, he can come bargain with you instead of killing you."

"What am I to say if by some wonder such a one should happen to come?" Laughter said. "Maybe you are too clever for your own good."

"It is your good I am thinking of," my mother said. "You will say to him that for a beautiful woman you must ask a price that he cannot possibly pay. You will say to him that your sister cannot wed outside of our own blood."

We had already eaten well that day, but my father took a charred gobbet of the venison that Esau had brought him and placed the whole of it in his mouth. He licked the fat off his thumb and forefinger. His eyes glazed over as he chewed.

"If I tell them you are my sister," he said when he had swallowed, "then who do I tell them is my wife? Are the men of Gerar supposed to believe that my two sons were born into the world without a mother?"

"Tell them their mother is dead. Tell them some other woman is their mother," my mother said. "It makes no difference who you tell them."

"I will tell them Zillah," my father said.

My mother laughed. She said, "No one will kill you for Zillah."

"You are not the only one who is clever," Laughter said.

So Zillah came to live with us on the city walls, the widow of one of the herders who had died of a wen in the throat. She had a squint in one eye and gobbled her words. If she had chosen to tell the whole city of my father's lie, they would have had no idea what she was saying.

It was because he had lied to them that my father came to dislike the people of Gerar so much even though they had saved us from starving. He could not look into their faces without being reminded of his cowardice. A brave man would not have pretended his wife was not his wife. He would not have shrugged and smiled at them the way Laughter did when he saw them eyeing my mother as she followed him down the street rattling with bracelets and trinkets. He was always discovering new reasons for finding fault with them.

"They are not of our blood," he said. "They have the sea in their blood. I have never seen the sea myself, but I have heard evil things of it. The sea is a monster. They say that like your mother it is never still. Why should I want to go see it? I wouldn't see it even if I went. Sometimes I can hardly see the toes on my own feet when the light is poor. Even if I saw the sea, I wouldn't like it. We have the Fear to thank that we are not sea people like the people of Gerar and that our blood is not tainted by monsters."

He said, "They do not even cut the foreskins of their male children. If you have ever seen one of them naked, you will understand what I mean. They do not cut their foreskins because for them the penis is only a plaything so why should they bother. For us it is the part we use for fathering the Fear's people. He told us to cut off our foreskins as a reminder of his promise. Every time a man of our people looks at his penis, he remembers the promise the Fear made."

Esau's shoulders shook. He covered his mouth with both hands.

"It is no laughing matter, darling," Laughter said.

"I laugh because every time I look at my penis," Esau said, "I think it looks like a plaything and I want to play with it."

"It is lucky for you that you were born simple-minded," my mother said. "He has ways of dealing with men who behave like beasts," she said, bulging out her eyes in her usual way, "but to the simple-minded, he is sometimes merciful."

It was not long afterward, in the spring, that Esau married a woman named Adah. She was not of the sea people, but she was not of our blood either. This caused my father the bitterest grief because it was Abraham's seed who were to bring luck and blessing to the world. Esau's wife was a drowsy-eyed woman who spoke a tongue that not even her own family seemed to understand very well when they spoke it to each other, and she was no kin to Abraham. Laughter was afraid that children of mixed blood might turn out to be the best he could offer the Fear for the carrying out of his purpose. He would never have dreamed of casting Esau out of his house, but my mother did not let him forget how it was his favorite who had risked the Fear's wrath by his unfortunate marriage.

Because of Adah, Laughter took to staying inside even when the coolness of evening came and there was some rest from the wind which serves only to blast the sun's heat hotter

the way bellows fan the fire of a forge. He sat outside the walls
in his tent drinking wine. He spoke little to anyone. Not even
Esau could rouse him. The sight of his son's red beard and
shaggy chest only reminded him of the woman of strange
blood that he had taken for a wife. He even turned his face
away from the gifts Esau brought him, the plump roebuck,
the plucked and gutted quail.

Then one day Adah bore her husband his first son, who
was also Laughter's first grandson. When the news reached
Laughter, he smiled his sad smile for the first time in months,
his well-dark eyes glistening. They named the child Eliphaz,
and though his blood was not pure, he bore the seed of Abraham in his fat little loins even so. When the time to cut him
came on the eighth day, Laughter put Abraham's ring on his
hand and came to be there with the rest of us.

He cannot have come with a light heart, but he came. He
came because he knew the sight of him would be as sweet to
his people as the coming of spring. They stomped with pleasure when he took the place they had prepared for him. They
had spread carpets out for him under a bower of wet green
rushes. They called out his name when they saw him. The
children ran forward to touch his beard. His bare scalp
gleamed like an old saddle. To his right and to his left he
crooned words of courtesy and greeting even to men he dis-
liked. Our people were there in a strange land among
strangers, but when Laughter joined them, he brought with
him home.

They unwrapped Eliphaz when the time came and laid
him at Laughter's feet on an overturned shield. They had
scattered it first with powdered sheep dung for softness. The
child was red as his father though such little hair as he had on

his ostrich eggshell of a skull was black. Adah, his mother, kneeled near him, and Esau near her with his arms crossed on his belly. An old man skilled in the art was there to do the cutting. He wore his headcloth pulled across his lower face though there was no sand to blow or any wind to blow it. Pressing forward from all around to see, the people clapped their hands when he drew his blade and flicked it to a fair edge back and forth across his arm. From his sleeve he took a pierced stone shard which he held in his left hand. With his right hand he reached down and took hold of the tiny foreskin of Eliphaz. Deft as a weaver he drew it through the shard and tied a thread about it. The baby howled. Adah covered the baby's eyes, murmuring things to it in her strange tongue. The baby quieted some. It blew bubbles of spit from its lips.

"Cut too much, darling, and I'll cut yours clean off," Esau said. His face was on fire with mirth and menace.

The old man severed the skin at the knot with such a light, swift stroke that Eliphaz felt nothing. He lay still now on the soft dung. Sweat dripped off the end of the old man's nose. He took the white wing feather of a dove and dabbled the end of it in the child's blood till it was red with it.

"He is handing you the feather," my mother said to Laughter. "For the love of heaven, take it."

"How can I take it if I can't see it?" my father said.

The old man was squatting by Eliphaz. He was holding the feather up for Laughter to take. Laughter groped for it and missed it so that my mother had to place it in his hand for him. He took it by the quill end and brought it close enough to his eyes to see.

"Don't drop it," my mother said.

"Am I a cripple," he said, "that a feather is too much for me to hold?"

In front of him, on the ground, the old man was powdering the baby's wound with charcoal.

"You are not a cripple, but you are going blind," my mother said.

Laughter held the feather out as far as his arm would reach so everybody could see how the white tip of it was stained crimson. The old man had handed the baby back to Adah, and she covered its ugly little face with her shawl. She had risen from her knees and was holding him in her arms. Esau had his arms around both of them. His head was thrown back. He was squawking like a raven.

At the sight of the blood of Eliphaz, the young women started clapping their palms together. Their unbound hair hung down about their shoulders and shone in the sun. Some of them had tambourines. The young men had flowers tucked behind their ears. They were dancing in a long row, each with his arm around the next one's shoulder. Sometimes the row came sweeping toward the bower where Laughter stood. Sometimes it swept the other way. Everybody was dancing now and shouting with high spirits. Tears of feeling rolled down Laughter's cheeks.

"Abraham, Isaac, and Esau!" he was calling out in his loudest voice.

Abraham's ring was bright on his finger, and the bloody feather was trembling in his hand. There was so much noise going on that nobody much was listening to him.

"The promise is to them and to Eliphaz and their people forever."

This time he called the way you call when you know that nobody much is listening.

"Listen to him! Listen to what he is telling you!" my mother cried. Her voice was so shrill that for a moment or two the people listened.

"Blessed be the Fear," my father said. At the sound of the Fear's name many of the women rolled their eyes up into their heads. Many of the men, as is their custom, put their fingertips to their lips and kissed them.

He said, "Blessed be the people the Fear has chosen for a blessing to all peoples, even to the people of the city of Gerar."

The bower's shadow cut off the top half of his face, so it could not be seen that the tears were still wet on his cheeks.

Later, at the feast that followed, he drank so much wine that he forgot his tears, and later still, when he and my mother were returning to their house on the wall, he looked at her for the first time in who knows how long the way a man looks at a woman. It was she herself who told me of it. I begged her not to.

"Your father has put all of us in great danger," she said. "You must hear for yourself how it happened. That way you will be ready for whatever may come of it."

She had awakened me before sunup where I slept out on the parapet. She had not combed her hair or painted her eyes. She spoke in a low voice, stopping from time to time to blow warmth into her cupped hands.

"Jacob," she said, pointing down from the wall, "I had just started up those very steps when he took hold of me from behind and pulled me into his arms. It has been years since the last time he touched me. He has touched no other woman for years either. Perhaps it is because his father tried to kill him once when he was a boy that he has never been like other men. Can you blame him for being so strange? I blame him in my heart although it was terrible for Abraham to do such a thing. Who should know better than I how strange your father is? But this is not what I woke you up to tell you. It is what happened down there by the steps that I want to tell you."

She pulled the folded cloak out from beneath my head and wrapped it about her shoulders. A breeze had freshened at the sun's first sign of rising.

"It was because of the wine. I know that well enough although for my age I am also a beautiful woman, and it was also because of my beauty. I have seen the eyes of the men of Gerar when I pass, and your father has seen it too. Jacob, he started fondling me," she said. "I let him have his way with me at first because it has been a long time for me too, and I am a woman like other women. But then he went further. I tried to stop him. You know that the moon was in her fullness last night. Anybody could have seen us plain as day. 'I am starving! Starving!' Your father kept telling me he was starving. I knew it wasn't me he was starving for. If it was me, at least I could understand it. Who knows what your father is starving for? Does your father know? He had me up against the wall. The man was like a rutting bull."

I put both my hands over my ears. I could not bear to think of his bald head in the moonlight. I could not bear to hear the bull sounds of his starving.

"Listen to me!" she said. She seized both my wrists in her hands. Her nails bit into my flesh. "What I am telling you is that someone came upon us. Now will you listen?"

She pulled my hands away from my ears.

"Over your father's shoulders I saw a man standing in the shadows though how I had eyes to see anything I cannot tell you. He had seen us from the bower on his roof and come down. That awful laugh he has. He said, 'Is this how the men of your people fondle their sisters?' Your father fell against me like stone. It is a wonder I have any breath left in me."

"The king?" I said.

"Who else has a laugh like a goat?" she said. "Your father was pale as death. I thought he was dead. 'I said she was my sister to save my life.' That is what he said to the king. He said, 'If you'd known she was my wife, you would have killed me.' What do you think the king said? 'I should kill you now.' That is what the king said. He said, 'Do you know what would have happened if one of our men had taken his way with this handsome woman thinking she was your sister?' There is no mirth in Abimelech's laugh. It is like the quacking of a duck. Then he named the name of their great fish. I will not soil my lips with the fish's name. The king said their god would slaughter them all for such a deed against strangers in his city. He said it was lucky for Gerar that their king had found out your father's foolish lie when he did."

"What did my father say?" I said.

"What could your father say?" she said. "He bowed to Abimelech. You know the way he can bow. The fringe of his sleeve swept the dust at the king's feet. Abimelech also bowed to your father. I will say that for him. He bowed because we are too many for the people of the sea to make enemies of. We are also too strong and too lucky. They know their fish is no match for *him*." She bulged her eyes.

I could hear my father's voice calling into the dawn from his high window. Who knows what he was calling for?

"We must be on guard from this time forth because of your father's strangeness. Who knows what disaster his folly may bring on us next," my mother said.

"The birthright is yours, Jacob. It is you more than all of us who must be on your guard."

6

THE WELLS

WHAT I WAS ON GUARD against were the thieves of Gerar. They came at night with their faces charcoaled and muffled in rags. I was on guard against the bear, the wolf, the fox, the thicket-dwelling lion. The sheep are so foolish and so helpless with their great fat tails. Their lives are spent nibbling and dropping dung and nibbling. I wore my club at my belt for clubbing off the world from them. I carried my staff in my hand for poking the lechers and laggers among them, the mad ones. I beat down leaves from branches beyond their reach with it so they could reach them. I scratched their rumps, their ears. Even when my bones ached to stretch out on the ground, I stood leaning on my staff because sheep take comfort from the standing figure of a man, especially at night when wolves howl and jackals circle with their smirks and terrible stench.

I have carried lambs the weight of fat Eliphaz, the dung dangling from them like grapes. Breathing the air like flames by day, frozen by night, I have scoured the moors for the strayed ones. I have lugged them to their feet when they fell because a sheep is too stupid when it falls to remember it has feet. I have cursed them through my teeth. I have held them to my heart. I have led them out of the furious sun into the shade of rocks and tall desert thorns. I have taught them the sound of my voice till at the sound of it they come when I call them for watering. While others' flocks come to others' calls, mine lie waiting for *hoo ha la, hoo ha la* and then come in a rushing torrent of wool to the trough or at dusk to the stone ring of their fold. I have counted them one by one at dusk. At dawn I have counted them again.

A shepherd does not sleep, a shepherd dreams. He sees things, hears things. Even on moonless nights a hill turns silver. Rocks sing like women. The lion dances. My grandfather Abraham's shoulders blot out the sky. His crimson beard rustles in the wind like leaves. The moon is a shepherd with a pitted face. He herds the stars. They flock to the cold fire of his call—*kah wee ay, koh see nah, nah.* The dead rise. Zillah's dead husband rises. His wen is blue lazuli. Old Abraham's milky seed floods the sky. It is our people drifting thick as dust in the sky as the Fear promised. Prayers shake even the timid lips of the sleeping sheep. "O Fear of Isaac!" they pray. "O Shield of Abraham! *Kah wee. Kah wee ay.*"

Under my care and others', the sheep multiplied, the goats also. Esau multiplied. He took more wives—among them our cousin Mahalath, of Abraham's blood, to please Laughter—and five more sons were born to him and cut like Eliphaz when the time came. Esau played with his boys the way a bear plays with its cubs. I have seen him knock them about with his great paws till they were half dizzy and more than half deaf from his huge laughter. Apart from Mahalath with her bitter mouth, Adah and his other wives drove my father to despair with their strange gods and strange ways. In time he became so nearly blind that he could not well see what they were up to, but my mother was always happy to tell him. She told him that Judith and Basemath made little cakes the shape of big-breasted women which they burned to Asherah, Queen of Heaven, who was herself hung with more breasts than a camel with baggage. Even when Oholibamah's time for bleeding was upon her, my mother said, she lured Esau into coupling with her. Adah laid curses on women she hated, including my mother herself and Esau's wife Mahalath.

"If I had eyes," my father said, "they would never stop weeping."

"Some of your tears should be tears of rejoicing," my mother said. "If you looked at other things besides those unspeakable women, you would know how much you have to be thankful for."

It takes more cleverness to move with the seasons across the land in tents than to nest like adders in the rubble of a city. Our people were far cleverer than the people of Gerar. We were better planters as well as herdsmen. We were sharper at trading. Our young men were lustier, their seed more abundant, our women more fruitful. My mother was right. We had much to be thankful for, and the more we had, the more the people of Gerar despised us. It was not many years before there were almost as many of our people as there were of theirs. If we met them in the narrow streets, it was they who flattened themselves against the mud walls to let us pass.

They mocked us at first for having a god nobody could see. Their Fish was to be seen everywhere. He had horns. He had crooked teeth. They hung the Queen of Heaven with beads and flowers and built a house for her larger than my father's where she was served by women with painted hands and feet who gave themselves to any man who came to them and by men who gave themselves as women. Nobody has ever seen the Fear. Not even Abraham ever saw him though he bargained with him like a man with his friend. The people of Gerar laughed at our folly. What good was a god who was only a name for frightening children? But they did not laugh when they saw how the Fear prospered us. The Fear they could not see, but they saw his power. They came to fear his power like a scorpion under a stone. They came to fear us who feared him. They cursed us the more in their hearts for not being bold enough to curse us to our faces.

When we were elsewhere, they took to destroying the wells where we watered our flocks. They crept out at night with their faces black as goats. They kicked in rocks, rubble, carrion, earth, their own dung, till the wells were filled to the lip. Abraham himself had had the wells dug when he too grazed his beasts in Gerar. The water was sweet and plentiful. To each of his wells Abraham had given a name.

Laughter went to speak of the wells to Abimelech in his own house. The king was sitting on a stone bench in the courtyard with some of his wives about him. He stuttered his laugh when I caught my father by the arm to keep him from tripping on the cobbles. He stuttered again at Esau with his jaw hanging slack. Esau always let his jaw hang slack in the presence of kings. Laughter stood before the king with sandals on his feet. He carried his staff in his hand.

"I hope that your sister is enjoying good health," Abimelech said. "Such a handsome woman."

"You are robbing us of our water," Laughter said. "Water is the life of the earth as blood is the life of a man. My father Abraham sank those wells at the cost of many months' digging. A man lost his life when the walls of one of them caved in. He had a harelip, which you'd think was trouble enough for a man, but he was killed anyway. I was only a child, but I saw it with my own eyes and remember it. Now our wells are choked with filth. It is the men of your city who have choked them."

Laughter looked more the king than Abimelech. He was twice the size of Abimelech. He did not stutter like a goat or have an absurd beard growing out of the knob of his chin.

"All water is from the Fear," Laughter said.

The Fear's name had power in it the way Laughter spoke it. The king held up his hands to ward off the power. I thought of the sheep praying to the Fear at night. Perhaps they were praying for water.

"The water in those wells is our water," Abimelech said. "The Fear is nothing to us here. He is only a visitor. You yourself are only a visitor."

"The people of Gerar treat their visitors no better than they do their beasts," my father said.

"They bugger their beasts," Esau said. "I have seen them at it with my own eyes. They grab a ewe by her hind legs."

My father held up his hand. "There are things that are as unseemly to speak, darling, as they are to do," he said. "You soil your lips with the filthiness of the men of Gerar."

"They do it even so," Esau said. "I have seen them with my own eyes."

"I am not a god. I am only a king," Abimelech said. "I cannot stand at every man's shoulder. Men do what they do. There are men who do it even with their own sisters."

Laughter said, "Abimelech, will you swear by the name of the Fish who is your god that from this time forth the wells of my father Abraham will be safe from the filthiness of your people?"

Abimelech's shaved cheeks were brown and creased. He had his hand under the cloak of one of his wives. She seemed to take as little pleasure from his hand as he did. She had hair on her upper lip.

"My city has grown weary of you and your people," Abimelech said. "They do not like the way you crowd them off their own streets. They do not like your cleverness. They do not like your luck. It is your luck especially that they do not like. I can swear anything you want me to swear, but it will mean nothing to my people. I know of only one way for you to make them stop doing these things which you have come here with your two sons to charge them with doing."

"I am a man of peace," Laughter said.

My mother would have said he was a man of weakness, but he was a man of peace as he said. At a word from him, our men would have fallen upon Abimelech's men like wolves. Ears would have been lopped and powdered with salt for trophies.

"I will not shed blood unless you force me to it," Laughter said. "All blood is from the Fear, even the blood of villains."

"It is we who are the villains?" Abimelech said.

"Even as I stand here listening to the words of your mouth," Laughter said, "our flocks are thirsting. Every second day they must be watered or their dugs dry up and their tongues blacken."

"It is the hearts of my people that blacken," Abimelech said. "How many years have you dwelled with us? How many children have been born to you in our city? Is it you who are strangers in our city, or is it we who have become strangers in the city that has become yours?"

When he stood up, the top of his head came no higher than my father's chest. His beard waggled as he spoke.

"If you go away from our city once and for all and leave us in peace," he said, "I swear by the horn of the Fish that your wells will be safe. May the dugs of our women dry up like your goats' if I lie. I do not lie like other men I have met. May I grow dugs like a woman myself and the nipples be black. May the seed dry up in my loins."

Abimelech didn't lie. Laughter put him to the test. He led us out of Gerar as he had led us in. He said that he had been planning to do so long before Abimelech suggested it. He said he had only been waiting for spring lambing to be over. Maybe it was so. Or maybe he feared that blood would be shed if he stayed. Our people rejoiced to leave the city. We complain of the wretchedness of living in the black tents. We bemoan the emptiness of heart and the weariness of herding. We curse the sun for withering our crops. We curse the rain for not raining or for raining with such madness that the new shoots are washed out or blasted with mildew. But by nature we are wanderers and belong in our black tents even so.

The Fear too is a wanderer. He does not dwell like the Fish in a house reeking of blood and rancid fat. He is not always in one place like the place of Asherah. The Fear comes when he comes. He goes when he goes. We listen for his words. Our days themselves are the Fear's words to us. The days of sorrow are the Fear's curse. The days of gladness are the Fear's blessing. The day we returned to our tents from the city of Gerar was a word of blessing that the Fear in his mercy spoke to our people.

We dug out the wells where Abimelech had filled them. Laughter came often. Sometimes he worked the winch that hauled out the stones. Someone would lead him to it, and he would handle the rope. There was no foulness they had not thrown in, so great was their envy at how we had prospered among them. There was the corpse of an old woman and the severed hands of thieves. There were swine. There were stones of cursing. But once the wells were cleared, they were not filled in again, and Laughter renamed them with the names that Abraham had given them. We dug new wells too and gave them new names. My mother named one of them.

"Its name will be Strife," she said because some of Abimelech's herdsmen had stood around as we dug it out, shouting that the water in it was rightly theirs, and thrown rocks.

"It is bad luck to give a well such a name as that," my father said. "The bad luck will be theirs," my mother said. "I am not the foolish woman you take me for."

Room was the name my father gave another of the wells because in its case there was no strife with anybody. He said that Room meant that now at last there would be room for us to dig wells wherever we chose. The water was a long time seeping up from the bottom, and when there was finally enough to drink, there was a bitter taste to it.

"What name do you think brings bad luck now?" my mother said. She spat what was left of the water in her mouth to the ground at Laughter's feet. "Even a camel would have enough sense not to drink such bitterness."

The camels drank from it nonetheless. They strained so much of it through the bristles that grow from their flabby lips that their bellies were swollen with it and they dribbled and moaned all through the night.

We moved east to Beersheba then where there is good winter pasturage. Abraham had planted a tamarisk there, and it had grown to a great height. The tree was so full of power that even when there was no wind, its small gray-green leaves trembled like feathers. There was power even in the shade it cast. It made the hairs of our arms rise. Laughter caused an altar to be built beneath the tree. The central stone was so heavy that it took four oxen to drag it into place.

The Fear spoke to Laughter at his new altar. I watched Laughter's face as he listened. His face was daubed gray with ashes. His body was naked to the waist though our tents were stiff with frost. His hairy breasts were plump as a woman's. His arms were stretched out wide. He whispered the Fear's words as one by one the Fear spoke to him.

We would be blessed above all peoples, the Fear said. Our daughters and sons would become as many as the stars. They would be like the dust that covers the earth. My father's lips wobbled around the Fear's promises like a camel's lips drinking. The Fear would be with us always, he promised. We would never need to fear any but him. My father's eyes filled with tears at the beauty of the words the Fear was speaking.

"All this I will do for my servant Abraham's sake," the Fear said through Laughter's lips. The tears that had filled his eyes overflowed them. They ran down his gray cheeks.

"It is always for his servant Abraham's sake. It is never for his servant Isaac's sake," my mother said. "It is no wonder the man weeps. He should stand up like a man and demand his just due."

She was speaking all of this into one of my ears while with the other ear I strained to catch Laughter's whispering.

My mother said, "It is because Abraham offered to slit your father's throat in honor of him that he loved him so." She bulged her eyes to show who she meant loved him. "I, myself, never loved Abraham. He always breathed in your face when he talked to you. His breath was like dung."

Two of the men held the calf down bleating and kicking. Esau struck the first blow. A thin song rose from the calf's mouth. Blood from its throat bubbled out onto the stone and spread over it. Esau severed the head. He slit the belly and flung the pink bowels aside. With Laughter's fumbling help, he skinned it and quartered it. Esau kept his teeth bared the whole time. Laughter's breasts were dark with blood. The fatty gut and chitterlings went into the fire with the rest of the fat and the liver. Smoke and flame carried it to the Fear up through the tamarisk's branches. What was left went into a pair of boiling cauldrons. Mahalath and my mother stirred them with sticks. My mother's face was red from the steam. Her hair was soaked flat to her skull.

"It is not for Abraham's sake I do this," she said to Mahalath. "It is for my husband's sake I do it. There are times when even I feel sorry for him."

It was several weeks later that Abimelech came to us. Ahuzzath, his counselor, came with him as well as Phicol, who commanded the warriors of Gerar. Laughter received them in his tent. It was I who told him who they were when he did not know them by their voices. He had carpets brought for them to sit on. He gave them barley cakes and bowls of warm milk scented with cloves. Ahuzzath was an old man. Several times he broke wind noisily but was too deaf to hear it. Phicol wore a helmet of goat's hide with a horn on top of it like the horn of the Fish. Abimelech limped from so many hours in his ox-drawn cart. Laughter was the first to speak.

"My eyes may be dim, but they see how you despise us, Abimelech. Did you not say that the streets of Gerar are not wide enough for both your people and my people?" he said. "As for my ears, they hunger to hear why a king would journey a night and a day and another night to visit a people he hates."

"We are neighbors, your people and mine, and between neighbors there must be true understanding," Abimelech said. "If neighbors are not careful to shake hands, the time may come when they shake fists."

My father said nothing. The burning thorns snapped and sent up a puff of blue smoke behind him.

"Let there be an oath between us, Isaac, son of Abraham. That is why I have come," Abimelech said. "Let us make an oath together that you will work us no mischief just as we have worked you none since the day we suffered you to leave our city in peace. Let our oath be that from henceforth there will be nothing but peace between your seed and mine."

Neither man spoke for a while. Laughter's shadow swelled and danced on the tenting over his head. He had looked for more strife, and the king was offering an end to strife. He had grown so used to speaking to people who wished him ill that he could find no words for a man who said he wished him well.

Finally Laughter spoke. There was a ring of white about his lips from the milk he had drunk.

"As the Fear is my witness, I will keep this oath," he said.

"May the Fish devour me in the night," Abimelech said, "if I do not keep it as well."

The king rose from where he was sitting then and limped over to Laughter. He put out his hand and touched Laughter's beard. Laughter put out his hand to find Abimelech's beard and touched it. They were of different blood, but each wanted peace for his own people just as each had a beard grown gray from leading them.

They swore their oath the next day. They swore it under Abraham's tree. Many of our people were there and so were the servants that Abimelech had brought, together with Phicol and Ahuzzath. First Laughter reached down between Abimelech's sinewy thighs and took hold of him.

Then Abimelech slipped his hand between my father's heavy thighs. They swore peace between each other's seed with each of them holding the other.

A milk white ox was slaughtered and cut in two. The head with its tongue lolling and its front quarters was hauled to one spot. The rump with its pizzle and tail was hauled to another. With the blood as thick on their necks and shoulders as shawls, Abimelech and Laughter passed together between the two parts of the white ox.

Several days after Abimelech departed, Esau came running to say that the digging of yet another well had at last been completed.

"Oh Father, the water is so lovely! It is so sweet and lovely this water in the new well we have dug!" he cried. "It is a well as deep as a mountain is high. Maybe it is deeper than a mountain even."

"Perhaps you will give your son Jacob the naming of this new well," my mother said. "It is time you gave him something."

"This well I have named already," Laughter said. "It will be called the Well of the Oath."

Then he said, "Jacob." He turned his head in my direction. "Jacob?" he said. He reached out to find which one of us it was who was standing beside him.

"The naming of the next well will be yours. I promise it," Laughter said. "Is it you, Jacob?"

"Yes," I said. "It is me. It is Jacob."

7
THE CAVE IN THE HILLS

M Y MOTHER RAN UP THE HILL in a half crouch.
She kept well below the ledge of rock so as not
to be seen against the sky. She gestured me to do the same.
She still painted her eyes as she had in Gerar, and the sweat
made them run. She was black under the eyes like a sick
woman. My father believed that he was the one who was
sick. He had told her so. He had told her he was dying.

"I told him he had been as good as dead for years," she
said when she stopped for breath. She leaned against the
rock. "He should beat me for my evil tongue. He should take
a stick to me for the things I say to him. It is what I would
do if I were in his place."

Beyond the hill we had climbed were two small round
hills with a narrow cleft between them. She pointed one finger at the cleft. The finger had three silver rings on it. I knew
where she was taking me. There was a shallow cave at the

head of the cleft hidden by the two round hills. I had found one of my rams there once. He was lying on his side staring at nothing and grinning. His ribs were heaving like a bellows.

"He has not lain with me for many years," my mother said. "That was the first of him to die. I cannot remember the last time he lay with me. Even the first time I hardly can remember. The first time I saw him I remember. I have told you about it often. Unless you do what I am going to tell you now, we will all be ruined. In the cave I will tell it."

She had told me often about the first time she saw my father. It was because of Abraham that she had seen him. It was because of Abraham that Esau and I were born and our children after us, with Joseph among them who saved us from starving when the time came, and our children's children after that. Abraham's hand reaches through the years. It is no wonder that I see him still. Sometimes I see his shoulders blotting out the stars. Sometimes I hear his crimson beard rustling.

Like my father, Abraham also once thought he was dying. Before he died he wanted to make sure that Laughter would marry a woman of his own kindred, so he sent a servant back to the land between the two rivers where he had been born to find one. It was the land where the Fear had first told him that he must go to a strange new land which the Fear would show him and father a strange new people there. I have never heard the name of the servant Abraham sent. He must have been very trusted to be honored with an errand of such weight. Perhaps his name has been forgotten because people wish to forget that Abraham didn't go on the search himself although he was very old by then and believed he would soon be dead. Perhaps Abraham was afraid that if he went himself, Laughter might marry a wife of foreign blood while he was gone. In any case, the old servant went as Abraham bade him, and in order to be certain that he would find the right woman, he prayed to the Fear to give him a sign. The sign the servant prayed for was this. When he came to a spring near the city of Abraham's kindred, he would ask a woman to draw him a jar of water to drink from. If the woman did what he asked her and offered to water his camels as well, he would know that she was the woman that the Fear had chosen. My mother, Rebekah, turned out to be that woman. It is hard for me to picture the Fear's choosing her.

I picture instead my mother's telling the servant to draw his own water. I picture her puffy cheeks and large front teeth. I hear her say that he must water the camels himself and then lead them off before they start mucking the place up with their urine. That is not what she said. Maybe she guessed the gifts that the servant had stowed in the baggage the camels were carrying. As soon as she finished pouring the camels' water into the trough, the old man rummaged around in his baggage and gave her a gold nose ring and two gold bracelets that he took from it. He told her that he had traveled many miles to find a woman for his master's son. He said that she was surely the woman. She told him that on a matter as serious as this she would have to consult with her father and brother first. That part I have no trouble picturing. She wanted time to think what she must do.

Her brother was Laban, my brick-faced uncle made like an ox whose gods my lovely Rachel stole long afterward. His face may not yet have turned the color of brick back when Abraham's servant saw him, but in every other way he must have already been the man I later knew. No sooner did my mother run home to show him her nose ring and bracelets than Laban ran back to the spring as fast as his ox legs would carry him. The servant can hardly have been prepared for the welcome Laban gave him.

"Why do you stand outside here, darling?" Laban said and threw his arms around him.

Laban could not do enough for the astonished old man. He took him back to his house. He ungirthed his camels for him with his own hands. He gave them fragrant straw for bedding and fodder to eat. He washed the old man's blistered feet. He washed the feet of the other servants who had traveled with him. He sent for his father, Bethuel, who was a nephew of Abraham's. He sent also, of course, for his sister Rebekah herself, who became my mother. The marriage with my father was quickly agreed upon among the four of them, and the old servant dug out still more gold and silver and rich clothing from his baggage. This time there were gifts not only for Rebekah but also for her father and for Laban. It was Laban who spoke the words of farewell to his sister. From his own lips I have heard them.

"Be the mother of thousands, gazelle of my heart," he said. "May the sons of your virginity seize the gate of all who hate them."

It was both my father and my mother themselves, though at different times and in different places, who told me of the day when the old servant without a name finally returned with my mother and of how my father and my mother saw each other for the first time.

"I was young then. You think long thoughts when you are young," my father said. "I had walked out into the fields to think some of them. It was evening. If you have thoughts, evening is a good time for thinking them. I heard the sound of a harness off in the downs somewhere, and I looked up. I had to shield my eyes from the sun. I saw camels coming."

"Your father was not fat then, but he was heavy. His flesh already hung on him," my mother said. "I saw him walking through the stubble toward us. He walked the way a heavy man walks, rolling from side to side because his thighs were too thick to fit together properly. My camel couched for me to dismount. I asked the old servant who the man was. He said it was your father. I covered my head with a veil. Jacob, when they told me the man I saw walking toward me with his flesh hanging was to be my husband, I covered my face."

"I brought her into my tent," my father said. He held his jaws between his two hands like a man with the toothache. "I removed the veil from her face with my own hands. She stood there like a little tree as I removed it. As soon as I looked into her face for the first time, I knew that I loved her."

When my father first told me the story, my mother still had more or less the same face, I suppose, as the one he had unveiled. There in the cave, it was smaller and sallower, the front teeth larger. There was the black under her eyes. Even when she smiled, her brows looked knotted in a frown. She was not smiling.

"Your father thinks he is going to die soon. He has been talking to your brother about it. I heard every word he said. He has asked your brother to do certain things for him, and he has promised to do certain things for your brother. These things must not be allowed to happen. You must listen carefully to what I am going to tell you," she said.

The cave was shadowy and low-roofed. I thought of the strayed ram with his ribs heaving. I had feared that his leg was broken, but he had only twisted it. Soon he was back nibbling with the rest of them.

"A word can never be unspoken once it has been spoken. Do you understand what I mean?" she said. "This is what I mean. If you speak a word with the strength of your heart in it, you can never get that word out of the ears of the one you speak it to and back into your mouth again. Once a word goes forth, it makes things happen for better or for worse. Nothing you do will ever make those things unhappen even though you live for a thousand years. Do you understand me? Don't speak till I'm finished."

I had started to speak. She laid her hand across my lips.

"Your father is getting ready to speak a word of great power to Esau. With my own ears I have heard him say so. Listen to me now," she said.

Even in the shelter of the cave she leaned close so no one else would hear her. There was no one else. I felt her breath on my cheek.

She said, "Jacob, unless you act quickly, unless you act with great cleverness, your father is going to give Esau the blessing and everything will be lost. Everything."

I had to look hard to find her fierce little face in the tumble of hair.

Blessing or no blessing, I would be father and first when Laughter died. I had bought Esau's promise with a bowl of red mush. Esau knew that. My mother knew that.

"It is only a blessing, Mother," I said.

Her slap stung my cheek like a wasp. She seized both my wrists.

"Only a blessing?" she said. "It is Abraham's blessing, that is the blessing it is. It is the blessing that Abraham had from the Fear himself."

I think it was the only time I ever heard her speak his name. She whispered it. For once she did not bulge her eyes.

"I was there when Abraham gave it to your father," she said. "I will remember it to my grave."

Her fingernails bit into my flesh. The cave smelled like a tomb. When I turned a stone, there were beetles under it.

"Abraham was so old I doubt there were a dozen breaths left in him," she said. "He had had them tie the pouch with the Two Stones around his belly. They had put so many rings on his fingers it was all he could do to raise his hand. The birds stopped in midflight when he raised it. All the camels made water at once. You've never heard such a splashing. They had him propped up under a tree, and the leaves of it rustled over his head though there wasn't so much as a breath of air stirring to rustle them. But all those wonders were nothing compared to your father's face."

She said, "Jacob, as the words of the blessing entered your father's heart, his face gave off light like the sun. It turned into a god's face. Seeing him today you wouldn't believe he was the same man."

She didn't want Esau's face to shine like a god's face. She wanted my face to shine like a god's face. It was for me, not for Esau, that she wanted the Fear's blessing. She was prepared to do anything to get it for me. She was prepared to have me do anything.

It is strange, remembering that time, that it is as if Esau had been with us there as we plotted against him. I can almost see him squatting on his heels at the cave's entrance looking in at us. He has his head cocked to one side, listening. His glazed eyes are fixed on us, but he doesn't have the faintest idea what we're saying. He is smiling. I am not smiling. Even as I am plotting his ruin, my heart goes out to him. Or did it go out to him only after I ruined him? My mother is talking to me like a child. I picture Esau listening like a child. Her plan has a child's cunning.

"Your father thinks he's dying, but still he wants to eat. You think even the fear of death can spoil hunger like his? But now especially he's hungry," she says. "He is like a pregnant woman. He is eating for the sake of giving strength to the blessing inside him. So he has told Esau to go catch him something and cook it the way he likes it. Instead it will be you, Jacob. You are the one who will catch him something. You will go catch him two fatlings from our own flocks. I will cook them the way he likes them. Who knows how he likes them after all these years better than I know it? When you bring him his meat, he will think you are Esau bringing it. He can hardly tell light from dark any more, and it is you, Jacob, he will give his blessing to, thinking you are Esau. That way our people will be spared the sight of Esau's face shining like a god. They will not have to endure Esau as Luck Bearer."

I can bear to hear again what my mother said just as I can bear to see again the way she looked crouching there like a child except for those black-ringed eyes staring out at me. It is only what I said myself that I cannot bear myself to hear again.

I said, "He will know that I'm Jacob."

"He will not know it," she said. "He has only his hands for eyes now. The skins of the kids you catch will make you hairy where you are not hairy. I will tie the skins around your arms and your neck, and your father's hands will tell him it is a bear he is touching. He will think it is Esau because Esau is a bear. He has the brawn of a bear. He has the ravenous, lustful heart of a bear. Your father will be so pleased with the meat that he will blubber all over the bear I will make of you. You have me to thank for your handsome, smooth skin, Jacob, but it will be well hidden by the skins. Haven't I said I will see to it?"

It was not deceiving my blind father that struck terror in me. It was not cheating my slow-witted brother. It was not even cheating the Fear, whose blessing it was that I was stealing as sure as a man steals sheep in the dark. What struck terror in me was only that my father would not be deceived. He would know I was Jacob. Instead of the blessing, from the strength of his heart he would speak a curse. My flesh crawled like the beetles under the stone.

"He will know who I am, and he will curse me."

"Never!" my mother said. "Never will such a thing happen. I will see to it that it cannot happen. If it happens, may the curse be on my own head, Jacob. Not on your head. My head, Jacob. Be sure the kids have the fattest tails. It is the tail your father likes best because it is fattest and sweetest. Who knows what he likes best better than his own wife? He should beat me every day for the way I am plotting against him. I would get down on my knees to thank him for it if he did. But I have always known what he likes."

I see myself squatting there in the cave like the ram with the twisted foot. I am staring at nothing and grinning. My ribs are heaving like a bellows.

8

THE BLESSING

LAUGHTER DIDN'T DIE FOR MANY years after he thought he was dying. First my beloved, Rachel, died giving birth to the second of our two sons. She died glittering with sweat in my arms on our way to Ephrath. Her hair was like leaves flattened by rain against her cheeks and throat. We were days piling stones for a pillar to mark where she lies. They tell me her voice can still be heard there now and then raised in lamentation and bitter weeping. I do not believe them. Even in life she never raised her voice. She lived just long enough to name her son Benoni, which is Son of my Sorrow. The sorrow was also mine who on the road to Ephrath lost her who was my moon by night and my shade by day.

From her pillar we went on to Hebron, and it was not long afterward that my father no longer had to fear dying because at last he also died. He lived to be older even than Abraham before him. It had been so many years since I'd seen him that I wouldn't have known him for my father if I hadn't known. His mouth had so caved in that his nose and chin met in front of it. He had lost so much of his flesh that it was like lifting a child when I carried him from one part of his tent to the other in search of air.

The last time I saw him as the father I had always known was the day I pulled the wool over his blind eyes. Rachel was not even a name I had heard of then. I was Jacob still—Heels, heel-grabber. I did not walk with a limp yet, one hip dipping deep with each new step. I did what my mother badgered me into doing. I did it because she badgered me, did it because if someone had turned the stone of my heart, he would have found beetles there. I moved from lie to lie like a jackal stalking his prey from bush to bush.

"Father," I said.

The flap of his tent was extended on poles. He sat cross-legged under it. One foot was bare where his slipper had fallen off. He was fumbling with a rope in his lap trying to splice it. Near him a small white spring-rat of pitiful beauty had crept out of her hole smelling dark in the air. She sat with her tiny hands clasped at her breast. I watched the rat's bright eye instead of Laughter's as I waited for him to answer. Laughter's eyes were liquid as always but cloudy now, starless.

"Here I am," he said.

There he was. My mother had dressed him for the blessing as she had also dressed me. He had a wool cap set crooked on his head. His purple shawl, stained with spilled food, was held in place by a topaz. His beard glistened with oil. I wore a cloak of Esau's that smelled of Esau, the neck of it dark with Esau's sweat, the very shape of it Esau's shape as it hung loose and heavy from my bony shoulders. The goatskins my mother had decked me out in were still slippery on the inside with blood. The coppery smell of the blood was part of the heavy, sour, sweet-grass, dung-foot, man-seed smell that was Esau's.

"Will you tell me which of my sons you are," my father said, "or must I heap still more shame on my head by having to ask you?"

"I am Esau, Father," I said. "I have done what you said. I have caught what you asked for and cooked it to your liking. I have come for your blessing."

I set the pot down at his bare foot and took off the lid. My mother had stewed the two kids with leeks and melon, stirring in coriander and black cumin to tingle the tongue. Laughter began to weep as the fragrance of it filled the air under the flap.

"That I should have to die in order to receive such kindness," he said.

He leaned forward into the fragrance. Testing first to see how hot it was, he stuck in his thumb. He placed his thumb in his mouth and sucked on it. His eyes were closed. The tears trickled down from his closed lids.

When he opened his eyes, he looked at me so directly that I couldn't believe he didn't see me as well as I saw him. My scalp turned cold.

"How did you manage to catch it so quickly when it's hardly been any time since I asked you?" he said. "You've grown yourself wings maybe? The game comes when you whistle?"

"It was the Fear. For your sake the Fear granted me luck," I said.

Thus I fouled the Fear's name with the filth of my lie and waited in terror. Already I felt the Fear strangling me. My tongue thickened in my mouth. I don't think my father even heard what I'd said. His arms were stretched out toward me. His cap had slipped over one eyebrow.

"Come let me touch you," he said.

The pressure of leaning so far forward over his paunch purpled his face dark as his shawl. He caught the back of my neck in one hand and pulled me to him. His other hand browsed and poked me like a lamb at its mother's bag.

"Can you be Esau and have Jacob's voice?" he said. "Can you be Jacob and have Esau's smell? Those hairy paws I'd know anywhere. As the Fear is your witness, tell me the truth."

He had such a grip on me that my words came out smothered against his chest.

"Ob blog glob," I said. "Stroof."

He took me by the shoulders and held me off at arm's length. He gently shook me. There was coriander and kid on his breath. I could smell the oil in his beard.

"Speak, boy, speak."

He did not say it, he crooned it. It was a lover speaking to his beloved. It was a child pleading with a man with a knife poised above him.

"I am Esau. It is the truth."

I do not know to this day if he believed me. I will never know. Maybe he himself did not know. Maybe he knew all along I was Jacob. Maybe though it was Esau he loved, it was Jacob he believed in his heart would be the luckier luck bearer and he only pretended to believe me. Maybe he was past caring which of his sons I was and wanted only to get on with his dying. And with the stew I had brought him.

"A man has to eat," he said.

I saw no sign that my mother was within earshot, but I knew in my heart that she was. She said she would see to it that no one approached my father's tent while I was there with him. If Esau came back from his hunting early, she would distract him somehow. Esau was not hard to distract. My father was sleeping, she would tell him. Or he must come see a two-headed lamb that one of the ewes had dropped. Even if Esau found me in spite of her efforts, I knew I could explain it to him somehow as a game I was playing. He liked games. He would get my head in the crook of his arm like a calf and drag me around for a while, twisting my nose and laughing.

It was Laughter I feared—the look in his sightless eyes as it dawned on him what I was up to. Unless of course he already knew what I was up to. Most of all it was the Fear I feared. The blessing I was stealing from my father was the Fear's blessing. I knew that the Fear too was within earshot. The sun had turned red. It was the Fear's angry eye. I heard the rustle of his wings behind me if the Fear has wings. If the Fear has leathery talons fierce enough to pinion a sheep or a man, has an eagle's creaking cackle.

My father had the stew all over his lips and in his beard. He sucked on the bones. If he came on a piece of melon rind that my mother had overlooked in her haste, he spewed it out of his mouth like poison. He picked gristle from his teeth with his thumb and forefinger. He had me fetch him wine, and when he had drunk it, he dipped his bread in the cup to sop up the last drops. He was not enjoying what he ate, but he was desperate to eat for strength in his dying. I have seen camels drink like that when they are laden for journeying. They suck up water till they are swollen and groaning, till their lovely eyes go crooked with pain.

When Laughter finally finished, he wiped his hands on his cloak and turned to me in such a seeing way that again I could not believe he did not see me.

"Are you afraid of me?" he said. "Come where I can put my arms around you. I will give you a father's kiss. It may be the last kiss I will ever give you. A man never knows how many kisses he has left."

He kissed me on my mouth. He buried his face in my neck, buried it in Esau's cloak which I had up over my ears against the chill that was already starting to rise with the red sun's darkening.

"The smell of my son is the smell of a field that the Fear has blessed," he said.

My eyes smarted with tears. It was Laughter who held me in his arms.

It was Laughter I held in mine with the bloody goatskins bound to them. If old Sarah had laughed herself into a fit when the bird-faced strangers first said she would bear Abraham a son, she would split her sides now to see her son gulled by a son of his own. A sob caught in my throat like a bone. Laughter put his hands on my shoulders and held me away from him at arm's length. He put his hands on my head where I knelt on the carpet in front of him.

"May the Shield of Abraham bless you with the dew of heaven," he said. "May the Fear of Isaac bless you with the fatness of the earth. May he bless you with grain and wine in great plenty."

My mother had more than once told me about the day when Abraham gave the blessing to Laughter. She said the camels had all made water at once. Flying birds had hung motionless in the air. Laughter's face had given off light. It had become a god's face. I could feel my own face burn as I knelt there with his hands upon me. My face did not burn with light like a god's. Shame was what burned it, a hot shame fragrant as kids stewed with leeks and melon. I was scorched. I was ashamed that Laughter was blessing the wrong twin. I was ashamed for my mother's cunning and my brother's dull wits. Most of all I was ashamed for myself. I prayed to feel the great claws sink into my flesh, the peck and dazzle of the merciless beak granting me the mercy of death.

"Let peoples serve you and nations bow down to you," Laughter said. "Be lord over your brothers, and may your mother's sons bow down to you."

I knew my mother had no son other than Esau to bow down to me yet he had spoken of sons instead of one son only. The words of Laughter's blessing must have been older than Abraham and gone back to a father with many sons. The words were as old as the Two Stones, each word a stone of crushing power. I felt the power of the words even stronger than I felt the shame. I felt it inside me hurling itself against my ribs like a caged bird. I felt it rise like a ram's horn between my thighs. It made me a live coal. My father's hands on my head burst into flame. I could hear the burning torment in his voice. Through closed eyes I could see the torment in his eyes.

"Cursed be everyone who curses you, and blessed be everyone who blesses you," he said.

I was doubly cursed then because I cursed myself. I made enemies of my father and brother. I became a fugitive. Twenty years I slaved for Laban. I lost my beloved on the road to Ephrath.

The blessing was more terrible still.

When the camel you're riding runs wild, nothing will stop it. You cling to its neck. You wrench at its beard and long lip. You cry into its soft ear for mercy. You threaten vengeance. Either you hurl yourself to death from its pitching back or you ride out its madness to the end.

It was not I who ran off with my father's blessing. It was my father's blessing that ran off with me. Often since then I have cried mercy with the sand in my teeth. I have cried *ikh-kh-kh* to make it fall with a sob to its ungainly knees to let me dismount at last. Its hind parts are crusted with urine as it races forward. Its long-legged, hump-swaying gait is clumsy and scattered like rags in the wind. I bury my face in its musky pelt. The blessing will take me where it will take me. It is beautiful and it is appalling. It races through the barren hills to an end of its own.

My father slumped back into his cushions. I could not bring myself to look at him. I looked back at the white spring rat instead. Another had joined her. They were whispering together. One of them glanced toward me and winked her small eye.

9
THE STONE STAIR

I OWE MY LIFE TO MY MOTHER TWICE. The first time she gave me my life, squatting on the birthstones as first Hairy dropped out and then, hard on his heels, Heels. The second time she saved my life, telling me that my twin was going to kill me. This time it was Hairy who was on Heels's heels.

"He is going to kill you, and then they will kill him for killing you," she said. "In one day both my sons will be killed. On the next day, I will kill myself."

Her small, pale face looked as though she had been killed already.

"Go to Laban in Haran," she said. "It is a long way. You will be safe there."

I had left my father to go count the sheep. I had a bit of a fire started. It was dark. My mother had her cloak over her head.

"You will have to keep your eye on Laban. I say it though he is my own brother. But at least at Laban's your life will be safe," she said. "You must leave tonight. If Esau sees you, he will kill you. He has found out everything."

"And Father?"

"I will tell you while you are making ready," she said. "Your brother is eating now. He is with that she-ass Basemath. When she has finished feeding him, she will make him pleasure her. If you are lucky, he will not think again about killing you until morning."

She stood close by me while I bundled together a few belongings along with a water skin, ash cakes, dried dates and the like, and bound them to a young black cow-camel my mother had found for me in her haste. The beast was wild and untaught and a great trial to me on my journey. She wasn't used to traveling with baggage on her back and a peg in her nose with a rope to guide her, so she would fall on her knees and couch whenever the notion took her. There was only a narrow moon as I loaded her. The tents were dark against the stars. My mother's whisper came muffled through the folds of her cloak.

She said that when Esau came to receive the blessing, he found Laughter dozing under the flap where I had left him. Esau woke him by taking a haunch of the deer he had roasted for him and wafting it back and forth under his nose. Laughter had already eaten himself into a stupor on the meat I had given him and had no idea why anyone would want to feed him again. He asked who it was, pushing the haunch away so roughly that he knocked it out of Esau's hand. Esau said he was Esau. He had come for the blessing. Laughter said he had already blessed Esau. They were two buffoons the way my mother told it. Then Esau started to cry, she said. He did not understand yet what I had done to him. He knew only that Laughter had knocked the venison out of his hand that he had been at such pains to catch and cook for Laughter. That Laughter had already given away the blessing.

"It was Jacob then! Jacob!" my father said.

My mother croaked my name like a raven to show me the sound of his voice. My fingers were stiff and cold from the saddle cords. The camel kept arching her long neck trying to bite me.

"Your father could hardly understand what Esau was saying, Esau was blubbering so. He wanted to know if there wasn't some blessing left over for him. That's what Esau was saying," my mother said. "He thinks a blessing is like beans. He thought there might still be some of it stuck to the sides of the pot that could be his if he asked for it."

What was stuck to the sides of the pot seemed so sad as my mother spoke it that I almost started blubbering myself— such a scorched, small remnant of blessing that even Esau must have heard it less as blessing than curse.

Laughter gave him what blessing he could.

Away from the fatness of the earth Esau's dwelling was to be, Laughter said as he blessed him, because the fatness of the earth was already to be Jacob's. Esau's dwelling was to be away also from the dew of heaven because that too the power of Laughter's words had already called down out of the sky for me. Esau would be second to Jacob. Esau would live by the power of the sword, and the sword would be his only power. Maybe someday things would go better for his people after him, Laughter told him, but that day would be a long time coming. It was the best Laughter could do for him,

Laughter said. Then he lay back exhausted, powerless, with his belly full of the stew I had plied him with.

He thought he was dying.

Only then, my mother said, did Esau seem to see what had happened.

Everything in him that had been puzzled, hurt, frightened, suddenly burst into a single flame. He pounded his temples with his fists. His beard dripped spittle. My mother said he would have found me out and slaughtered me then and there except that he thought Laughter might die any minute and he had better wait around till that minute came. Who could tell? Laughter might still find some scrap of blessing crusted to the sides of the pot, and Esau wanted to be on hand if he did.

"Maybe it's true your father is dying," my mother said to me. "If you don't get out of here in a hurry, before daybreak I may lose my husband as well as my two sons. It is the least I deserve for my meddling and scheming. I have meddled and schemed for your good, Jacob. Why should you thank me for it? You wish I had never been born. I deserve that too. Go now, before I have your death on my head along with everything else."

She unwrapped just enough of her face to give me a quick, fierce kiss.

"Watch out for Laban," she said.

It was the last time I ever saw her. It was the last time I ever heard her voice.

For the first days I traveled, my eyes were fixed only inward. I saw nothing of the land I passed through. If a lion had sprung into the path before me, I wouldn't have seen him. Hills and valleys were one and the same to me. Was it a train of merchants I passed or a flock of ostriches with their dawn-colored shins and dusty plumes? It was not shrubs, clouds, earth I saw. I saw faces.

I saw the fat, milky-eyed face of my father. I saw Laughter's face with stew all over his mouth and chin, tears running down his cheeks. His face was telling me my smell was the smell of a field that the Fear had blessed. The nose of his face was smelling me.

I saw Esau's face. I saw the wet teeth of his tilted grin. I saw his red mane. All that my brother was at any moment was in his face for as long as that moment lasted, unlike me whose face is what I hide who I am behind. There is nothing ever in my face except what I choose to have in it. All the fullness of his anger was in Esau's face when he was angry, or of his lust when he was lustful. When he loved you, his love for you was in his face to overflowing. You drew back to avoid being drowned by it. His bent eyes flooded you with love, his parted lips, the way he cocked his head at you calling you darling, darling, staring at you so hard that it was as if there was never a delight under the sun or the moon like the delight of you.

My mother's face I had to part the thicket of her curls to see, brushing them to right and left with my hands like a man brushing leaves aside to drink from a puddle. What I drank from the small, pale puddle of my mother's face—the painted eyes and puffed cheeks, the rabbity teeth—was bitter as death although down through the years I think I never found another, except for my beloved, who meant everything she did to be so much for my life's sweetening.

They say the Fear has no face a man can see, and I did not see it. But on starless nights as I traveled north with my black camel I saw over my head an emptiness that had no end. I saw darkness. I heard silence deeper than the kingdom of the dead. I knew that this was the way the face of the Fear appears to those who have committed abominations in his sight, and I shuddered beneath it.

Toward the end of one day my way took me over the shoulder of a steep hill. The hill was covered with bare rock. Some of the rocks were upright like the markers of graves. They stood black against the sky, leaning at different angles. Some of the rocks were as tall as trees and some the height of a man or less. There was a cruel pounding in my head as I climbed. Each time my foot struck the ground, it was as if a peg was being driven deeper into my head. Perhaps I was feverish. I was sweating and had an appalling thirst. Sometimes the pain inside my head was dull and heavy as a mallet, sometimes auger sharp. Sometimes it didn't seem inside my head at all but outside. The pain was a voice telling me over and over again that I had made some stupid mistake—I was following the wrong path; there had been no reason for leaving home; my uncle had died and there would be no one to take me in if I should ever arrive where I was going. Sometimes the pain was a face. It was Esau's face. He was watching me as I climbed. When I got to a certain place he would kill me. He would hurl me to the ground and crush my skull with his foot. He would force my head down on a sheet of rock and stomp on it. The pain in my head was his foot stomping on it. I hoped he would finish with me as soon as possible. Then I could stop climbing and the pain in my head would stop and the pain of the rope cutting into my shoulder, the rope I dragged the camel behind me by, which was tied to the peg in her nose.

I reached a level place finally. The mountainside rose in terraces beyond me. The hills I had left behind were a cloudier gray than the gray rock all about me. I tethered my camel to one of the standing rocks. I found a flat stone. I lay down beside it with my head on the stone for a pillow. My tongue was as dry as a stone in my mouth, but I was too tired to drink. There was little left in my water skin. I waited for Esau's foot to fall. I fell asleep.

I dreamed of a long flight of stone stairs that began near where I was lying and rose into the sky. I could not see to the top of it. They were stone stairs, or it was a stone ramp such as I have seen since leading to the high places that men build for raising themselves closer to the stars who are their gods. There were stars moving all the length of the flight of stairs. Some were moving up the stairs toward Heaven. Some were moving down the stairs. They were dressed in light. It was the Fear that the stars served. It was the Fear's light that fell from their shoulders, their wrists.

They made no sound the way the stars in the heavens make no sound. The hush of their moving was the hush of the stars when you see them scattered across the night like sand. I knew in my dream that the Fear was at the top of the stairs above where I could see. I buried my face in my hands.

"I am the Shield of Abraham," he said. He whispered the words. "I am the Fear of Isaac. The land you lie asleep on is your land. I give it to you and to your children who will come after you. I give it to their children. To the east and to the west, to the north and to the south, they will cover the earth like dust. They will be the earth's best luck and blessing."

I uncovered my face. The stars were still moving both up and down the stone stairs. The stars moving down overflowed the stairs. All about me the earth, the rocks, the stone beneath my head, shone with their light. The voice out of the dark was Light's voice. The words the voice spoke were the stars.

The voice said, "I am with you, Jacob."

When I opened my mouth to speak, light filled my mouth.

The voice said, "I will be with you where you are going, and I will keep you. I will bring you here again. I will bring you home."

Light welled up in my eyes.

It said, "I will not leave you until I have done what I have said. I will not leave you. I will keep my promise to you."

The camel woke me. She had slipped her tether. It was just before dawn. She looked at me as I spoke to her—her lovely eyes, her long, fanned lashes.

"I am afraid, camel. I am afraid of this place," I said.

The shadows of the rocks were all around us. In the east, the sky had lightened to the color of rock.

"It is God's place," I said. "Camel, this is God's house. It is the Fear's stone stair and gate."

She flung back her head, burning my hand with the rope. She shot out her terror in a long, green string of spittle. I tried to gentle her. I pressed my cheek against her black neck. I whispered words of comfort. It was mostly myself that my words comforted as I whispered them.

I set up a pillar before I left. At the cost of a fingernail torn backward and two split thumbs, I wedged the flat stone loose that I had slept on for a pillow. I set it upright with smaller stones about the base to hold it fast. I poured upon it half of what little oil I had. The oil gave the stone life. It made it glisten. I thought how the stone was like my head that had rested on it and how the glistening of it was like the dream my stone head had dreamed.

What I spoke to the Fear then at that pillar I have shuddered often to remember. Instead of the anger I awaited, what his star words brought me down the stone stairs was promise. He promised me the land I lay on.

He promised that from Haran he would bring me home. He promised to be with me and to keep me all my days.

What I spoke to him at his altar was IF.

"If you will be with me and will keep me in this way that I go," I said, "if you will give me bread to eat and clothing to wear so that I come again to my father's house in peace, then you shall be my God, and this stone that I have set up for a pillar shall be yours, and of all that you give me I will give the tenth part to you." Those were my words. Even with him I hedged and bargained.

But ever since, in my heart, the stone stairs have stood no less for my hedging and bargaining, and it was my beloved's firstborn who many years later told me the best and deepest of the stairs' meaning. It was far from home, in the Black Land, that my son Joseph told me, teller of dreams to the Shepherd King.

Heaven has to do with earth, Joseph said, and earth with Heaven. As prayers and offerings rise, the God descends.

The end is light.

At such as that I become all camel. The beauty and the terror of it are too much to hold. I shoot them from me in a string of spittle.

10

THE STRING OF SCARLET

THE NEXT TWENTY YEARS of my life were as cluttered and yammering as Laban's house.

The walls of his house were kiln-baked brick sealed with mortar and whitewash. The roof was brushwood overlaid with earth and clay. We rolled it after every rain and still it leaked. When the weather was fair, the women worked their looms up there, dried the wash there, sometimes baked there. Evenings we often gathered there. We spoke to the Fear there. We watched and waited for the Fear to speak. We watched for Sin there as well. Sin is the moon. He is the god of the city of Haran. His beard is dark and flecked with stars like lapis lazuli. At night he sails his crescent barge across the sky.

Beneath the roof, the floor was mud packed hard as stone by years of feet. A ladder led to the cellar where Laban kept his gods. Winters, the fire of dung or thorn stung the eyes and made them water. The rooms were shadowy. They stank. They stank of life. They stank of the ailing goats and

disowned lambs we stabled there. They stank of the burning
oil of lamps, of garlic and onions, of sweat, of moldy straw, of
piss, of coupling, of smoke, of women. Most of all they stank
of children. Eleven sons were born to me in that teeming
house of twenty years and a twelfth and last on the road we finally left it by. The last and Joseph were from my beloved,
Rachel, two from her maid Bilhah, six from Leah, my
beloved's sister. From Zilpah, Leah's fat maid, there were two
more still who were fat and quarrelsome. Dinah, my daughter, was from Leah too.

The children crawled naked among the ashes and got
burned. They tumbled cheeses off the shelf. Laban stepped
on them. Their mothers rubbed them with salt and swaddled
them, suckled them, switched them. Their small brown bodies were everywhere like mice. The house became their house.
They punched each other's heads and howled. They were as
shrill in laughter as they were in pain or rage. Laban took to
stuffing his ears with lamb's wool against their clamoring.
The women squabbled with each other and with Laban over
them. They sent the women into fits of exasperation and
cow-eyed doting. Child rivaled child with the mothers judg-
ing. Many a night, for peace, I slept with my flocks beneath
the silver beard of Sin. Many a day I dragged back to the
house like a sheep to his slaughterers.

But the children were the Fear's. All the time I knew it,
even so. They were the seed of the seed of the seed of Abraham, who was his friend. My sons' pert, jouncing little
parts, which they snatched at like monkeys when they wrestled on the hard-packed floor, were bearers of the earth's
best luck and blessing. Theirs was the seed that would cover
the earth like dust. They were the promise to me and to my

fathers before me. They were the message from the stone
stairs, with stars to bear the words to me and other stars to
bear my wonder back.

If the twenty years were a house, my beloved's kiss was the
door through which I entered it. Kisses were also the door by
which I left it. There at the end Laban kissed everybody. He
kissed the two daughters who were leaving him, my wives.
He called them his does, his little heifers. Each of my eleven
sons he kissed in turn, his grandsons. Some were as tall as
he by then, as lean and straight as he was jowled, beefy. His
face shone with sweat as he kissed them. His cheeks ran
tears. One after another he flung his arms around them
starting with Reuben, the oldest and proudest, and crushed
the wind clear out of them. Dinah he held at arm's length a
moment first. She was slender and blue-eyed, her gold hair
fine as spider's silk. He took her face between his hands and
kissed her mouth. Even me he kissed. As he moved from one
to the next he found me in his path and was in such a state
by then he could not stop himself. I remember still the feel of
him in my arms. It was like feeling a boulder in my arms. It
was like being hugged by a tree.

But it was through the door of a single kiss that I entered
the house of the years. I did not know what awaited me, but
it was all gathered like shade there by the well in the north
near Haran where the door opened. All the sons and the one
daughter I was to father were gathered there. So were the
four women I was to father them by, and Laban from whom
I was to steal the four women even as he was plotting what
he could steal next from me. All the years beyond the twenty
with Laban were gathered there too—the stranger at the
dark river whose face I never saw, the three deaths, the pit

and the famine, the years in the Black Land. But I saw none of it at the well. I saw only the young woman coming to water her father's sheep. Her hair was dark and gathered at her nape in a scarlet string.

I had already talked to the shepherds I'd found waiting there. They were as hairy as Esau, most of them. They seemed about as slow of wit. Their clothes were filthy. They wore breechclouts only and rags tied around their heads. They spoke another tongue—slurred and softer, swifter than ours—but I knew a few words of it and eked the words out with hands and shrugs.

There was one shepherd who had lost an eye and spoke our tongue a little. From him I learned that they were men of Haran. They were waiting for the other flocks to gather. With one bare foot he scuffed the heavy, flat stone that was set over the well's mouth. When all the shepherds were there at once, he meant, they would together lift its great weight off and do their watering.

Then he made water himself. He didn't turn his back the way our people do but puddled the earth right there between us. I saw he wasn't cut like us, and more than anything else on all that long trek north it was the sight of his uncut part between his thumb and finger that told me how far I'd come from home. The Fear was not known among those hairy, ragged men. Their parts were hooded, not shorn bare like ours to keep us mindful of the promise. The only name they knew to call on in the night were names like Sin's. Sometimes Sin was in the sky for them to see. Sometimes dark was all they saw. It is the way with gods.

I spoke the name of Laban to the one-eyed shepherd. Did the shepherd know of him?

The man was short of teeth as well as eyes. He bared his gums. His laughter cracked his rutted face from ear to ear. He cackled the name of Laban over his shoulder to his friends. Some laughed. Some rolled their eyes. One filled his cheeks with air and thrust out his belly.

Then a boy among them reached out one arm and pointed to something I couldn't see behind me. He called out something in words I didn't know. One-eye slapped his bony knee and laughed still harder. They were all of them laughing now. He held me by the shoulder so I couldn't turn. He knew our word for sheep and spoke it with his nose to mine. I felt his spittle in my face. He put our name for sheep together with the name of Laban.

"Laban sheep." he said.

By now he had me by the ears. He also knew our word for woman. "Laban woman," he said.

He cocked his head at me like Esau. He held me with his stare.

"Laban woman sheep," he said. He was gaping his mouth and clicking his tongue like a lizard.

"Sheep woman Laban," he said.

I saw her first in the eyes of the pointing boy who stood there seeing her. He had narrowed his eyes to shut out every sight but her. Then one-eye spun me around so I could see her for myself.

She was walking through the shadow of a crooked tree. I could see the string of scarlet in her hair. Her flock was bleating and bumbling along behind her. In place of a staff she had a branch of willow. She had trimmed it to a clump of leaves at the far end and shook it as she walked to make the leaves flutter. Now and then she flicked some straying ewe with them. She wore her skirts tucked high. From the knees down, her legs were flecked with mud. She stopped when she was near enough for me to see her face. Her chin was faintly cleft. She held one hand at her throat. Shy as a doe she was. She watched me through her lashes.

I do not know why I did then what I did. What I did was this. I tore off my shirt so I was as nearly naked as the shepherds. Compared with theirs, my flesh was as white as curds. My chest was bare and bony as a shield where theirs were matted. I ran to the well and kneeled down beside it. Bending forward over it, I circled with my arms the heavy stone that covered it. At first I thought the heft of it would never budge. I could feel the sinews in my back and shoulders pull tight as tent cords in a storm. Sweat dripped off the end of my nose.

I pressed my cheek flat against the stone's warm roughness and clasped it to me as if it was a woman made of stone. My breath came quick and deep, my stomach working like a bellows. I felt the weight move beneath me. Fire shot up my thighs. I gave another heave. I had the stone about a handsbreadth in the air, then set it down again.

I heard a sobbing in my chest as though some other life inside my life was sobbing. I slowly lifted till my back came straight. My whole body was shuddering like a man with fever. I didn't dare to let my burden go for fear it would fall and cripple me. I couldn't breathe. My salty sweat had blinded me. I had my eyes screwed tight. My teeth were clenched. With one last heave, I cast it to the side. The well was clear.

I went to her where she was standing with her father's sheep. She raised her eyes. Her eyes were bright with tears. I had no breath for speaking. I showed her with my arm that she could draw water now. Then for the second time that day I did something I hardly knew I'd do until I'd done it. I placed my hands on either side of her waist and drew her to me. I kissed her lips. The door of the years opened. I buried my face in her neck and wept on her.

11

THE DANCE BEGINS

I HAVE GROWN ALL BUT BLIND in the Black Land like Laughter. My sons have grown old. My sons have sons. The runaway blessing careens down the years with all of us. Even in a land of painted rooms and tombs that rise from the sand like white clouds the luck lasts.

I have seen the people carry their god in his golden house to a barge on the blue river. Their garments are sheer as spider webs. When they cover their nakedness, they do not hide it. Often they go naked through the streets without shame. They bandage their dead with linen and set stone beetles in among the bandages. My son Joseph is lord over them. Their king pulled the seal off his own finger and gave it to him. He hung a gold chain of eagles wing to wing around his neck. No man dares lift a hand or raise a foot in the Black Land until my gold son has nodded at him first.

Sometimes he asks me to tell him about his mother. She died so young he remembers her only in glimpses. Old as I am, I cannot forget her. I remember the tilt of her elbows when she combed out her hair in back and gathered it. I remember her shyness and the cleft in her chin. I remember her sister Leah with legs as heavy as Laban's. I remember Laban and the clay-roofed house. Most of all, I remember the dance of madness that Laban and I danced.

I have seen men dance that way in the desert. They slap hand to hand and hand to cheek so hard that they nearly knock each other off their feet. They spin. They howl. They brandish knives. They sing and hug. Sometimes they draw blood. I have seen them fall exhausted to the ground still singing, still hugging. It is a drumming, tricking dance of love and savagery. Half the time the dancers don't know which. Their cloaks fly out. Their flying beards fling sweat. They hurl fistfuls of sand into the air, kick sand into each other's eyes and roar with laughter, roar with rage. Faster and faster they go. Sometimes they go honey slow. They pick up their feet high like wading birds. Their heads are turned aside. They watch each other from the corners of their eyes. So it was with Laban and me. I have told Joseph about it because he is the only son I have who asks. I tell it as a dance his grandfather and I danced for twenty years. Perhaps something like love between us was the drum we danced to. Cunning and guile were the sand we kicked into each other's eyes.

We started dancing the day I heaved the great stone off the well for Rachel. The madness of it was the only way I knew to show her the madness that the sight of her had stirred in me. I would have shown it to her by putting out one eye, or both my eyes, with a charred stick if she had asked me to. For days afterward I suffered in my back, my gut, my thighs. Speaking our tongue easily but with something of the shepherds' soft, slurred way, she asked me why I had wept when I kissed her. I told her it was her beauty made me weep. I told her there was ugliness inside me and that was why I had to touch her beauty with my mouth. I asked her why she had wept. She said it was for the pain inside me. All this was while the shepherds gawked at us, while with her willow branch she flicked the rams about the eyes to make them give room at the trough for the ewes. She brought my camel water in her leather pail. She swabbed her about the eyes where they were gummed and sore from travel-dust.

She took me home with her. Laban was there as if he'd known I was coming. He covered me with kisses, his sister's son. Our dance began.

He said, "How handsome you are! Of course you will deny it. You are not boastful and foolish like most of the young men who come prancing around. See what a strong young neck you have! A man can be proud of a neck like that. How I adore you for being so modest."

With one of his hands he had grasped the nape of my neck. With his other on Rachel's chin, he tipped her face so I could see it better. Her eyes welled up again.

He said, "She is my second daughter, but she is first in my heart. She is first in everybody's heart. Show me a woman half so beautiful and I will let you wrench my two arms out of their sockets one by one. Was there ever a lovelier name than Rachel? It means ewe. She is my own ewe-lamb. She is my rising moon. She is the sweetness of water that quenches my heart's deep thirst."

His arms stuck out through two slits in his billowing tent of a cloak and his head through another. He wore string upon string of bright blue beads about his neck. He was clean shaven like many in Haran. He was bald in front but, behind, his hair hung down in a braid. His eyes bulged like a man showing you how long he could hold his breath without fainting.

"What is mine is yours, Jacob," he said. "Name it, and you will have it. Abraham was my uncle. Only think of it! You are bone of my bone and flesh of my flesh. Isn't it a wonderful thing? You will live in my house. You will be as a son to me. You will be as a brother to my little ewe. See how beautiful she is when she blushes. I would blush too if I were a girl. It is not often we see a young man with a fine, strong neck like yours. How proud my sister must be to have such a son. Someday you must tell me all about her though not just now. Your father I have never seen. Someday you must tell me all about your father too. He gave many rich gifts for your mother's hand, for my sister Rebekah. I was there when Abraham's servant laid the gifts before us. What price do you suppose a man would pay for a woman like Rachel, whose beauty compared with your mother's is as the sun compared with a smoking lamp?"

He punched me lightly on the arm and then again not so lightly.

"If we can't joke with each other, my darling," he said, "what is the point of living at all?"

It was a month later that we agreed on the price I would pay.

Up until then I helped with Laban's flocks. I put back a tumbled wall. I rolled the roof after rains. I mended Leah's loom.

You would never have guessed that Leah was my timid Rachel's sister. If you said the day was hot, Leah said the day was cold. If you knew a cure for warts, Leah knew a better cure. If you told Leah you had gone out of the house three times in the night to make water, she would tell you it was only two. She had small, pink-rimmed eyes which were so weak that when she wove, she touched the warp with her nose. Laban's wife had died young, and Leah had so long had charge of Rachel that she still told her what to do like a child, and like a child Rachel did it.

When I finished mending the loom, Leah threw herself upon me and clasped me so tight that I almost drowned in the mountainous swell of her breasts. Trying to be Leah's friend for Rachel's sake was not the least of my tasks that first month.

"It is not just that you should work so hard without wages," Laban said one day. He had come up from talking to his gods in the cellar. You could see from his face that whatever they said had pleased him well.

"Is Laban a man to cheat his own sister's son?" he said.

He clapped me so hard across the shoulders that it snapped my neck.

"Tell me the wages I must pay, and I will pay them."

"Pay me Rachel," I said. "Just Rachel is all the wages I ask."

He jumped back as if a snake had fastened its teeth into his heel.

"Just Rachel? Rachel is all you are asking?" he said. "You mean you do not want me to add the shirt off my back for good measure? You do not ask me to part also with my testicles as well?"

With his hands on my shoulders, he held me off at arm's length as if to see better what manner of man he was bargaining with. He cocked his head.

"Jacob, Jacob," he said slowly. His voice was suddenly deep and full of sadness. He gave me a sorrowing smile. "Be serious, Jacob. Do us both a kindness and be serious. Don't try to get the better of an old man just because he has taken you into his heart like a son."

I said, "Five years. I will work for you five years for the hand of your daughter in marriage."

"Five years for a hand with five fingers. At least now you are beginning to talk like a man of good sense. One year for one finger," he said. "Now you are beginning to be serious."

He held his own five fingers out before him as he spoke and waggled them.

"Perhaps you have noticed that my daughter has two hands with five fingers on each," he said without looking up. "Surely you are asking for both of her hands. What is the price of all ten fingers at one year apiece?"

He had all of his fingers waggling in front of him now to study them. He winked at me.

He said, "Ten years you will work for the ten fingers. What could be fairer? Then my chief treasure will be yours. For a young man like you, ten years is like a single day. In return you will receive the treasure of her father's heart for all the days of your life."

He clasped his hands at his chin and beamed at me over them.

"Stop!" he said, breaking in upon himself. "For you I will take off one year. I will make it nine years. Only for my sister's son would I commit such madness."

"Seven years," I said.

Laban was puffing like a bull through his nostrils. His brow was drawn into a black frown. For a moment I thought he was going to raise his clasped hands above his head and bludgeon me. Instead he reached out and patted my cheek.

"Only seven years for ten fingers? For three of her lovely, young fingers you pay nothing at all? But what are three fingers between men who love each other?"

He had both hands on my face now. With the thumb and forefinger of each he pinched my cheeks hard.

"My daughter will be yours at the end of the seventh year," he said. "Why should I complain? At least you have left me my testicles."

I have long since forgotten the seven years, but the wedding at the end of the seventh I cannot forget. For two days the men feasted. Down to the lowliest water-carrier, Laban left no man out. The dung-gatherers were there, the plough-makers, the brick-makers, the winnowers who with their forks tossed grain and chaff into the sky for the wind to sift them, the shepherds and goatherds, the one-legged man Laban sent into the city for bartering because he thought the merchants might be less apt to cheat anyone so pitiable. Laban's sons from an earlier wife were there who lived away from the clay-roofed house and were almost strangers. They were lesser Labans to a man—brick faced, thick necked—except for one named Obal. Obal was slender and soft-mannered as a woman and the butt of his brothers' japeries. Like Rachel's, his chin was cleft.

All manner of races and dances and hand-clapping there were, the whining and mooning of pipes and windy rams' horns, the slap of goatskin drums, the dithering of baked-clay rattles filled with pebbles. There were fires of brush piled sky-high to shatter the night into flickering shards. Beer and date wine poured heavy as winter rain. Whole oxen were turned on spits. Wheat loaves overflowed panniers. Ash cakes kneaded with olive oil jostled honey cakes dusted with cinnamon. Laban was everywhere at once—hugging and punching, beer-breathed, sweat-stained. One night he did a high-stepping, thigh-slapping dance next to naked in front of one of the fires with his dugs heaving while overhead the god Sin hid half his pitted face for shame or envy.

The women in the meanwhile had prepared the bridal tent. They lined it with deep carpeting and strewed it with cedar boughs and sprays of minty hyssop around the walls. Garlands of cyclamen and white pimpernel hung at the door. Inside they scattered caper berries about the bed for fruitfulness and a basket of figs. They spread the forked roots of mandrakes under the cushions to flame our desire though they might have known that mine, like my love, needed no flaming.

When the time came, it was Laban who fetched the bride from his house where she had been waiting with the women. He led the procession. He had ropes of flowers around his neck. He waved his arms from side to side and swung his hips. He shouted greetings. The night was starless. There were torch-bearers. The pipes wailed in a high-pitched frenzy. The women, who had kept out of sight all during the men's feasting, were so relieved at being allowed to come out at last that many of them spun like tops as they moved. Some of them had tambourines. Children and stray goats ran along beside them.

The bride came last. She rode on a white ass. I had given her a mantle for which I had traded dear—a blue wool mantle stitched with linen—and she wore it over her head to show that no man except her husband would ever cover her. Her half-brothers' wives led the ass by the bridle and waved branches in the air to ward off any evil gods who might have been attracted by the noise. Laban had made a gift to her of a timid little plump-cheeked woman named Zilpah to be her maid, and Zilpah too was among the branch-wavers.

I waited in the dark bridal tent alone. I was naked except for a shift.

I was half blind with desire as well as with wine. Like one of the torches, my flesh was on fire. When they brought her in to me, all night I burned like a flame with the bride whom my eyes could not see through the darkness.

Early the next day I searched out Laban. He was waiting by the sheepfold. He knew I would be coming. There was a flat rock that we used for slaughtering, and he was sitting on it like a man waiting to be slaughtered. He held his head in his hands. He had a knife in his belt. When he saw me coming, he took it from his belt and held it out to me.

"Take the knife. Kill me," he said. "I deserve no less. I will kill myself if you don't want my blood on your hands. I have been hoping you would come and do me this kindness."

Tears ran down his cheeks.

"What have you done to me?" I said.

"Jacob, I didn't do it. I did it, yes, but I could not help myself. I did it for my daughter. I did it for Leah, my oldest daughter. I did it to honor the ways of our fathers before us. Here," he said, pulling his cloak apart and baring the hairs on his chest. "Strike me on this spot. I will not even cry out. I will bite my off tongue to keep from offending your ears with the cry of my pain."

"You made me a promise before the Fear," I said.

"Not before the Fear," Laban said. He held up one finger. "I don't say that excuses what I did, but perhaps it is worth mentioning. Whatever else I may be, I am not a blasphemer. We didn't swear on each other's seed. I didn't call on any of the gods. I am not deaf, darling. I would have heard my own voice if I had called on one."

"Seven years of my life I served you for Rachel," I said.

"I said I would give you my daughter in return," Laban said. "Did I say which daughter? I am only asking, Jacob. Did I speak the name of the daughter I promised?"

"I spoke it," I said. "My eyes spoke it. Everything you knew about me spoke it and everything I knew about myself. For seven years you have known which of your daughters was my heart's desire whether you spoke her name to me when you made me the promise or not."

"Of course you are right. Anyone could see which of my daughters was your heart's desire," he said, "but you did not name her. I mention it only because in matters like this the judges of Haran set great store by the actual words that were spoken or not spoken. I myself set no store by them at all."

He thumped his bare chest with the pommel of his knife.

"Please take it," he said, holding the knife out to me again. "Only, I beg of you, get it over with as quickly as you can although you have every right to make me suffer as long as you want."

He shifted from one buttock to another on the rock. He brushed his tears away with the back of his hand.

"I trusted you, Laban," I said.

I had trusted my nakedness. I had trusted her nakedness. Surely my flesh should have told me whose flesh I was grasping. Surely her flesh should have told me. But our flesh was as dumb as the clay that the Fear fashioned it from on the day when he slew the great dragon and fashioned all things. Together we wrestled and tossed in the dark tent with the scent of the hyssop and the cedar in our nostrils. The power of the wine thrashed in my head like the wings of a bird. We crushed the caper berries with our bodies. We sent the mandrake roots spinning.

Outside, the goatskin drums kept at it far into the night. Faster and wilder they went. Faster and wilder we went. I swam her like the fierce white billows of the sea. Together we braved the swells. Together, in each other's arms, we drowned only to wake in each other's arms and drown again. And when dawn came ruddy through the walls of the tent, we awoke in each other's arms and my eyes beheld at last the woman I had drowned with.

I saw the sleepy, pink-rimmed eyes. I saw Leah. With her tongue she touched the tip of my nose. As I drew my arm out from under her, one of her breasts came at me with a blue snout. She pressed the heel of her hand against her mouth to stifle her laughter. She ogled me through the fingers.

I buried my face in the hot pit of her throat and wept.

"I betrayed you, Jacob," Laban said, "but only because I had no choice. Does a man give the younger daughter in marriage before the elder? It has never been so, darling. But you are going to see how I will make everything up to you. I will give you the younger as well as the elder although I am an old man now with few comforts left and it breaks my heart even to think of parting with her."

His tears began to run again even though he had already started to smile and wink. He placed the knife back in his belt. There were some loose pebbles on the rock near him, and he picked up a handful.

"After this unspeakable thing I have done, I will not ask

you ten years for Rachel." He lined up seven pebbles on one broad knee as he spoke and threw the rest away. "I will ask only seven."

He dabbed at his eyes.

"She is the red rose of my heart, Jacob," he said. "I will have nobody left when you take her."

The tears in his bulging, bloodshot eyes were real tears, and as he looked up at me through them from the rock like a sheep awaiting the knife, for a moment I felt almost as sorry for him as he felt for himself.

12

A Storm of Children

To the last moment Rachel expected to be the bride. To the last moment Leah expected to be shamed by Rachel's being the bride. I believe Laban astonished even himself. He was a cunning man and one to be watched out for as my mother said the last time in my life I ever saw her. But even the most cunning are not cunning every hour of the day.

I believe Laban truly hated losing Rachel, his favorite. I believe he dreaded to think of Leah's attacking him all the days of his life for having married off Rachel before her. I believe he had been scheming for months how he might be able to get some more years' work out of me. I think that as he went swaggering back from the feast to his house where the women were waiting for him, these thoughts simply all came together in his wine-fogged mind at once. Bursting in upon his daughters with a torch in one hand and the blue mantle with linen stitching in the other, he threw the mantle over Leah's head instead of her sister's. The moment before, he hadn't planned to do it. When the moment came, he did it. When he woke up the next morning, I believe he was as dumbfounded as everybody else by what he had done.

I was the one who was cunning. For the seven years that I slept with Leah and dreamed of Rachel, every time I took pleasure in her voluminous embrace, I withdrew myself just in time to avoid getting her with child. It is not the easiest thing in the world for a man to manage, but with only an occasional lapse I managed it and was richly rewarded for my effort because as the result I was able to work a threefold revenge.

First, Leah wanted children to complete her victory over Rachel, and thus I revenged myself on her for her small-mindedness as well as for not being the sister I loved. In her innocence she did not understand what I was up to but believed that all men withdrew themselves as I did and that her childlessness came about because she was barren.

Second, Laban wanted more heirs to carry on his name the way he wanted more flocks and servants, more feasts, more gods, more everything, and thus I also revenged myself on him for the way he had made me the butt of a thousand jokes not to mention also for the way he had caused Rachel seven years' suffering at the thought of me lying in Leah's arms. Little did he know.

But third and last, it was my revenge upon the Fear that was sweetest.

From my father I had the Fear's blessing, and it had become a curse. From Esau I had the Fear's promise to make me the father of a great people, and it had sent me fleeing for my life. In the terrible light of the Fear's beauty, I had seen my own ugliness, but the Fear himself I did not see because he did not choose to let me see him. The ravaged face of Sin is in the night sky for any dung-footed shepherd to gape at. The men of Gerar paint the gnarled and smoking snout of their Fish on walls and carve it in wood for all the world to see. But not even the keenest eye can pick out the distant shimmer of the Fear's promises. You cannot parade him through the streets in his golden house as they do their gods in the Black Land. You can go blind searching the night for the sight of him. You can go deaf straining to catch just the echo of his footfall through the burning emptiness of day. It was to spite him for this that I withheld my seed from Leah's womb.

In my dream of the stone stair he had promised me children thick as dust for the world's sake. I would deny the luckless world those children. One day I watched ants at work, marveling how they could not see my face watching them, and I thought of the Fear's great face, unseen in the sky above me, running with the tears I had caused him.

Then after seven years, for the second time I awoke in the bridal tent, only this time with my beloved asleep in my arms. I could see us in the polished copper they had hung from the ridge pole over us. She was a girl still. Her flesh was lily pale and fragrant. Her hair was a dark tangle at her throat and cheeks. I had become a bird. My eyes were a bird's eyes, furtive and glittering. My nose was a curved and narrow beak shadowing the wry scar of my mouth. I was beardless except for the shaved blue sheen of my bony jaw. The fingers of one of my hands were splayed like talons on her breast. My other arm was thrown across her belly like a dark wing. My seed was in her belly.

My seed was in her belly, but her belly proved to be barren. Terrible are the ways of the Fear and more cunning even than mine. The bitterness of Leah at having no children became now barren Rachel's bitterness and mine. It was the Fear's revenge.

My seed was in my power, but the power of my seed to stir life was in his. Months went by without Rachel's conceiving. By rights I should have spent one night with her and the next night with her sister, but instead I spent six nights out of every seven with Rachel and only the one with Leah. It was not only that Rachel was the one I loved, but I did not want to waste my seed on anyone else. Leah was enraged. She spat on the ground whenever Rachel showed her face. On the one night out of seven when I came to her, she kept me awake for hours either railing at me for my neglect or trying to win me from her sister by various desperate wiles. She anointed herself with sweet-smelling oils. Clad only in a child's shift, she danced for me with her breasts swinging heavily from side to side or sang songs of passion to me in a quavering, high voice which she hoped would enflame me. She disposed her milky limbs in various grotesque ways which she hoped would add zest to our coupling. She painted around her pink-rimmed eyes to make them look larger. By custom she had the right to take a sheep or a goat from my flocks for every night that was rightfully hers which I spent with Rachel, and she took them. She gave the beasts to Laban, thinking that would be an added sting to my punishment, but then from time to time she would be overcome with remorse and infuriate her father by taking them back again so she could return them to me as a token of her slavish devotion.

We were all of us at odds with each other. Rachel grew
thinner and thinner thinking that she was barren and that
her sister hated her. Leah in her humiliation grew fatter and
fatter, stuffing herself with food to make up for all the ways
she charged me with starving her. Perhaps she did it as well
to make people think—perhaps also to make herself think—
that the reason her belly was so fat was that at last she had a
child inside it. Laban was angry with all three of us for giving
him no grandchildren and with me in particular both because Leah kept returning to me the beasts that were rightfully his as forfeit and because in his heart he felt so guilty for
having cheated me of seven years that the very sight of me
was jarring and distasteful. He was happiest when everybody
was hugging everybody else and calling each other darling.
When he called me darling, it was as a reproach. His mouth
went slack when he said it. His eyes went crooked.

"Maybe there is something wrong with you, darling," he
said one day. "Two healthy young wives and not a single child
to show from either of them. Maybe there is something
wrong with your manhood the way they say there is something wrong with my son Obal's. Or maybe you have angered Sin or the Fear or some other god. Gods can be quick
to take offense, may every last one of their names be praised.
I would think things over very carefully if I were you and
see if there is anything you can do to make it up to them. A
little gift of some kind is never out of place."

Laban knew there was nothing wrong with my manhood.
He must have heard sounds in the night to reassure him of
that. His reference to Obal was just a way of taunting me—
poor Obal, who blushed as easily as a girl and ran with his

knees together and his arms flopping out at the sides. But what Laban said about angering the gods gave me pause.

Maybe the Fear had laid his curse on Rachel's womb because out of spite I withheld my seed from Leah. Maybe the gift he wanted from me was not a gift for himself but the gift of a child for Leah, whom I had for so long mistreated. I thought of all the ways she had tried to please me and of her bitterness. I thought of all the times I had leapt free of her billowing thighs like a man stung by an adder just in time to spill myself elsewhere. If I did right by Leah, I thought, then maybe the Fear would do right by my beloved and open her womb.

On the very day Laban spoke to me, I went up to the roof when darkness fell and spoke to the Fear. Only an ashen sliver of Sin's face was to be seen. It was like the face of a man listening at the slit of a tent. I bared my chest and drummed upon it with my fists. I touched my forehead to the roof's rolled clay.

"I have been spiteful and cruel to my wife Leah," I said. "Her only fault is not to be beautiful, not to be Rachel, yet for that I have hurt her grievously. I have tried to hurt you grievously as well though you visited me with a holy dream when I was fleeing Esau's rage on a black camel. I have spat in your face though you brought tears to my eyes with your mercy when it was you who should have spat in my face. Now you are punishing me. I cannot blame you. Rachel is wasting away for want of a child. Her grief is a torment to me because it is I who have brought it upon her. O punish me any other way. Strike me with blindness like my father. Let me die in a strange land among strangers. But for her sake, open the womb of my beloved."

Somewhere off in the dark hills I could hear a shepherd calling. It is the loneliest of all lonely sounds. You call though there is no one to answer you and because you are lonely. The dark is only the dark until you call into it, and then your call makes the dark the answer to your call. Then you are lonelier still.

"If you will open the womb of Rachel, I will no longer withhold my seed from Leah," I said. "I will be a true husband to her if only you will cause the heart of my beloved to rejoice by giving her a son. This very night I will fill Leah with my seed if only you will remember your promise to make me the father of a great people, I who am now the father of no one at all."

I would have spoken longer except that suddenly I started hearing my voice as the skreek of a crow squabbling for carrion. The way I was speaking to the Fear, I could have been bargaining with Laban, and I was filled with shame. I stopped speaking. I listened to the silence.

If there was a stone stair, I could not see it. There were no lights going up, no lights going down. There was only the glimmer of Sin's ailing face. I reached my arms up into the darkness. Then I went down to where Leah lay and that very night, with loneliness in my heart, begot her first son.

Leah called his name Reuben which means See, a Son! Rachel was the one she particularly wanted to have see him. She wanted Rachel to see the boy and to see also that it was to her, Leah, that the Fear had given the boy. She wanted her to see that it was she, Leah, who was the fruitful wife while Rachel remained barren as stone. Her next son she called Simeon, because Simeon means Hear, or so she said, and the Fear had finally heard how long her husband had hated and neglected her and that was why he had taken pity on her at last. Levi she named Levi or Joined because the birth of yet another son was sure to join me to Leah in a bond too strong for Rachel or anyone else to break. Judah became Judah, Praise, because the Fear was to be endlessly praised for raising her high over the heads of her enemies.

The names were like so many arrows shot into Rachel's tender flesh, and Laban as well as I thought that she would die. He was always bringing her medicines that he had bartered from the merchants of such things in Haran, or burning foul-smelling herbs under her nose, or spending hours in the cellar pleading with his gods for her health. She almost never spoke, and when she did, it was with great bitterness. She ate little or nothing. She made me couple with her every night we were together, but there was no love in it, only desperation. The yammering of Leah's four small boys were as music to her ears compared with the song of triumph that was in every word Leah spoke.

Rachel told me at last that I must have a child by Bilhah. Bilhah was the maid Laban had given her at the time of our marriage the way he had given Zilpah to Leah seven years earlier. Bilhah was close to a head taller than I was. She had large hands and feet. She had eyes that swelled in their sockets beneath the sweeping brows of an owl. Her hair was red, and she wore it, like many of the women of Haran, combed tightly into a band on top of her head where it sprang out of the band like plumage. Her hair made her even taller still. I had no desire for this towering woman whose eyes and brows gave her the look of perpetual outrage, but for Rachel's sake I did as she asked me. A child born of Bilhah would become Rachel's child, and Bilhah's fruitfulness, if indeed she proved fruitful, would also become Rachel's, or so all the women believed. Laban believed it. He spent much time in his cellar cajoling the most ancient of his gods down there, the bald and beardless one who held his member out before him in both hands and had only a crack in the stone for his mouth. He rubbed the god with oil. He hung him with foul-smelling pouches of dried meat. He said that when and if Bilhah bore me a child, the child should be born into Rachel's lap because that way the fluids and vapors of fruitfulness would flow from Bilhah's fertile womb into Rachel's empty one.

In time Bilhah had the child—a boy, red-headed like his mother, whom Rachel named Dan—and the women who were present at the birth said that as he slowly emerged from between his mother's thighs, he seemed to be trying to make his way in between Rachel's. This was seen as an excellent omen, but it did not prove so. Rachel remained childless, and when at her urging Bilhah bore me yet another son—Naphtali, who grew to be the handsomest of the twelve and also the dullest—she remained so still.

There is no telling the wretchedness and turmoil of those child-begetting years. Rachel and Leah despised each other more and more. Rachel was jealous of Bilhah. Bilhah cast dark looks at Rachel for treating Dan and Naphtali as her own. Rachel, in turn, would hardly let Bilhah near them. Almost as tall as a tree herself, the poor woman would hide behind a tree, her lofty topknot trembling with sorrow, and watch Rachel play with them.

To make matters worse, after the birth of her fourth son, Judah, Leah could no longer conceive, and so, following her sister's example, she would give me no peace until I agreed to lie with her maid Zilpah. Zilpah was a plump little mole-rat

of a woman who gave a startled cry if you so much as glanced
her way, so that the only way I was able to beget a child of
her was to make her drunk first. Pot after pot of beer I all
but poured into her frightened mouth until in the end I am
not sure she even knew that she was lying with a man. I was
afraid that when her child was born, the beer would turn out
to have made him soft in the head, but that was not so. Gad
was what we called him, and far from being soft-headed, he
grew up to be as bold as his mother was bashful, a shrewd
and cold-blooded raider and thief of his neighbors' sheep.
The second son Zilpah bore me we called Asher, who even
as a child was as fat as his grandfather Laban. Both these boys
were born on Leah's lap as Bilhah's were born on Rachel's,
and this time the magic was successful because Leah bore
me not only two more sons—gentle Issachar and Zebulun
the sea-farer—but also my only daughter, Dinah, whose
beauty was to cost many brave men their lives.

In all I had ten sons and one daughter by Leah and the two
maids. Even with the building of several new rooms, Laban's
house was as crowded as a sheepfold. The children were
everywhere. They were into everything. One by one they
learned to crawl and walk. They learned to talk after a fashion
as well as to scream and to make your ears ring with their
shrill laughter. They learned to poke and pinch and slap. Before they learned to take care of their needs outside, the
house stank worse than the narrow, sun-baked streets of
Haran with their little mounds and puddles. They shattered
the nights with their wails. I had begotten them all, but there
had been no tenderness, no joy, in their begetting. Zilpah and
Bilhah were strangers to me. Leah, once she established victory over her sister, became a kind of overpowering friend

though she was so caught up with her children that we had little time for friendship, and when there was time, I had to be careful that Rachel did not see us together. Rachel's beauty returned with the birth of Dan and Naphtali, but she gave as much of herself to them as though they had been truly hers, and we were seldom alone together.

I was like a man caught out in a storm with the wind squalling, the sand flailing me across the eyes, the chilled rain pelting me. The children were the storm, I thought, until one day, right in the thick of it, I saw the truth of what the children were.

One boy was pounding another boy's head against the hard-packed floor. Another was drowsing at his mother's teat. Three of them were trying to shove a fourth into a basket. Dinah was fitting her foot into her mouth. The air was foul with the smell of them.

They were the Fear's promise. That is what I suddenly saw the children were. I had forgotten it. They were the dust that would cover the earth. The great people would spring from their scrawny loins. Kicking and howling and crowing and pissing and slobbering food all over their faces, they were the world's best luck.

I started to weep. Just a trickle at first, the tears hot on my cheeks, salty at the corners of my mouth. Then it was as if I couldn't catch my breath for weeping. Laban came over and pounded me between the shoulders. He thought I was choking to death. Rachel took my head in her arms. Leah held my feet. It was as close as the two sisters had come to each other for years.

A deep hush fell over the children. They stopped whatever they were doing. Their eyes grew round in their heads.

"You are so—so noisy," I choked out at them.

They were the Fear's promise to Abraham, and I had forgotten it.

It was with Abraham's ancient eyes that they were watching me.

"You are—so hopeless,"I said. "So important."

Their silence, as they listened to my sobs, was Abraham's silence as he waited all those years for the Fear to keep his promise.

A month or so later, my firstborn son Reuben of all people was the one who saved the day for us, the same Reuben who when he grew to manhood lay with Bilhah not because he had any more desire for that chill-fleshed, red-haired woman than I had but because he hoped that by taking the mother of two of my sons he would also take my place. But at the time I speak of he was only a beardless, bird-voiced boy.

One morning he found some mandrakes in a field and showed them to his mother, Leah. When Rachel heard of it, she swallowed her pride and asked Leah for them. Leah refused at first.

"For years you have tried to take my husband from me," Leah said. "Now you want to take my mandrakes from me as well to rekindle his fire."

But then Leah relented. She had borne me six sons and one daughter. Rachel had borne me nothing. Maybe in some corner of her heart she pitied Rachel, pitied me even. Or maybe it was because Rachel promised that in return for the mandrakes she would persuade me to spend more nights each week with Leah. In any case, she gave Rachel the mandrakes Reuben had found. Rachel made me a brew of them, and I drank it down gagging on its bitterness.

Rachel's womb was opened at last, and when she gave birth to my son Joseph, I told her it was Reuben and his mandrakes that she had to thank. Still exhausted from her labor, she reached out and placed her hand across my lips. "No," she said. "No, no, my dear."

They had laid the child at her breast though it was still too weak to drink from her. Her cheek was grazing his round, bald head. His head looked too big for him, as though already it was full of dreams.

"I thought he had forgotten me, but he remembered me," she said. "At last he remembered Rachel."

Like my mother, she rarely if ever named his name, but I knew the one she was thanking without naming him.

13

THE END OF THE DANCE

MAYBE IT IS TRUE that the Fear remembered
Rachel. How could even a god forget her?
Or maybe it was the mandrakes.

Or maybe the mandrakes were the Fear's way of remembering her. For all I know, it was the Fear who led Reuben to the place where they were growing. He was a scattered, wild-eyed child. It is hard to imagine his finding them by himself or even knowing or caring what they were if he found them.

Who knows about the mandrake magic of the earth, the hidden roots of things? Who knows what makes leaves stir when there is no air to stir them, makes the calf seek the udder before it knows there are udders, makes the Two Stones rattle out the secrets of yesterday and tomorrow? Who can say what causes women to bleed and the members of men to rise unbidden or, full of shame and sadness, to fall unbidden? Who knows about dreams? In dreams the living and the dead meet and talk like wanderers in the night. Stone stairs slant up into the dark to draw down light from the very well of light and send it tumbling earthward like a cataract over the stairs, then draw it skyward again together with the light-filled hearts of men.

Who knows about the Fear? Abraham was his friend, but not even Abraham knew where to find him when he needed him. All through the years of Sarah's barrenness, I picture the old man with his crimson beard tramping the scrubby planes with his flocks and his women. I see him searching the sky with scorched eyes for some sign that the promise has not been forgotten.

The Fear came to him at last. He came to him through the bird-faced strangers who foretold the birth of Laughter. He came to him through the gold-eyed ram to knife and burn in Laughter's place. But did such gifts as those make up to him for all the years of giftless searching? A gift can come too late. Did Abraham die a man at peace?

As far as I have heard, he never said. They buried him with the secret still untold in the cave of Machpelah, in the field of Ephron. I have seen that cave and the stones they heaped over him in it. It was there that Esau and I buried Laughter. It is there where they will doubtless bury me though I would rather lie near my beloved on the way to Ephrath.

Abraham flattens under the stones in the cave, his jaws sprung. The wells of my father's eyes have long since gone dry. Esau sobbed over his spade as we covered him. He tucked an ashcake under each of Laughter's cold, braceleted arms. He said, "You'll get so hungry, *hungry* there!" What will they tuck under my arms? The lock of my beloved's hair that for years I've worn strung in a goatskin pouch around my neck? It is of small matter. I will have only bandaged fingers by then to pluck it out with, only waxed lips to press it to. I have seen how they prepare the bodies of the dead in the Black Land. Bats will hang like withered fruit from the cave's roof. All I ever was will be undone and dead.

It was thoughts of death that drove me from Laban's. I had grown rich at Haran. My flocks already outnumbered Laban's flocks. I had more sons than he had sons. I had more wives, more honor. Each year I grew richer. The merchants of Haran came out from behind their heaped stalls to duck their heads to me. The gelded priests of Sin raised their plucked brows to see me pass. It was a scandal to them that though I did not feed burned beasts to the moon, I fattened like the moon. I waxed there at Laban's, but through death's eyes I saw also how life is always on the wane.

Before the light of me went out for good, I wanted to go home. I wanted to see again the land that Light's voice had promised me from the stone stair. I wanted to be known there for the promise he had promised to the world. So I went to Laban.

He had a ewe between his knees. Her woolly flanks were quivering with terror. With one hand he held her head wrenched back. With the other he was working to pluck out piece by piece a blood-bloated beetle all but buried in her throat. Her eyes were white and rolling.

"The time has come to give me my wives and children, Uncle," I said. "The gods well know I've paid for them, slaving for you fourteen years and then some, but it's the way of things to ask your leave, so I'm asking it. Give me my leave, Laban. I'm going home."

Laban had stopped picking at the beetle as soon as I started talking. He held the ewe in both arms now, hugging her. He pressed his nose into her deep curls as if she was yet another loved one I was threatening to rob him of. He looked up at me with moist eyes.

"I was a boy when I came," I said, "on the day when I almost broke my back heaving the stone off the well, the day when Rachel watered my black camel. I'm not a boy any more. I've become a bird. I've grown a vulture's talons tramping your fields for you. My nose is a beak from pecking and pulling your weeds. Who knows what welcome I'll find when I get home? Who knows who is still alive to welcome me if any of them are still alive? But home is where I mean to fly to, Laban, and I mean to take my hens and nestlings with me."

Laban gave the ewe one final hug and let her go. She leapt away from him, shaking her head and bleating. Still sitting, he stretched out both his arms toward me.

"You a vulture, darling?" he said. "A bird of prey, taking what doesn't belong to you? An offense to the eyes of all decent people?"

He shook his head from side to side, laughing with disbelief.

"You are too handsome for a vulture. You are an honest man who always wants to do things the way it is fitting to do them. Everyone adores you, especially the women. It is no wonder. I adore you myself."

"I want to leave before the rains," I said. "I am a bird, not a fish. You will perhaps want to give me gifts to take to your sister, my mother, whom you haven't seen for so many years."

Laban held up one hand to silence me.

"More than anyone else adores you, the Fear adores you," he said. "Don't think I haven't noticed. How could anyone not notice the way he has prospered you? Eleven fine sons and a daughter of rare beauty. Flocks that fatten and breed like locusts while other men's pule and dwindle. Of his mercy, the Fear has prospered me also because of you. I have spoken to the other gods about it, and they all agree it has been the Fear's doing. Stay with me just a little while longer, darling, and we will both be the richer for it. Name any wage you want."

I think what made me listen to him at all instead of just leaving then and there, with or without his leave, was the sheer sport of it. Any wage I wanted. I knew full well that he intended it to be any wage he wanted. I had seen him play at dice or squares or ring-the-rod that way. *You choose. You go first. We use your rules. Any way you like, darling*—all of this with his arm around your shoulders, crushing you to him, or patting your cheek with his big hand, or holding you off at arm's length, his face aflame with admiration and encouragement. And then of course you lost your heifer to him, or your wool shirt, or fourteen years of your precious youth. He sat there now among his baggy ewes and boulder-ballocked rams, that impossible and irresistible man. I could not resist him.

"How about this then?" I said. "How about letting me pass through your flocks this very day and take all the speckled and spotted sheep and goats for myself?" I knew there were more than a few of them and Laban knew it too. I said,

"Maybe you will throw in all the black lambs too for good measure, because I am so dear to your heart. That is a wage that might tempt me to nursemaid your beasts for another year or so."

"It is no wonder the gods all adore you. They have told me so themselves in the cellar where they tell me things," Laban said.

There was a flickering about his eyes that could have been a wink. The muscles of his jaw tightened. I could see that many matters were stirring beneath the surface of his face the way water stirs when it is about to boil. He heaved himself to his feet.

"Done!" he cried. "Done!" His face was radiant now as the setting sun.

I never dreamed that he would accept such an offer, nor did I dream how he would turn it to his advantage. It was Obal who told me, shy Obal, looking up at me through his lashes as he spoke. The way Laban turned it to his advantage was this.

Before the flocks returned to the fold on the day I was to cull them, Laban managed to get to them first. He rounded up as many herdsmen as he could lay his hands on, wherever he could find them keeping watch with their sleep-starved eyes. Together with them he scampered up and down the stubbled hills with his cloak tucked up to his thighs and the braid of his hair flying. He sweated. He gasped. He shouted instructions to the herders, threats and endearments to the beasts. Obal's chin trembled with laughter. The tale as he told it brought tears to his lovely eyes.

As many speckled and black beasts as they stumbled on they did their best to draw off into a freakish flock by itself

with one ancient, lop-eared ram, pied as a lizard, for bell-
wether. They scrambled after strays. They coaxed and prod-
ded jet weanlings from their creamy dams. Swooping down
on one of them, Laban slipped on a shoulder of rock and
went sprawling. It left him with a red knob on the end of
his nose and a thumb bent backward that he couldn't
straighten. His roars sent skittering a dozen or more of them
to be caught and corralled again a second time. It took them
hours.

They didn't get all the dark and spotted ones, but by dusk
they had a great many of them. Then Laban sent them off
with the old ram and a pair of herdsmen to lead them on a
three days' journey to where his sons lived. Laban's sons
lived among the olive groves and bee swarms beyond the
tall east gate of Haran. It is there that stone-bearded Sin,
keeper of time, stands watch with his wife Ningal and wears
chiseled on his apron the task he was given when the world
was new: *At the month's beginning to shine on earth thou shalt
show two horns to mark the six days, on the seventh day di-
vide the crown in two, on the fourteenth day turn thy full face.*

When Laban came staggering back to his house at nightfall more dead then alive, the face he turned full on me was
pale as Sin's except for the red knob. But it was flashing triumph. He well knew that the bleating wages which I had
found in the fold at watering time were scarcely enough to
fill the room where we stood. He beamed at me innocent as
a rosy-footed dove.

"Were they less than you thought, darling?" he said. He
kissed my mouth. "No matter, no matter. Maybe the Fear
forgot to prosper you for once. Sometimes the gods are ab-
sent-minded. Perhaps I'll give you other cullings as time

goes by. I want you to have all the brindled ones you can find. I want you to be happy because then I am happy too. If we cannot live in happiness, my heart's delight, why bother to live at all?"

It was weeks before his bent thumb was straight again. He had Zilpah give it a tug to snap it back into the socket and let fly such a yelp as she did it that it made her gasp with terror.

Rachel taught me the magic I finally got the better of him by. Like begets like, she said. Crouch and glower like the crouched gray rain clouds glowering over the hills, and rain comes. Make a clay doll in the likeness of your enemy, then break it, and your enemy breaks. Slip a drop of your blood into the cup of the one your heart desires, and her heart will come to desire you.

"Dearest, you must take fresh-cut poplar rods," she said. "Take some of almond and some of plane too because they are lucky."

Leah would as soon have swallowed fire as call me dearest the way Rachel did although in her rough-tongued way she was my friend by then. Husband she called me, or Jacob. Sometimes she called me Heels because I had told her of Esau and how I had snatched at his heels as he led our way out of the stillness of Rebekah's belly into the noisy world. I did not speak often of Esau even to myself, but I spoke of him to Leah. Perhaps it was because I had wronged her for many years the way I had also wronged him.

"Peel the rods," Rachel said. "Do not peel them all the way. Just part of the way."

She had brought an almond rod to show me.

"Like this," she said.

Her lashes were no longer than Obal's, but her eyes were shyer and softer. With her thumbnail she loosened a bit of bark and peeled it enough to show the glistening white almond flesh beneath. Below that she peeled another bit and then another, first on one side of the rod and then the other side. Streaked dark and light the rod was, like sheep streaked dark and light, like a brindled goat.

"Make more like this. I'll help you. I'll do them all if you want. Then stick them in the ground by the watering troughs."

She blushed. She lowered her soft glance to the ground. She said, "You know what beasts do at the watering troughs. While they are doing it, their eyes will be on the rods."

I took her chin in my hand and tipped her face to me. I kissed her lowered lids.

"I know what beasts do," I said.

I kissed her just above where her breasts began. They were still the cool, pert breasts of a girl though it wasn't long since she had weaned Joseph. While the ewes nibbled sweet water, the rams mounted them. The eyes of the rams were cool slits and furious. The ewes seemed always more lost in the water's mystery than in the mystery of what the rams were doing.

"Then you will see what you will see," she said.

I saw.

Year after year for six years the striped rods worked their striped magic. The brindled beasts grew almost to outnumber the one-colored brown, black, white ones. I separated them out and penned them apart before Laban could get to them. At each lambing I scratched their new number on the lintel of Laban's house where he could see the number, and I could see him see it, and he could see me seeing him. Each evening I counted them. I had Reuben keep watch over them at night when I was elsewhere.

It was on one of those nights that I made an enemy of my son Reuben. I found him sitting with his shirt pulled up over his belly milking himself into the dark. I struck him across one cheek with the full strength of my hand and then across the other cheek. I told him his seed was Abraham's seed. I told him every drop of it was to be treasured like the richest treasure so when the time came he could sow sons to the world's saving. I made no mention of the seed that over many years I had spilled for spite on Leah's thighs. Reuben wept with shame and anger, covering his nakedness. From that day on, I think, he hated me.

Simeon and Levi I set to watch as well once they were old enough to tell goat and sheep from shadows. The goats and sheep multiplied under our watching, everything did. The shadows multiplied.

So it was that we danced our dance, Laban and I. He circled me, I circled him. We kicked sand into each other's faces, all the while singing. We clapped palm to palm and clasped and hugged. We scuttled apart like rats in a granary only to come together again slow and high-stepping as herons. We brandished like knives the stealth there was between us and the stealthy love, if you could call whatever else there was between us love. Laban loved to call it love. Perhaps it was.

Seven years I danced for what turned out to be Leah. Seven years more I danced for my beloved. Add six to that for the years I danced growing rich to the scattered music of flocks, of shepherds' piping, the jangle of bracelets and ankle rings. I danced to the soughing of wind through the tall grain, to the shouting of my dark-eyed, lean-limbed sons—except for fat Asher—growing tall.

The brindled beasts were my wealth to start with, but wealth begets wealth as like does like. I bartered the beasts for slaves and servants. When times are lean, men barter their sons to keep from starving and to keep their sons from starving. Daughters and wives they will barter too and even themselves if it comes to that. In time my slaves begot more slaves for me. Some of them were from Haran. Others were from foreign peoples taken in skirmish, leather-skinned hunting and raiding men, naked, with shaved heads and magic patterns pricked out on their cheeks, their women kept muffled with their quick, frightened eyes and heavy breasts.

Once I had slaves and servants to work the ground, I worked more ground, grew more wheat, more millet. I took it on camelback in sacks into the stench of the great city to barter it there for vessels of hammered and welded copper, for rich cloths, for honey. I decked my two wives with gold, with silver—nose rings and earrings, necklaces that tinkled their coming when they moved about among the trees, among the children, Leah heavy-footed and loud as her father, Rachel pattering light as rain.

I bartered also for gods, wood gods carved and painted in the likeness of creatures to be met only in dreams, gods of baked clay, of plaited straw and feathers. One was a silver god. He stood tall as my knee with an owl's body and a face more human than a human face. His silver eyes were closed. His silver lips were parted in a whisper I could never hear. He held out one seven-fingered hand, palm up and fingers cupped to take the gifts I gave him. Sometimes all I gave him was my hand in his. His silver hand was cool even in the summer heat. When I held it, it was like when the air stands still at evening and the birds stand still and you stand still inside your own cool skin. He had no name I knew. When our hands were clasped like that, I also had no name I knew.

I also built myself a house. The roof was brushwood overlaid with clay like Laban's, the walls of mortared brick, but it was larger than Laban's and built around a court. There was a spring-fed pool in the court. By the pool there was a stone bench. You could sit there in the darkness and watch Sin sail the sky. The women sometimes did their weaving there. Inside, the servants kept the floor strewn with fresh rushes. In the room where my sons slept, the windows were barred. There are thieves of sons as there are thieves of tombs and treasure. If my sons took a mind to go thieving themselves, or scavenging for women when that time came, their only unbarred way led past my door. Dinah slept in a room with Zilpah and Bilhah and the other maids. Her hair was reddish like the hair of Esau, her uncle, but with more of gold in it. Her eyes were blue as they say Abraham's were. She was too young then to have a secret, but deep in her blue eyes you could see where she would keep it when she found one worth keeping. I would never have guessed then the terrible one she finally found.

Finally, at the end of the last six years, I left. It was Laban himself who brought me to it. He could endure my being more rich than he was—more sons, more flocks, a bigger house—but he could not endure my being more cunning. He could not endure having all Haran see I was more cunning

as my brindled flocks continued to grow. So he started pouring poison into the ears of all who would listen to him.

He said that I was a thief. That out of the kindness of his
heart he had taken me in when I first appeared like a beggar
at his door, and I had played him false. That I had stolen his
flocks. That I had cheated him of his daughters. He remained as lavish as always with his embraces and honeyed
words, but the words of the ones he poisoned against me
were not honeyed. There were children who threw stones at
my children and told them that the demon Resheph had
come to dwell in me and work his ways through my wicked-
ness. There were men who bit their thumbs at me when I
passed. There were rumors that Laban's sons were plotting
a raid to recover the flocks they believed should rightly be
theirs.

I have already told how I waited till Laban was off at a
shearing one day to make my escape. My wives and my children, my camels, my servants, all the beasts, the baggage, the
tenting—I took everything there was to take. Without my
knowledge, as I have also told earlier, it was Rachel who took
her father's gods. She placed them carefully in a sack and had
it loaded onto her own camel so she would have them near
her whenever she might need them. She was afraid of the
dangers we might run into on our journey and believed that
Laban's gods might help the Fear shield us against them.
She was afraid of the danger that awaited us at the end of our
journey when at long last I came face to face again with Esau.
I had not told her all there was to tell about how I had used
him, but I had told her enough. She read the fear in my face,
and it frightened her. I told her that surely twenty years had

been enough to quench the fire of Esau's rage, but even as I spoke, I wondered if they had only served to fan it.

We had made our slow way across a wide river amidst such a bellowing and caterwauling as could scarcely be believed—men, women, children, beasts, all in an uproar as the tawny waters tumbled around us—and we had already reached the hill country when some days after our departure Laban overtook us. He had his sons with him and all of them armed with spears. He took hold of me by the ears and wagged my head first one way, then the other, in time to his words.

"Tambourines!" he said. "Lyres! Pipes! Drums! What music and dancing we could have had if I'd known you were leaving! What laughter! What feasting! What songs full of sorrow and love! Instead you stole off like a thief in the dark. You carried away my daughters as if they were slaves taken in battle. You robbed me of the chance to kiss the lips of my grandsons in farewell and to throw my arms around the neck of Dinah, my life's jewel. You even made off with my gods, the gods of Bethuel, my father, and of his father, Nahor, before him. Did it cause you no pain to rob me of the very ones to whom I have poured out the secrets of my heart in the cellar where for years I have fed them and honored them? Oh Jacob, how could you do it?"

All of this he said while his sons stood around with their faces set and their eyes narrowed except for Obal, who had slipped away to talk to Issachar. Issachar was Obal's favorite among my children and also the gentlest among them although when the time came he was not gentle with his brother Joseph. Laban's face shook with anger as he spoke. He let go of my ears in order to shake his fist in the air.

I told him that he was welcome to search for his gods wherever he chose. I said if they were found, I would have the thief's throat cut as a gift to them. Almost before the words were out of my mouth, he and his sons were off poking and prying into everything. There is no need to tell again how Rachel succeeded in hiding them from her father. She sat on the sack that contained them, pale both with fear and with the pain of their pointed caps and sharp elbows sticking into her. She said it was her time for bleeding, as indeed it was though not in the way Laban understood her to mean. He kissed her brow because he pitied her and because of all the treasure he saw me making off with, I think it was she whom in his heart he most treasured.

When he returned from his search empty-handed, you could see that his anger was spent. He looked winded and old. His small eyes were startled like the eyes of a hare that does not know where to run next. By this time a number of my men had joined the group around us. They carried heavy staffs and had their headcloths pulled across their faces against the chill that rises suddenly in those wooded hills as dusk approaches. It was my turn to be angry.

"Ask them," I said, pointing to all of them, including his sons. "Let these men be the ones to decide between us. Let them hear how I have spent my youth in your service. Your ewes and she-goats did not miscarry under my care. I did not eat of your rams though it was my right. The ones that were torn by wild beasts I did not lug to your door so you could see it was not I who had torn and devoured them. I bore the loss myself. I bore the loss also not just for the ones stolen by day, as custom requires, but for the ones stolen also in the dark of night when no man should be held accountable."

I was so heated by my own words that I had to stop and wipe my brow though others were shivering.

I said, "I have been scalded by sun, my eyeballs parched, the skin of my neck and face broken and peeling. On winter nights I have writhed on the frozen ground with my knees drawn up to my chin like a corpse and my lips clattering. For years sleep has fled from my eyes. You have called me a thief, Laban. As the Fear and these men are my witness, I say you have thieved me of twenty years of my life."

Laban lowered himself down onto a rock and sat there with his shoulders hunched about his ears.

"What can I say?" he said. He shrugged his hands. "What hope has an old man against a young man's eloquence?"

He pointed toward where our tents were pitched and our herds grazing.

"All that you are taking is mine. Is there any man who will deny it? Any god?" he said. "The daughters are my daughters. The children are my children. The flocks are my flocks. But what can I do, darling? What do you expect me to do? I'll tell you what I will do."

He smiled his most radiant smile, but tears had started trickling down his brick cheeks.

He said, "Why make people angry and sorrowful when it is so easy to make them happy?"

Issachar was nearby, standing beside Obal, and Laban pulled the child toward him and set him between his knees. Issachar flushed with embarrassment when Laban spoke to him.

"I would give you the moon, Issachar, if I had it in my bag. Why not? If they were mine, I would let your father steal the stars without complaining." He waved one hand skyward. "Always remember what a generous man your grandfather Laban was. You remember it too, Jacob." He clasped the child's head to his stomach before letting him run back to Obal.

"What can I do? Now I will tell you. I will give all of you peace between your people and my people. That is what I will do," he said. "I will also give all of you yourselves. Tomorrow we will pile up stones and make it as an oath between us."

Reaching out for my hand, he pulled himself up from the rock where he was sitting. It nearly knocked me off my feet. He stretched out both arms as far as they would reach to show how great was the gift he was giving us. He threw back his head and made a gargling sound at the sky.

Taller than Issachar was tall was the pile of stones we raised the next day. There were round ones and flat ones, some dusty and dry. Some of them were damp from where we had pried them out of the ground with bits of earth still clinging to them and here and there a worm. We found a stone as thick and long as a man's thigh to fix for a pillar on the top. It had moss on one side, the other side all cracked and scarred.

With his own hands Laban slew a white lamb, catching the blood from its throat in a bowl while its hind legs were still weakly thrashing, its eyes rolled up in its head. Together we sprinkled the blood on the top stone. Together we burned the carcass, saving nothing for ourselves. Men, women, children, beasts, there were enough looking on to cover the whole crown of the hill where we did it soon after sunrise. There was mist in the valley like a smoking gray sea.

Laban said, "These stones are a witness, and this pillar is a witness, that I will not pass beyond these stones to you, and you will not pass beyond these stones to me, for harm."

He spoke the words in a slow and solemn voice. He had marked his face with ashes from the lamb's charred carcass. His mantle hung crooked from his thick shoulders. Then he winked at me and spoke in his own voice.

"Good-bye, darling," he said so that only those standing nearest could hear. All I could do was nod my head good-bye.

"The God of Abraham watch between us till our paths cross again," Laban said. "Who knows? Perhaps our paths will cross again."

Again I nodded.

He threw his arms about me. He kissed my mouth. The people clapped and shouted. Someone started playing a pipe. It was high pitched and strident, like a woman having fits.

By the time the sun was high enough to cast shadows, all the piping and clapping were over, and Laban and his sons were gone.

14
THE FACE OF LIGHT

NO ONE ELSE SAW THEM, but I saw them. If I had had no eyes, I would have seen them.

"Look," I said to my beloved. She was beside me on her knock-kneed camel. I was on foot leading it by the tether. I thought if I divided with another pair of eyes the sight of what I saw, I might escape blinding.

"I am afraid," she said. "I am afraid of what awaits us beyond the hills."

"Look between the hills," I said. "It is like a river."

It was not like a river. A river has to make its way between hills. Even as I looked these hills instead had to draw back to make way for what was moving between them. It was an army. There were as many marching in it as there are stars. They were stars. Rank upon rank they were moving silent as light. The hills were drawing their dark skirts close to let them pass as I have seen people do to let the king of the Black Land pass because the power of the life in a king's touch can bring death. The silence of the stars was like thunder. They were helmeted with light. They were shod with light.

"Will your brother try to kill you, Jacob?" my beloved said. Her fear was all she could see between the hills.

"They are here to keep us safe," I said. She must have thought I meant her father's gods. "It is why they have come."

"Your brother hasn't seen you for many years," she said, "but there are things a man does not forget easily."

I said, "You mustn't be afraid, Rachel."

I had halted the camel to watch the stars. They were moving south as we also were moving south. Shadows fled before them, scrambling up the flanks of the hills, scuttling for refuge into caves and gullies. As the stars marched, they were singing without sound. Their song was my name—not Jacob, Jacob, Jacob, over and over again, but one endless and unbroken Jacob the way light is endless and unbroken. It was the fullness of my name as I had never heard it, and they were scattering my path with its fullness the way I have seen the people of the Black Land scatter flowers, rushes, garments, before the golden feet of their king. I told myself the Fear had sent them. They were making me a highway home. Many times afterward I looked for them, but I never saw them.

When we reached the mountains of Seir, I knew we didn't have many days to go. My sons were too exhausted by the long hours of climbing even to quarrel with each other. Levi and Judah lay curled asleep almost on top of Reuben, whom they adored and followed everywhere though he paid little attention to them and seldom had a kind word for them when he did. Leah was cross as a bear. She said it had been a grievous mistake to leave Haran. We had been happy and prosperous in Haran, she said, and for all we knew, Esau and his men would fall on us as soon as he got word of our approach. What was there to prevent his killing every last one of us, she said, the mothers with the children? It was not too late to change our minds and go back. Laban would forget all his grievances in the joy of our reunion. It was madness to continue the way we were going. Rachel was of the same mind, Leah said, only Rachel was too timid and tongue-tied to say so.

Leah sat down then near a brazier of burning thorns with her elbows on her knees and her chin in her hand. She said that she would not go a step farther unless the safety of her sons could be assured. Even when a breeze came up and started blowing the thick smoke into her face, she remained there coughing and rubbing her eyes and making terrible grimaces to show that she meant what she said.

It was Rachel's red-headed maid Bilhah, the mother of Dan and Naphtali, who suggested I send messengers ahead to Esau. They could tell him that we were on our way, she said. At the same time they could smell out how he might receive us once we arrived. Maybe Leah was right in her fears and maybe she was not, Bilhah said. This way we would know for sure. Bilhah was such an imposing woman with her owlish brows and towering topknot that everyone thought highly of her counsel and I decided to follow it.

The messengers I sent were two boys barely older than Reuben whom I chose not only because they would be able to make the journey with the speed of gazelles but also because they were so fresh-faced and young that the sight of them might persuade Esau that my intentions in returning were peaceful. I told them that when they saw him they must be sure to address him with great courtesy and deference. His servant Jacob, they were to say, had been living for the past twenty years with Laban and was returning home now in hope that he might find favor in his brother's eyes. They must be sure to say that I was his servant Jacob. Would he give his cavernous, wet-toothed smile at that? Or would it send a murderous growl rumbling out of his red beard? Maybe he was the same Esau who had smothered me with kisses even when I had bought the moon and stars from him for a pot of beans. Or maybe my treachery had festered in him all these years like an arrowhead so that when he finally got his hands on me, he would break my back over his knees like a dry stick.

It took the two boys the better part of a week to return. They had seen Esau. He had just come back from the hunt with six quail hung from his belt, they said, and the bloody brush of a fox like a plume in his headband. When they gave him their message, he let out such a roar that they thought their hour had come. Then he took one of them in the crook of each arm and almost crushed the breath out of them against his chest. "Tell him I will come meet him," he said. They told me his whole body shook as if from fever. "I will start out tomorrow," he said. "Tell him I will bring a hundred men with me. Tell him," he said, "that I will bring four hundred men with me."

He started laughing and clapping his hands at that. He clapped them together with his palms cupped to make it like the pounding of drums. His men clapped too. He had to shout to make himself heard over the din of it.

"Tell him I have never forgotten him!" he cried. "Never! Never!"

They said his eyes were bloodshot and teary. There was spittle on his lips. They said when he reached out to grab them again, they ducked and ran. They thought he had gone mad.

Leah, when she heard what they said, took up two fistfuls of ashes and scattered them over her head. Rachel clutched Joseph to her breast and wept. I swore both my wives and the two boys not to breathe a word of what they had seen. I was afraid to strike terror in the hearts of the others as well. I divided the whole long train of us into two groups. My wives and children I kept in one group with me. The other group I would send out a day ahead of us so that if Esau attacked them, our group could still escape. I said that this was the Fear's will. The Fear hadn't said that it was his will, but I was the luck bearer. He wouldn't have willed it otherwise.

That night I spoke to him for the first time in many months.

I said, "O God of Abraham, God of my father Isaac."

Were the stars that I saw above me as I spoke the same stars that I had seen marching between the hills or were they other stars? They were hushed and unmoving. If they knew my name, they were no longer singing it. I did not know their names.

"I had only my black camel and my staff when I left home to escape my brother's wrath," I said to the Fear. "Now I return like a great merchant. If it was your doing, I did not deserve it. You know what I deserve. Esau knows."

I thought of the seven-fingered hand of my silver god and how the Fear has no hand a man can touch. Does the Fear have an ear to hear? Were the guttering stars his eyes? Was the moon his thin smile?

"Save me from the hand of my brother Esau," I said. "Save my children and their mothers. Wasn't it you who saved

Isaac from the knife of Abraham, and Sarah from her barrenness? Wasn't it from the beginning your promise to save us all?"

As I spoke, a single star came loose. It is always the stillness of the stars that astonishes me. There was not so much as a whisper from it as it fell. It fell slantwise across the dark tent of the sky. It vanished as silent as light.

"Hear me," I said. Then I said it again, as a star does, in my heart, without speaking it. *Hear,* I said. I said *Hear me. Save me.*

Would he?

In my tent I took the silver hand in mine of flesh and said the words once more to the silver god. Rachel murmured in her sleep. Joseph was dreaming beside her, Joseph who was her dream, her life, as she was his. My heart drummed like Esau's cupped palms. The sack of Laban's gods lay at Rachel's feet. There were more gods than people in the tent. Not one of them answered me. I thought I could not let the safety of my sleeping sons depend only on gods.

The group that was to leave a day ahead of us was one thing I could do to save them. The next morning, before that group was to leave, I did another thing. I set apart five herds. The first was two hundred female goats and twenty males; the second, two hundred ewes and twenty rams; the third, thirty she-camels with their calves; the fourth, forty cows and ten bulls; the fifth, twenty she-asses and ten he-asses. I put a seasoned man in charge of each and told them to keep enough space between them so that everyone could see that they were five separate herds. As one after another of the five herdsmen came upon Esau and his four hundred men, each was to speak to him the same words.

"My brother will ask you whose flocks you are leading and where you are leading them," I said.

I thought maybe he would ask them nothing. Maybe he would simply crack their skulls with his stick, knowing they served me, and take the beasts.

"You are to tell him this," I said. "Each of you is to tell him that your herd belongs to his servant Jacob. Those are the words you must speak. That is what you are to call me. You are to tell him that his servant Jacob is following behind you. You are to call him my lord Esau and say, each one of you, that your herd is a gift to him from me. A gift from his servant Jacob."

Even if he cracked their skulls one by one as they came out of the hills, at least it would serve to slow him. The advance group would slow him still more. Word would travel back to me, and with the gods' help I would escape. With the Fear's help I would save my eleven sons and their sons and grandsons after them. The Fear would remember what he had promised. With the help of my cunning, he would save my sons for the world's sake.

When the time came and everyone else had left, I started out with Rachel and Leah, Bilhah and Zilpah and the children. It was just at nightfall and the darkness so thick that we had to light our way with torches. The ground was steep and uneven. We traveled slowly. Zilpah was so full of fear that she could not speak words. Instead she spoke small chirping noises as she picked her way forward between her two sons, Asher the younger and Gad, who was as lean as his brother was fat. Leah still believed that despite my safeguards we would all be murdered, but she had decided to make the best of it. She spoke words of comfort to Rachel. She let her daughter Dinah wear her best sandals as a way of taking her mind off the danger. She helped keep the pack animals moving forward with her prod. I led the way, holding my torch over my head to cast as much light as I could on the path ahead. I told them all to keep quiet as we went, and except for the creaking of the harness and the sounds of the beasts, we did little to disturb the night's silence.

We thought at first that what we heard was voices. The voices grew louder and fiercer as we drew nearer. There was some great matter they were trying to tell us, but we could not understand a single word of it. They were like voices in a dream. Even the beasts grew quiet to listen. In time, the voices were lost in another sound so deep-throated that I took it at first for the voice of silence. I have heard the winter rains sound that way when they fall heavy out of the sullen sky, or the wind when it blows through grain. There was something of thunder about it too. But I knew it was none of those. Nor was it the marching stars again because there were no lights to be seen except for our torches snaking off into the dark behind me. There was no singing of the fullness of my name.

Finally I heard that it was water. It was a swift surge of water shouldering its way around a bend through steep rocks and scattering the air with spray. It was the river Jabbok. When we came to the ford, it was scrambling and frothing over a flat, stony bed. We halted at the ford, and I had to shout to make myself heard over the roar of it. I told them that they were all to cross over to the far bank ahead of me. I told them I would stay on the near bank until morning. I did not tell them why. I did not know why.

The fording was easier in the dark because the beasts could not see much of the river, but it was not easy. There was bellowing and balking, bleating and lowing. The camels skittered sideways under their cumbersome loads. The children screeched with fear and excitement. The torches' fire shone back at them from the black torrent as the men waded through it with their clothes hiked up to their hips, the women for modesty staggering across under the weight of their sodden skirts. Goats and sheep strayed and scattered. The current took several off wailing into the night when they lost their footing. Dinah carried a ewe lamb that was almost as big as she was across in her arms. Rachel begged to stay with me, but I sent her across with the rest of them. I said that we would rest the few hours that remained of the night. I said I would stay alone and rejoin them at daylight. I wanted to be able to see Esau when he came. I wanted Esau to be able to see me.

I knew what lay behind me. I did not know what lay ahead of me. The river lay between. In the meantime I wanted to be alone with the river.

The water's sound drowned out all other sounds as the darkness soon swallowed up the torches of my people. I could have been the first man who ever was as I sat there. I could have been the last man who ever will be.

To comfort myself, I thought about Haran—the shuttered balconies and peeling red mud walls, the rooftops where men play at dice or squares at sundown, the flimsy hovels of the poor pitched under the city walls for shelter. I thought of the noises of the streets, the cries of the water-sellers banging their metal cups together to catch the ears of buyers, the ring of iron-bound wheels on cobbles, the shouts of children whose eyes and mouths were rimmed with flies. The stench of Haran was everywhere. The gutters were choked with excrement, dead leaves and flowers, carrion, scraps of food floating in pools of darkened urine. The rich breathed through pomanders as they hurried past, pressing them to their faces as if they were sobbing. There was much to sob at in Haran—the lepers and beggars, the mad ones among them gibbering under the pepper trees that grow behind the temple of Sin, the felons with their cropped ears or noses, some of them with their hands cut off at the wrist, some with an eye socket puckered and empty.

There was a house with thick walls that kept it cooler inside than most and an earthen floor alive with rats. Wicks floating in oil cast a dim light. An old woman whose hair was full of the blood of ticks sold beer with slices of sweet onion and olives so salty that they made the inside of your mouth raw. Laban and I sometimes went there together when he was too tired from a long day of haggling to be anything but my friend. We would drink our beer in silence and watch the rats. We had sworn an oath never to pass beyond the pillar to work the other's harm. I thought how I would probably never pass beyond it to drink the old woman's beer with him again either. It was the last thought of him that I had time to think.

Out of the dark someone leaped at me with such force that it knocked me onto my back. It was a man. I could not see his face. His naked shoulder was pressed so hard against my jaw I thought he would break it. His flesh was chill and wet as the river. He was the god of the river. My bulls had raped him. My flocks had fouled him and my children pissed on him. He would not let me cross without a battle. I got my elbow into the pit of his throat and forced him off. I threw him over onto his back. His breath was hot in my face as I straddled him. My breath came in gasps. Quick as a serpent he twisted loose, and I was caught between his thighs. The grip was so tight I could not move. He had both hands pressed to my cheek. He was pushing my face into the mud, grunting with the effort. Then he got me on my belly with his knee in the small of my back. He was tugging my head up toward him. He was breaking my neck.

He was not the god of the river. He was Esau. He had slain all my sons. He had forded the river to slay me. Just as my neck was about to snap, I butted my head upward with the last of my strength and caught him square. For an instant his grip loosened and I was free. Over and over we rolled together into the reeds at the water's edge. We struggled in each other's arms. He was on top. Then I was on top. I knew that they were not Esau's arms. It was not Esau. I did not know who it was. I did not know who I was. I knew only my terror and that it was dark as death. I knew only that what the stranger wanted was my life.

For the rest of the night we battled in the reeds with the Jabbok roaring down through the gorge above us. Each time I thought I was lost, I escaped somehow. There were moments when we lay exhausted in each other's arms the way a man and a woman lie exhausted from passion. There were moments when I seemed to be prevailing. It was as if he was letting me prevail. Then he was at me with new fury. But he did not prevail. For hours it went on that way. Our bodies were slippery with mud. We were panting like beasts. We could not see each other. We spoke no words. I did not know why we were fighting. It was like fighting in a dream.

He outweighed me, he out-wrestled me, but he did not overpower me. He did not overpower me until the moment came to overpower me. When the moment came, I knew that he could have made it come whenever he wanted. I knew that all through the night he had been waiting for that moment. He had his knee under my hip. The rest of his weight was on top of my hip. Then the moment came, and he gave a fierce downward thrust. I felt a fierce pain.

It was less a pain I felt than a pain I saw. I saw it as light. I saw the pain as a dazzling bird-shape of light. The pain's beak impaled me with light. It blinded me with the light of its wings. I knew I was crippled and done for. I could do nothing but cling now. I clung for dear life. I clung for dear death. My arms trussed him. My legs locked him. For the first time he spoke.

He said, "Let me go."

The words were more breath than sound. They scalded my neck where his mouth was touching.

He said, "Let me go, for the day is breaking."

Only then did I see it, the first faint shudder of light behind the farthest hills.

I said, "I will not let you go."

I would not let him go for fear that the day would take him as the dark had given him. It was my life I clung to. My enemy was my life. My life was my enemy.

I said, "I will not let you go unless you bless me." Even if his blessing meant death, I wanted it more than life.

"Bless me," I said. "I will not let you go unless you bless me."

He said, "Who are you?"

There was mud in my eyes, my ears and nostrils, my hair. My name tasted of mud when I spoke it.

"Jacob," I said. "My name is Jacob."

"It is Jacob no longer," he said. "Now you are Israel. You have wrestled with God and with men. You have prevailed. That is the meaning of the name Israel."

I was no longer Jacob. I was no longer myself. Israel was who I was. The stranger had said it. I tried to say it the way he had said it: *Yees-rah-ail.* I tried to say the new name I was to the new self I was. I could not see him. He was too close to me to see. I could see only the curve of his shoulders above me. I saw the first glimmer of dawn on his shoulders like a wound.

I said, "What is your name?" I could only whisper it.

"Why do you ask me my name?"

We were both of us whispering. He did not wait for my answer. He blessed me as I had asked him. I do not remember the words of his blessing or even if there were words. I remember the blessing of his arms holding me and the blessing of his arms letting me go. I remember as blessing the black shape of him against the rose-colored sky.

I remember as blessing the one glimpse I had of his face. It was more terrible than the face of dark, or of pain, or of terror. It was the face of light. No words can tell of it. Silence cannot tell of it. Sometimes I cannot believe that I saw it and lived but that I only dreamed I saw it. Sometimes I believe I saw it and that I only dream I live.

He never told me his name. The Fear of Isaac, the Shield of Abraham, and others like them are names we use because we do not know his true name. He did not tell me his true name. Perhaps he did not tell it because he knew I would never stop calling on it. But I gave the place where I saw him a name. I named it Peniel. It means the face of God.

The sun's rim was just starting to show over the top of the gorge by the time I finally crossed the Jabbok. Bands of gold fanned across the sky. I staggered through the rocky shallows, one hip dipping deep at each new step and my head bobbing. It is the way I have walked ever since.

From that day to this I have moved through the world like a cripple with the new name the Fear gave me that night by the river when he gave me his blessing and crippled me.

15
THE FACE OF ESAU

ESAU WAS COMING. As soon as I rejoined my people on the other side, we all of us saw him and his four hundred with him. They were still a way off, moving along the side of a hill with another hill and a field of rocks and thornbush still left between us. There was a cloud of dust in the air from their feet. Then I did a thing that still causes me shame to remember it.

I divided my children among their mothers. I put Bilhah and Zilpah and their children together. I put Leah and her children together. I put Rachel and Joseph together, just the two of them. I told Bilhah and Zilpah that they were to take their children and start out ahead of the others. They were the group that Esau and his men would come upon first. If he killed them, maybe he would spare the ones that came next. Everyone understood my meaning. I could tell that they did from their silence. Bilhah stood holding Dan by one hand and Naphtali by the other while I told them what they were to do. There was a look of scorn in her swelling eyes. Zilpah was too terrified even to chirp. She was ashen. When Gad and Asher tried to hide in her skirts, she didn't notice them.

As soon as Bilhah and Zilpah were halfway to the field, I nodded to Leah that she was to go next. Was it the only time I ever saw her weep? I do not know whether she wept from grief that I had placed her and her children second to be slaughtered or from gratitude that I hadn't placed them first. She put her son Reuben in front and told the others to stay close behind him no matter what happened. Her eyes were pink and swollen.

Only Rachel and Joseph were left then. Joseph was round-eyed from fear. He was making a breathy, whistling sound through his lips. Rachel was holding her camel by its tether with the sack of Laban's gods lashed to its back. We said nothing to each other. With a nod of my head I sent them off last so that all who had gone ahead of them would be their shield. If any were to be saved, Rachel and Joseph were to be saved. Everyone saw what I was doing, and no one spoke of it. Then I mounted the swiftest of my camels and loped ahead till I was well out in front of Bilhah and Zilpah. I wanted to be the first to meet my brother.

He was at the head of his people as I was at the head of mine. He was on foot. Before I was close enough to see his face, I knew him by the rolling way he walked. He was throwing his arms and shoulders about as if he was pushing through a crowd. As soon as he saw who I was, he stopped. In one hand he held a spear. A bow and quiver were slung across his back. He was bare-headed, and the early sun flamed in his bush of red hair and flying beard. I had raised one arm to stop those behind me. I had also stopped. I called *ikh-kh-kh* to my camel who couched so I could dismount.

There was only half of the field now between my brother and me. With his legs planted wide apart, half crouching, he shifted his weight to his heels and drew back his right arm to hurl the spear. It was not the spear I saw, the long shaft of it trembling in his grasp, the barbed point of it hovering for flight not far from his ear. I saw his face. I saw the fullness of his life in his face. I saw the fullness of my death in his face. Our eyes met for the first time in twenty years. A great stillness filled me so that there was no place left in me for anything except the stillness. There was no place left anywhere for the twenty years, no place left in my eyes for anything except his face.

It was fuller and redder than the face I remembered. It looked crumbled, like old brick. The eyes were not on a line with each other. The mouth hung loose. His face looked broken in pieces once and then mended. Had the sight of me broken it? Had the sight of me mended it? The brow was spangled with sweat beneath the matted hair. He was shouting something I could not hear through the stillness. Several of his teeth were missing.

He was hurling the spear. He hurled it up into the air so that when it slowed at the zenith, arced, and came down, it came down with a clatter somewhere between us. He was running toward me. His arms were outstretched. His arms were around me. His face, his beard, his sweat, were in my face. I heard myself speak as though it was someone else speaking.

I said, "To see your face is like seeing the face of God."

That broken and mended face. He did not hear what I said. It is possible I had not said it so he could hear it. I heard it.

"You are limping, darling!" he cried. "If someone has hurt you, I will kill him."

He said, "All those beasts you sent ahead of you. Why did you send them?"

The missing teeth gave him a fierce and mirthful look. His eyes swelled in his head as they fed on me. I thought I was laughing. Perhaps I was weeping or half weeping.

"I sent them to find favor in your sight," I said. "The Fear has been gracious to me. They are yours."

He stood scratching his head. The thongs of his sandals were broken. His cloak was torn at the hem and covered with stains.

"Now we will go home," he said. "I will show you the way."

He took hold of the gold neck-chain I wore and pulled me close enough to kiss. He kissed me first on one cheek and then on the other. He held me in his arms.

"Mother is dead," he said. "She shriveled up like a little nut and just died. How she missed you, darling. How we all missed you."

He could have been telling me a calf was dead or a shriveled nut fallen from the branch for all it meant to me. I understood the words as they came from him one by one but not the sense of the words strung together like beads. I understood *dead*. I understood *mother*.

"The beasts are my gift, and you must take them," I said. *Beasts* I understood. I understood *gift*.

When he smiled, I could see the gaps where his teeth had been.

"Anything you want," he said. "Anything is fine, Jacob. What a limp you have! You will ride, and I will ride with you. Maybe I will ride a little ahead of you. That way I will be ahead of you if trouble comes."

"We will be too slow for you," I said. "My children are young. They travel slowly. I have a daughter. Her eyes are blue like your eyes."

They were not Jacob's words. I heard them as Israel's words, the words of Israel who had wrestled with God and with men and had prevailed. It was for Israel to travel alone through the worst the world could dream, through the worst that God could do and the best.

I said, "Some of my beasts are with young. If they are overdriven, they will die. You go ahead of me. I will match my pace to the beasts and the children. At the end of the journey I will meet you."

"Take some of my men with you," Esau said.

Some of his men had gathered about us. My people were still where I had halted them. For all they could see, already I lay dead among the thorns.

"Take a hundred," he said. "Take two hundred. They will see you are safe."

"There is no need," I said. "I need only to find favor in your sight, my lord. I have found it."

"My lord, my lord," he said. He was grinning.

He made as if to do battle with me. He circled me, bobbing and feinting. He jabbed at the air all around me with his fists. Once or twice he slapped at my cheeks lightly, like a girl, with his open palms.

"You'll have your way, won't you, darling?" he said. "Nobody ever got the better of you yet. Nobody is ever going to get the better of you." It was some queer, tremendous tenderness that had knocked his eyes crooked and loosened the hinges of his mouth.

To see your face is like seeing the face of God. They had been Israel's words, not Jacob's words, and I searched my brother's crumbled face for their meaning.

16

THE CUTTING OF SHECHEM

"ABRAHAM?" I SAID. I said, "Grandfather?" Abraham had stood where I was standing on the high slopes of Mount Ebal. It was all gorse and rock. Hills were everywhere, vast, gray-green waves of hills heaving and sinking like the sea. Nearest to the north was Mount Gerizim. She lay like a woman on her side said my son Reuben— the swell of her hip, one dark, tree-covered breast cresting. Even then Reuben thought overmuch about women. What had Abraham thought as he stood there?

It was where Abraham had halted when he first entered the land of the Fear's promise, tenting near the city of Shechem, whose high stone walls rise from the saddle between Gerizim and Ebal. From the slope I could look down on it. It is not so great a city as Haran but great enough even in Abraham's time with the broad highways converging near it bringing merchants with their treasure. My grandfather had more than half his long life ahead of him then and almost all but a year or two of his long waiting for the promise to be kept. He wasn't young then but not old either. His eyes were not hooded yet against the sting of sand to come. His cheeks were not seamed and sunken, his nose not unfleshed to the bony beak-shape it became with hairy nostrils gaping like caves.

It was the Fear that Abraham thought about. What else, with the Fear's hook tearing at his mouth, the Fear's words flaming and fuddling him like a woman's? It was here among the crowding hills that the Fear spoke to him again.

"Everything," the Fear said, "everything you can see both here and southward is to be for everyone whom you father and for everyone whom they father and their fathering sons father after them. I have promised it. I am promising it."

Sarah was barren as a stick. Abraham had fathered no one. But he built an altar to mark the place where the Fear had spoken anyway. It stands near the great oak where later I buried Laban's gods and the small gods of my people and my own small gods, together with him of the silver hand tumbled in among them and reaching his hand out into darkness to this day as far as I have reason to know. The stones of the altar are unhewn so as not to hew the power out of them. Some of them have tumbled to the ground. Some are leprous with lichen and bird droppings.

I lay on my back on Ebal's stubbly ribs to search for Abraham among the clouds—a wisp of his beard here, there his ragged jaw slowly chomping down, a gout of his seed floating deep into the sky's barren, blue womb.

"Grandfather?" I said.

Abraham knew the nethermost caverns of grief if any man has ever known them. Maybe it takes a god to know them. I wanted him to know also the grief that had befallen me there at Shechem because it was he who had fathered it. He had fathered Laughter, who fathered me, who fathered Simeon and Levi, whose hands still smoked with innocent blood, all of us following the path that Abraham had set us, the path that the Fear had set Abraham. I wanted to tell him the tale of my grief backward, putting the worst of it behind me first.

The worst of it was Hamor and his sons bludgeoned, their skulls broken, lying on their pallets where my sons had fallen on them in their pain and broken them. The worst of the worst was that Hamor's son Shechem was among them. He was not much older than Simeon and Levi, who broke him. He was a boy still, beardless. He had a boy's brave eyes, a boy's quick smile. I do not believe he took my daughter against her will, as a ram in rut takes what he can, humped and thrusting, the beads of dried dung dancing on his hams. I believe his heart went out to her as hers to him. I believe their beauty took each other by surprise, my blue-eyed Dinah's beauty and the brave-eyed boy's. The beautiful always surprise us. Everything else in the world we expect as we expect weariness at the day's end and sun at waking. Shechem no more ravished her than she ravished him. A boy is as frail with his big feet and strong hands, his lean, long legs, as any girl with her fingers in her hair stringing flowers. A boy is as helpless at least against the heart's fury, which is as terrible as an army with banners.

Somewhere outside the high walls, Shechem and Dinah met and fell. Beauty felled them together. Afterward—

heartsick, all bravery fled from his eyes—the boy told Hamor, his father. He said that he must have her as his bride or die without her. Hamor was king of the city for whom his son, to be king after him, was named. Hamor was a small, thin man, blind in one eye from battle. He was a proud and kingly man as well with his heart set on his son's happiness. His heart was set also on forging a bond between his people and mine. He had seen our herds and flocks as we paused for pasturage and rest on our way south after Esau. He had seen the servants and slaves, the laden camels.

Hamor came to treat with me and brought along his son, Shechem, who was as crippled by his love as I by my wrestling in the dark of Jabbok. My sons and I were roasting a spitted lamb on the green plain that lies east of the city where we had pitched our tents, and the two of them met us there. Shechem stood beside him as his father spoke, his young eyes listless with dread and longing. Hamor made up for his small stature by his grave and stately manner. He carried the tall staff of his office and around his headcloth wore a gold fillet.

His words were of such elegance that it was not plain at first what homely matter it was that he was using them to tell. He was telling that between his son and my daughter it was already as it is between a man and his wife. He was saying that surely the gods smiled on their union because in the few days that had followed it the new grain had already doubled in height and a spring, dry for years, had again started flowing. It could have been a treaty of kings that Hamor was describing rather than how a boy and a girl had taken pleasure in each other's arms, but in spite of the courtly way he wove it, you could see while the words were still hot on his lips that already they had enflamed Simeon and Levi.

Next after Reuben, Simeon and Levi were Leah's sons and thus also the full brothers of Dinah. Simeon was a gangling, weasel-faced boy who had reached his full height in such a rush that it was still a puzzle to him and he stumbled about as loose-limbed and clumsy as a new calf. Levi, the younger and shorter, was in everything his brother's rival, so when he saw Simeon's anger mounting at what Hamor, the king, was saying, his anger mounted higher and hotter still. Their virgin sister had been dishonored. That was the long and the short of what Hamor was saying. His son, standing brazenly beside him, had taken her by stealth. Gauging Shechem's lechery by their own, they saw him overpowering her, thrusting himself between her thighs. For all they knew, he had taken her on the green grass of the very field where now he stood inwardly mocking them. They saw him entering her with a bull's brute member. His member was uncut because what did his barbarous people know of the Fear's command to Abraham to cut it in honor of the Fear's promise? Shechem had defiled the Fear himself. Our whole people had been raped.

Already Simeon and Levi were muttering these things by the fire with the lamb's fat flaring it, but Hamor paid them no mind. He could have been talking of mending the city gates to a council of elders.

"The soul of my son longs for your daughter," he was saying. "See how pale is his brow. Read the great yearning of his heart in the way he sighs even now as I speak. Give him your daughter, Dinah, in marriage. That is my prayer to you."

All this while Dinah was off somewhere with the women, I suppose. I picture her eyes soft with what she believed was her secret. She knew nothing of Hamor and Shechem's visit. She knew nothing of what was to come of it.

"Make marriages with our whole people," Hamor was saying. He spread his arms like wings to show how great a people they were. "Give your daughters to us and take our daughters for yourselves. You shall remain with us, and the land shall be open to you as if it is your own land. Dwell and trade in it so that we may grow and prosper together like brothers."

He turned to Shechem then, touching him on the shoulder with his bone-headed staff. The heartsick boy stepped a little forward, a smile faltering on his lips.

"Let me find favor in your eyes," Shechem said. "Whatever you ask of me, I will give."

For all his shyness, he was so stalwart and comely that I thought I would be proud to have him for a son. His eyes were upon me, his dark brows knit with pleading.

Shechem said, "Ask of me whatever you want as a marriage gift, and I will give it. Only give me in return—" He paused as if thinking whether he could trust himself to speak her name. "Give me your daughter in return. To be my wife."

It was not a matter to be decided in haste, but I was on the point of making an answer when without warning Simeon leapt to his feet. He had been crouching on his haunches by the fire. He stood in front of me now so that I had to step aside to see. I could see that he was trembling. The smell of his sweat was sour with fear.

"We cannot do this thing," Simeon said.

His voice came out shaken and high-pitched. His rage had carried him that far and then stranded him. For a moment I thought he was about to bolt. His brothers were as silent as death. The only sound was the spitted lamb's hissing. He shot a panicked glance at me over his shoulder.

"We cannot give our sister to a man who is not cut," he said. He was speaking to Shechem now, his voice still shaking and shrill. "You must be cut where we have all been cut. Every man of you must be cut there because it is the way of our people. It is the Fear's way. If you refuse, your words are a disgrace to her and to the Fear as well. They are an insult to us all."

"Should I have struck him across the mouth, Grandfather?" I said when I told it to Abraham on the slopes of Ebal.

There was a tiny thread of ants disappearing down a hole where I was gazing. Deeper down still, at the roots of the mountains, deeper than the freshets of the sea, they say the dead dwell. They say they have a thirst that is never slaked. They move like shadows, unspeaking, unknowing. They say that even the Fear forgets them there though perhaps he does not forget Abraham there because Abraham was his friend. Perhaps he does not forget Rachel there either because Rachel was Israel's friend and his beloved. Perhaps when you speak to the dead, they hear you though they do not answer.

I did not strike Simeon across the mouth. He had dared to answer in my place, but his answer had power in it. I could see its power in the eyes of Hamor and Shechem. For the first time Hamor nodded and smiled as though the thought of letting himself be cut was not distasteful to him. Perhaps he had heard how they say that it heightens a man's pleasure with a woman as well as his fruitfulness. Perhaps he had heard of the Fear and thought it might be a way to win the Fear's favor. As for Shechem, if Simeon had told him that he must cut off both legs beneath the knee as well, he would have thought it too little to pay. He stood with his lips slightly parted, his eyes shining with the bravery that had returned to them.

"Simeon persuaded the king to let himself and his people be cut, Grandfather," I said.

I sealed the ants' hole with my thumb. I wondered if they would bear my words to him one by one like crumbs.

"Hamor went back to his people and summoned all the men to the gate," I said. "He told them that if they did what Simeon asked, all would be well with them. He said all our flocks would be as if they were their flocks and so would all our servants and our treasure. We would stand as one people against any who came against either of us. They would grow fat on our bartering. Our women were fair and would make them excellent wives. I am told there was a man among them who had already been cut as we are, and Hamor made him show himself. He stood on top of a cistern with his shirt pulled up, and they all crowded around to gape at what they saw. They laughed and poked each other in the ribs. They made jokes about how it is said to add heat to a woman's desire for a man as well as a man's for a woman and even a man's for a man because there were not a few among them who like beasts took their pleasure where they found it.

"They suffered it to be done to them, Grandfather," I said. "I sent some six or seven of our men into the city to cut them. Simeon and Levi went with them to make sure it was done properly. With their own eyes they saw it done upon Shechem. It is my guess they hoped to hear him cry out in pain. I have been told he did not cry out. It was three days later that he cried out and then for another cause. His blood is on my head, Grandfather. His blood is on your head."

I did not know what it was that even then my sons were planning. I have sworn my innocence to the Fear. I swore it also to the silver one who had only a few weeks more by then to hear my blubbering before I buried him. If I had any part in my sons' evil, may my eyes be struck with blindness. May my tongue cleave to the roof of my mouth. I had no part in it, but they were my sons. It was on their homeward journey with me that they did it. If I had struck Simeon across the mouth when he leapt up from the fire and spoke in my place without leave, it would never have happened.

Simeon was the leader in it, that tall, stumble-footed boy with small, sharp eyes like his mother's and a cruel mouth. And in all the evil he worked that day, Levi tried to outdo him though left to himself he would never have dreamed it. They persuaded a number of our men to go with them. They told them that as Dinah had been ravished already, so would their own daughters and wives be ravished soon enough. They told them not one of our women was safe from the lust of the men of Shechem. They armed themselves with knives and bludgeons. They heated their blood with beer.

It was on the third day that they struck because it is on the third day after a man has been cut that the pain of healing is sharpest. They waited till nightfall. Many of the men of Shechem were already asleep. Others were drugged with wine to ease their soreness. Some were moving about but holding themselves and moaning.

"The worst of the tale is not yet behind me, Grandfather," I said. "The worst is still to tell. It was Simeon himself who slew Shechem. Levi helped him. They found the boy lying naked and in pain on his bed with only his cloak covering him. Levi sat on his legs. Simeon knelt on his chest and gelded him. They held up the boy's bloody parts before his eyes. Then they blinded him so it would be the last sight he would see. There were other things they did to him as well, dragging old Hamor in to watch them at it. I cannot bring myself to tell those things. Only then did they bludgeon him."

The way the shadows fell on Gerizim as the sun moved westward made it look as though the woman Reuben saw her to be had turned slightly where she lay to whisper to someone who lay beside her. Maybe it was to Abraham she whispered. He was lucky to have no ears for hearing if it is true that the dead have no ears. He was lucky to have no eyes for seeing.

By the time Simeon and Levi's work was done, there was not a house in the city where there were not women with ashes in their hair beating their breasts and wailing. Children wandered dazed and speechless through the narrow streets. All the booths of the merchants were tumbled and shattered. Fruit lay in the gutters. Cloths lay torn and trampled underfoot. Rats gibbered and scuttled through the wreckage that my sons had left.

Dinah did not speak for many days. She would not eat or drink. She lay on her pallet with her thumb in her mouth. Leah slept with her in her arms, but Dinah herself did not sleep. Night and day her eyes were open. Her eyes were blue and clear as a cloudless sky. She lay with her knees curled up against her chest. When we were striking our tents to continue our journey southward and the air was loud with the cries of men and the clamoring of beasts, she put her hands to her ears. It was the only sign she gave of living anywhere other than in the secret inside herself on which her gaze was fixed. I would come sometimes and sit by her and speak her name many times over. I do not think she knew her name even if she heard me as I was speaking it.

I had Simeon bound to a tree with his brother Levi. They were tied back to back with their arms tight against their sides and their legs trussed. Their feet were puddled with their own urine. I allowed them only water. Leah, their mother, brought it to them and held the cup to their cracked lips. For three days I kept them there, and the wonder of it was how little pain it seemed to cause them. I think they were as drunk on the blood they had shed as men can be drunk on wine. For hours on end they would call out loud and boastfully to each other in words so jumbled that there was no understanding them. Perhaps they understood each other. Sometimes they sang broken scraps of songs. Their hoarse laughter was brother to weeping. By the third day, Levi's lips were blue. Leah came to me and said they were dying.

She padded into my tent just at dawn and said it quietly, crouching down beside me and taking my hands in hers. Her hair hung uncombed about her heavy cheeks. Her weak eyes blinked in the dimness.

"It is yourself you are killing, Jacob," she said.

I alone knew I was not Jacob but Israel. I had told no one of what had happened at the Jabbok. I explained my limp by saying I had twisted my foot on a stone in the fording.

She said, "A woman can outlive her children and stay alive inside herself, but when a man's sons die, the man dies with them. Even if he lives to father other sons, inside himself he is dead. Many times I have seen it happen, Jacob."

I touched her lips with my fingers for their kindness and thought again of Abraham. Was it himself he was killing when he raised his knife over Laughter bound like a beast to the dry sticks? By commanding Abraham to do it, and to die of doing it, was it the Fear himself that the Fear was killing? Tears flooded my eyes. It was not just Simeon and Levi I wept for, but for all the sadness there is between fathers and sons. I wept for my father, Isaac. I wept for Jacob, my father's son. I wept for Abraham, and for Hamor and his son Shechem. With more tenderness than I had ever felt for her before, I kissed the hands of Leah and left the tent.

I limped out to the tree where my two sons were bound and with my own knife cut the ropes that bound them. They crumpled to the ground and lay there whimpering.

I said, "You have put us all in great danger by this thing that you have done. You have made us an abomination to all who live in this land. If ever they gather together against us, not one of us will be spared."

I said, "You are my sons, and I must spare your lives because they are my life, but this thing you have done is a stench before the heavens."

It was Simeon who reached up and took hold of my cloak. His chin was wet with spittle and his voice like a frog croaking. "Was it right for him to use our sister like a harlot?" he said.

I said, "The Fear chose us to be a blessing to this world, and you have made of us a curse."

17
THE RED HEIFER

THE BLOOD OF THEIR BUTCHERY was caked on their hands. It got under their nails and into their hair and into the hair of their arms and legs and bony chests. The life in the blood got into their life, their blood. Their clothes were fouled by it. Everyone they touched was fouled by it. They touched their wives and small children the way men will after battle, grabbing them close and covering them with kisses, burying their faces in the warmth and fragrance of their embraces. They were desperate to wash their foulness away in innocence, but it was rather the innocent who were fouled and who in turn fouled still other innocents until there was not one of us left innocent and clean. Even the clear and innocent-eyed beasts were tainted. When Simeon reached up from where he lay to touch the hem of my cloak, I was tainted. The bitterness and terror that was in the blood of the slain men of Shechem seeped through their skin and into the blood of their slayers and into all of us. It became our bitterness and terror and taint. We were an abomination in the sight of the Fear. We were an abomination in our own sight. We avoided each other's eyes and touch like the eyes and touch of lepers. We were like rats gibbering and scuttling through the wreckage we had made of ourselves.

I was lying awake in my tent next to Rachel when the Fear spoke to me. The darkness was the darkness not just of night but of the dark blood and broken skulls of the slain men. It filled my eyes so that I could see nothing and filled my ears so that I could hear nothing. But the heart has ears, and it was with them that I heard the words of the Fear as clearly as though it was Rachel who had whispered them. I held my breath to hear them.

"Arise," he said.

I thought how can a man arise when the darkness fetters and fills him? I thought why does a god speak to a tainted man? It was as if a man should speak to a rat telling it to rise when it is trapped in its own filth beyond rising or hearing.

The Fear said, "Arise."

I was a rat listening. I was a rat with its rat heart arising.

He said, "Go to the place where you slept in your flight from your brother, Esau. Go to the place where I spoke to you from the top of the stone stair."

I remembered the place though it was twenty years back and I was a man still though rat-hearted even then, a rat man scuttling from the rage of a brother, from the grief and despair of a blind father. I remembered the stone stair, the stars moving up, the stars moving down.

"Make me an altar there," the Fear said. "Build me an altar there where the stone stair stood."

The small mouth of a rat is speechless. I could not answer him. The small hands of a rat are helpless. What can they build? I knew that before I could do the Fear's bidding I had to gnaw a way for us out of the foulness. I had to be a man again, had to be Israel. I had to be clean again and my people clean with me. I reached out my small hands. I bared my rat teeth in the dark.

When morning came, we found a heifer without blemish. Sleek she was and glossy with her hair in flat curls between her ears and creamy at her chest and fetlocks and tasseled tail. She had never borne the yoke. Except for the creamy parts, her color was red, the fire-color that drives off demons and the gods' ill-will. Red is the color of luck. We felled her with a blow between her round, moist eyes and slaughtered her. We burned her carcass in a storm of fire, throwing in cedar branches and hyssop. We threw in cochineal such as Abraham used for dying his red beard red. Hours it took as we watched her crack and blacken, piling on dried dung and dead branches to make the hot flames dance and devour her. When she was all ashes, we cast them, still smoking, into seven basins of water which we placed in a circle, and through that circle every man, every child and woman of us, passed—I first among them—to be sprinkled and cleansed of the tainted blood until there was nothing left in the basins but a gray sludge. With my own hands I forced the sludge into the gaping mouths of Simeon first, then of his brother Levi, making them swallow it down, gagging, until they retched out all that was left of their uncleanness. The skinny, ashen boys lay in their vomit on the sobbing ground. My bowels stirred for them. They were my unlucky, luck-bearing boys. They were cruel and cleansed.

The unclean blood no longer clung to our hands, but the small gods clung still to our hearts. They clung with silver fingers, with fingerless hands of wood and baked clay. Like rats, the gods gibbered in our hearts about the rich gifts they have for giving to us. The gods give rain. The swelling udder they give and the sweet fig, the plump ear of grain, the ooze of oil. They give sons. To Laban they gave cunning. They give their names as the Fear, at the Jabbok, refused me his when I asked it, and a god named is a god summoned. The Fear comes when he comes. It is the Fear who summons. The gods give in return for your gifts to them: the strangled dove, the burnt ox, the first fruit. There are those who give them their firstborn even, the child bound to the altar for knifing as Abraham bound Isaac till the Fear of his mercy bade the urine-soaked old man unbind him. The Fear gives to the empty-handed, the empty-hearted, as to me from the stone stair he gave promise and blessing, and gave them also to Isaac before me, to Abraham before Isaac, all of us wanderers only, herdsmen and planters moving with the seasons as gales of dry sand move with the wind. In return it is only the heart's trust that the Fear asks. Trust him though you cannot see him and he has no silver hand to hold. Trust him though you have no name to call him by, though out of the black night he leaps like a stranger to cripple and bless.

It was to cleanse our hearts of every other trust but trust in the Fear that I made them bury their gods and Laban's gods in the hole under the oak near Abraham's tumbled altar limed with bird droppings. Rachel stood by weeping. She had conceived again. She leaned with her back to the oak, round-bellied and wretched. She had looked to her father's gods to make her mother of another son like her heart's treasure,

Joseph. I laid my silver god in on top of the others and covered them with earth. I stamped the earth down. I put on more earth and stamped it. Before we left, I strew what remained of the cleansing sludge on the gods' raw grave.

The gods took their revenge soon enough. With what power they had left—the earth stopping their eyes and mouths—they reached out of their grave and touched an old woman with the shadows of their hands. Deborah was her name. She was almost a dwarf. She wore what little hair she had left in two thin braids that hung down her back. Her eyes were always squinnied and her toothless gums bared in a sneezelike grimace that could have been either mirth or anguish. She was the oldest one among us and so frail that I would have left her behind at Laban's except that she pleaded so piteously to go with us that I had to take her. She had been my mother's nurse in the distant days of my mother's childhood before she was carried off to be my father's bride, and Deborah had her heart set on seeing her again before she died. She did not know that by then my mother had already died herself. I had spoken of her death to no one since Esau told me. I had all but forgotten it myself in the welter of other dark matters to think about.

Nor did Deborah know that my mother had ever ceased to be the child she remembered. She never tired of saying how her heart longed to take her into her lap again, to cuddle the child's curly head against her shriveled breasts and gobble the old tales to her and cackle the old songs that she had weaned her on years before. If she had lived to meet the grown woman Rebekah as I had last seen her, I wondered what she would have made of her. Perhaps she was too blind to have seen her as she was at all—the puffy small face and rabbity teeth, the eyes ringed with antimony peering out of the tangled mane. Or perhaps in Deborah's arms all the years of my mother's scheming and fretting and badgering would have fallen from her like a garment and she would have become again the fresh-faced child the old woman remembered. Such a meeting was never to happen.

Our journey to the stone stair was fearsome, and we made it with all the haste we could, prepared for battle. There were many in the land we passed through who were hot to revenge the slaughter at Shechem. We kept the children and women together and sent outriders before us and behind us to warn of danger. Much of the baggage and many of the flocks I ordered to follow at their own pace. I placed only a handful of men in charge, telling them they would have to fend for themselves if trouble came. Too feeble to walk, old Deborah rode up with us lashed to the back of an ass so she would not fall. Her eyes glinted at the thought of feasting again on her heart's darling. The hoops in her long earlobes swayed and her head bobbed to the beast's rough plodding. Her legs stuck out to either side like sticks.

My mother was all stone when Deborah found her. Deborah thought my mother was the pillar I had set up on the rocky hillside where twenty years earlier I had dreamed of the stair and the climbing stars. The flat stone I had slept on loomed still where I had placed it on end with packed earth and smaller stones about the base to hold it. It was Rebekah that Deborah saw waiting to welcome her at last into her stone arms.

She called out to her hoarse as a crow. She flapped her arms. She clawed at the cords that held her. Her rutted face leapt and sputtered like fire. She kicked the sandals off her feet. I untied her myself and helped her to the ground. She lurched forward with hands grabbing out at the air like talons. She fouled herself in her frenzy, her beads rattling, her stained skirt hiked. Her bare feet faltered through pebbles and stubble.

She was almost within reach of the stone child she had nursed when the shadow hands of the gods touched her. For gods, they touched her not unkindly considering their wrath at the earth that choked them. She didn't fall like a beast felled. She crumbled like earth. She made such a small, still heap with the breath gone out of her that it was hard to believe she had ever breathed.

18
THE TWELFTH SON

"**B**ENONI," MY BELOVED SAID.
Her hair was moist with sweat on her cheeks, her throat. The child, no bigger than a squirrel, lay at her shoulder. Its eyes had not opened yet to see light. Its fists, the size of pigeon eggs, were clenched at either side of its tiny, swollen face. It was swathed and salted. We were on the road to Ephrath, some few days south of the place of the stone stair where at the Fear's command we had set up an altar next to the pillar where Deborah died. They have come to call the place of the stone stair Bethel, which means the house of God. Benoni means Son of My Sorrow.

"His name will be Benoni," my beloved whispered, naming him for his mother's tears as my father was named for his mother's laughter and Abraham's. Rachel's tears were because she knew that the child would be motherless. Hours she had labored, bearing him. She was bleeding and torn.

She knew she was dying. Hers was the second and hardest of the three deaths that followed on the gods' burying. Benoni is a sad, unlucky name, but I said nothing. I lifted a strand of moist hair from her throat.

We had set up the altar at Bethel in sadness because of the old woman. Simeon and Levi stood by sullen as I anointed it. Simeon looked bloodless. His cloak flapped around his long white legs. Reuben as firstborn held the cruse. He had Joseph beside him because Joseph was the brother he was most drawn to though the two were as different as winter and spring. Reuben was winter, full of coldness and gusty anger. Sometimes I would find him staring at me as though already he dreamed of the day when he would be father and first in my place. Joseph was spring. He had the cleft chin of Rachel, his mother, and her brother Obal. He had soft eyes and down on his upper lip. He was a thoughtful, inward-looking boy. When Reuben took the cruse back from me, Joseph stood at his elbow with a cloth for me to wipe the oil from my fingers. The other boys were often rough with him because they knew I favored his mother over theirs and thought I also favored him. I favored him. I had not yet given him the cursed, red-striped mantle, but I had given him other things.

Rachel called for Joseph when she was dying. He stood on one side of where she and the baby lay in the tent. I stood on the other. He had brought her blue windflowers which he laid across her stomach. The flowers moved with her breathing.

"He is your full brother, Joseph. You must watch out for him," she said. "He will need somebody to teach him to walk."

Joseph reached out and touched one of the tiny fists with his finger.

"Somebody must teach him words and talking," she said.

She was frowning. I thought how I had labored seven years for her and then another seven. I thought how I had moved the great stone from the well for her with the shepherds standing around gawking and laughing. She had worn a string of scarlet in her hair and watched me through her lashes. There had been tears in her eyes.

"His name is Benoni," she said.

Joseph crouched down on his heels and put his face close to his brother's.

"Hello, Benoni," he said. "He is very small."

I said, "See the flowers Joseph has brought you."

She said to Joseph, "Teach him to say his name and your name. He will never learn anything unless somebody teaches him."

"I am Joseph," Joseph said. "You are Benoni, and I am your brother."

"I am Israel," I said.

It was the first time I had ever said it to anybody. She turned her face to me. Her glance was shadowed, puzzled.

"Your limp is no better," she said. "You walk like an old man."

"I am not a young man," I said.

"Use balsam leaves," she said. "Make a poultice."

The baby was making sounds. It was not a cry. It was more like the sound of locusts, of bees.

"See, he is starting to learn already," Joseph said. He was a slender, brown boy then. There was down on his upper lip where soon his beard would be. "Say Benoni," he said. "Say Joseph."

"Teach him about Laban," she said. "Teach him about Abraham."

Would she see Abraham where she was going? Did the dead in their kingdom have eyes for seeing? I thought of the thread of ants disappearing down their hole on the slopes of Ebal. Would Abraham see Rachel's eyes and know she was Rachel he was seeing? Did the dead have speech? Was there any remembering among them? Did the Fear forget them?

"There are women who will suckle him," she said. "There is Shammah's wife. There is Zillah, the wife of Elam."

Joseph buried his face in the blue flowers. The baby was crying now the way a baby cries. He was batting the air with his fists.

She died in the night. It was still and warm. Her maid Bilhah was with her and her sister Leah. Unknown to me, Leah had kept out one of her father's gods from the sack we had buried. He had a flat, square head and a crooked mouth. She stood him on the ground where Rachel could see him. I do not think she saw him. The tent was hung with lamps, but I do not think there was anything by then that she could see. The last word she spoke was a question. It was my name.

"Israel?" she said.

I was the only one who heard it.

I did not name the child Benoni. I named him Benjamin. Benjamin means Son of the South, not of My Sorrow. South was where our way was taking us. The farther south we went, the nearer we came to the heart of the land of the Fear's promise. Benjamin is a name with hope in it. Part of the hope was that my beloved would have forgiven me if she had lived to know that I chose against the name she gave him or that she forgives me now if she has come to know it since in the land where death took her.

As to the sorrow she named him for, it clings to him still. I have never looked at Benjamin without remembering it. I have never looked at the life of my twelfth, last son without remembering the death that his life sprang from.

I have never looked at anything in this world—the moon, the hills, my people dwelling in their tents—without remembering that it is a world bereft of her who when she lived was my heart's deepest delight and when she died its deepest sorrow.

19

THE THIRD DEATH

THE LIGHT OF A DEATH, for the living, is like rain-light. All colors show richer. The green of leaves shows greener, the tawny swells of sand tawnier, browns browner, blues bluer. It is as if, with no sun to light them, they are lit from within. In the rain-light of Rachel's death, the grief of Bilhah glowed as red as her hair. It was an ember of grief that glinted in her eyes. She set her big feet carefully one before the other as she walked. She undid her topknot and let her hair hang loose about her shoulders with a rough cloth covering it. She spoke little. Even when her two sons were by her—Naphtali as dull-witted as he was beautiful and Dan with hair fierier than hers—she hardly noticed them.

It was not red grief that Rachel's death brought out in Reuben. It was a cool, silvery anger. His lean cheeks were pale with it. It filmed his eyes like the onset of blindness. He didn't speak less, like Bilhah. He spoke more. He spoke cruelly to

Levi and Judah, who followed him like a god. He told Levi he had brought down a curse on all our heads by the blood he had shed at Shechem. He cursed Judah for being hairy like a beast from coupling with beasts. He shouted for all to hear that he had caught him with a plump ewe between his thighs and his bared teeth grinning like a wolf's, Judah who worshiped him and was full of gentleness. In his heart I think it was death that angered Reuben. Death did not anger him for taking Rachel. It angered him for not taking me who loved Rachel as I did not love his mother, Leah. If I was to die, Reuben would be father and first next after me.

Perhaps he was angry as well at himself for thinking such evil. Perhaps it was for not taking himself that death most angered him. Perhaps it was because he needed to warm his cool rage at the ember of Bilhah's grief that he went to Bilhah. And because it was a way also to dishonor me by taking the mother of two of my sons as if I was dead already and himself in my place.

It was Joseph who told me what Reuben had done. The rain-light of Rachel's death showed the shadowed gray of Joseph's missing her. His soft gaze was turned in upon the places where his dreams came from and where his mother was remembered. Who knows what he dreamed about when he was a boy. Who knows whether already he was dreaming about the king of the Black Land and the falcon-headed god whose eyes are the sun and the moon and whose breath is the north wind.

It was Rachel Joseph remembered. He did not often name her, but his silence named her. He remembered how she had told him to watch out for Benjamin, his only full brother. He was with the child many times a day, whispering his name to him. *Benjamin, Benjamin,* he would whisper because I had told him I had changed it. He had a harp of ivory from Haran that I had given him, and sometimes he would pluck music from its three strings and sing to the child. He watched out also for me because he thought his mother had charged him with that as well, as perhaps she had. He made me balsam poultices for my limp. At night I lay alone in my tent because I had no desire for women, and sometimes he would come and lie by me. Sometimes he brought me wine. Sometimes he brought water to wash the soil of travel from my feet and ease their burning.

It was not to harm Reuben that he told me about him and Bilhah. Reuben was his friend. I think he told me because I was alone and he pitied me. I think he told me for fear of losing his father as well as his mother if taking Bilhah was only the start of Reuben's dream to supplant me.

"There is no evil in him. There is just pain in him," Joseph said. "Please don't harm him. He's harm enough to himself. Only be on guard, Father. His pain is a danger."

At first I could not believe the story. Bilhah was the age of Rueben's mother. I could not picture her chill, unyielding flesh kindling a man's desire or even suffering it. Dan and Naphtali, both, I had begotten of her, but there was never less fire in a mating since the world began. It must have been her grief that drew Reuben to her as warmer and more alive than anything he had of his own. Perhaps she saw his silver anger as a way to cool her grief's red embers.

I did not speak to Reuben of what I knew. If he had made a show of it in front of others, I would have had to speak, and who knows what sad battle of father against son would have come of it. But when eyes were upon them, Reuben and

Bilhah met as strangers. When and where they sought comfort in each other's arms at night was the night's secret. Who would have guessed it, seeing them?

Just once I saw him touch her. She was carrying a pannier of unbaked loaves to the fire when she stumbled and dropped one of them. Reuben picked it up and gave it to her. Their hands met, hers wide across as a bear's paw and white, his brown and long-fingered. "Thank you," she said with not a trace in her grave voice of all she had to thank him for, but not drawing back her hand either. "Only a loaf," he said with a boy's curt laugh. That was all, but it was much. Their hands struck like flints which I knew might spark a blaze that in the end would consume me. To my wonderment I found I did not greatly care. If Reuben wanted my place, it was his to take. The only place I coveted was deeper than the roots of mountains where Rachel, whom I do not forget, dwells among the forgotten like a shadow. The color that the rain-light of her death brought out in me was the cloud-color, the no color, of hopelessness.

We journeyed on, less wary than before as we headed farther southward. Night after night we heaved their burdens onto the kneeling camels, their drivers squatting by them to rest out the last few moments on their heels before we started off. We moved by night to escape the burning day. We carried iron cages of fire set on poles to light our way, the air breathing more chilly from the highlands as the dark deepened. By day we took our ease, scraping out holes for hearths so there was room beneath the pots for cooking fires of desert brush. Sometimes, by day, there was some singing to the beat of drums and soft fluting, but mostly the people found whatever shade they could and slept with headcloths bound about their eyes against the sun. Wells were sparse, and such rain pools as we came upon were foul with fever, stale and mantled. The herders beat the lagging cattle forward, goading them with the heels of spears, cursing them and wailing. The camel drivers had the worst of it because any sandy place a camel comes to, he will fall on his knees and wallow in it to ease his itching pelt and send the baggage tumbling. Any white stones that catch their long-lashed eyes they take for blanched bones and halt at them, thinking to grasp them in their mouths and chomp for salt. It was Leah's voice that would rise above all the others like a ram's horn threatening them with torments if they loitered.

"Arise," the Fear had told me. Did he know in his high heavens the weariness of rising? Lord as they say he is of all the living, can he guess the bitterness of death and dying? The flaming, footsore men? The camels' burden? "Go," he told me. Can he without shame bid a man go and then cripple him for going? Can he show him the face of light and then leave him in darkness without even a silver hand to hold to?

How Esau carried on when he saw us coming! He was out with his sons hunting and in such a rush to show them to me one by one that he almost knocked them off their feet grabbing them by the shoulders and shoving them forward. Adah's son, Eliphaz, was the oldest of them. I had seen him last in Gerar when he lay little bigger than his father's hand in powdered dung on an overturned shield waiting for the old man to come cut him. He stood taller than his father now with a bear-colored beard and legs like trees wrapped around with the thongs of his sandals. Reuel was next, whose mother was Basemath, then Oholibamah's boys, Jeush, Jalem, and Korah. There were only six of them all told, compared with the twelve of mine. The eyes that counted their number were mine, not Esau's. "I get twice what you get. Twice everything," I had told him when I bought his birthright for a bowl of red beans, and twice I had gotten. Only six of them there might be, but to Esau they were the match of a hundred.

He made them flex the bulging muscles of their arms and open their mouths wide to show their strong, white teeth. He cupped his hand between their thighs so I might gauge their manhood for myself, and all the while prodding them, thumping them, thumping me and laughing with his head thrown back like a man trading oxen.

Only when I told him about Rachel did his face fall. Maybe it was to make it fall that I told him. Once only, beyond the Jabbok, had he seen her and hardly long enough then to know her again if they had met a second time. It was out of pity for me, I suppose, that his face fell. Then it fell farther.

"Grief follows grief like sheep through a gate," he said. It was the closest to song I ever heard from him.

"Father is dying," he said. "He'd have been in his grave long since, but he wanted to wait till you came."

Laughter was my father no longer when I saw him. He was lying on a pile of carpets in his tent, the side flaps lashed back to let in air. His flesh was gone. He was toothless. He was shimmering with sweat, his face, his scrawny chest and ribs. His eyes were patches of blue cloud and sightless. He turned his head toward me as I entered.

"It's Jacob," I told him, giving him the name that he had given me. "It's Heels. I'm home."

His first words to me were a long time coming. When they came, it was as if they had started so deep that by the time they reached his lips they were only unshaped air. He seemed to be gathering power to shape them.

"I'm older than Abraham," he said. "I do not sleep. I do not wake. I thought you were dead."

His breath was fluttering his lips.

"They say you are rich. You smell rich," he said. "I can still smell smells."

I said, "I have twelve sons. You will see them for yourself."

"Will I?" he said. He gave what I took for a laugh deep in his throat. "Your mother died. It was like having a thorn drawn from my foot. Sometimes I weep for her in the night."

"My wife died too," I said.

"Are they the lucky ones?" he said. "If you are so rich, tell me. No, don't tell me."

The air in the tent was stifling. There was a basket of dates at his side and a ewer of milk. A fan of sunlight lay across his lap.

"Take me where I can breathe," he said. "Maybe your sons will take me."

"I will take you," I said.

I slipped one arm behind his shoulders, the other one beneath the crook of his knees and lifted him. It was like lifting a child. He smelled of urine like a child.

"My father lifted me," he said. "First he bound my legs and arms."

There was a pile of cushions which, still holding him, I was able to kick nearer to the open flaps where I thought some air might be stirring.

"There were green sticks for smoke," he said. "There were dry sticks for fire."

His cloudy eyes were on my eyes as I lowered him. He touched my cheek with his fingers.

"Your mother said I knew it was you when I blessed you," he said. "Don't ask me what I knew. I don't even know if I'm sleeping or waking."

"Did you forgive me?" I said.

"Maybe I did. Maybe I didn't," he said. "You think I can remember all that?"

"Have you forgiven me since in your heart, Father?" I said. I placed a cushion underneath his head to raise it. He closed his eyes.

"I see better with my eyes closed," he said. "Who knows about my heart? I don't even know if it's day or night."

"It's day," I said. "I'm Jacob."

"You're not Esau," he said. "Esau smells of game."

"I cheated Esau too," I said.

"A rich man should worry about cheating?"

He coughed, choked, then lay silent a while, his eyes still closed.

"Sometimes at night I wept for you too," he said. "Tears. Urine. At my age, they come when they come."

He spoke unshaped words of air again. There was the thin sound of goats bleating outside, an axe chopping wood. He lay so still that I thought he was dead. His cheeks were full of shadow. Then he opened his eyes.

"The Two Stones are yours to keep safe," he said. "They were Abraham's before me, before Abraham Terah's, before Terah Nahor's, before Nahor Serug's and Reu's and Peleg's. Who cares who had them before? They are yours now. One black for the night, one white for the day. They say they are the Fear's lips, if the Fear has lips."

"He has lips," I said. "I have heard them speak."

"He was Abraham's friend," he said. "Maybe Abraham would have been better off friendless."

He coughed again and tried to spit. I held a cup of the milk to his mouth. It ran down his chin and onto his chest.

"It is better here. Thank you for moving me," he said.

There were shapeless words again. The milk had gathered like a jewel in the pit of his chest.

"I could have done worse," he said. "I could have given Esau the blessing."

He took me by the wrist in a grip as strong as a boy's. For a moment the clouds seemed to lift from his eyes so they were eyes again. I would swear that he saw me. He tightened his grip on my wrist.

"Go now," he said. "Go away."

"Let me find favor in my father's sight," I said.

I wiped the milk from his chin with my sleeve. Before I left, I kissed the hand that held me and laid it with the other hand just above where the milk jewel glistened.

Esau and I buried him together in the cave of Machpelah in the field of Ephron, Esau sobbing as he placed the ash cakes under his dead arms. Abraham lies there as well with Sarah, his wife. Rebekah, my mother, lies there. It is where, when the time came, I buried Leah. It is where they will doubtless bury me too except for my heart, which was buried long since on the road to Ephrath.

It was not long afterward that Esau left. There wasn't pasturage enough for his large flocks and also mine, and I was father now and first. I was keeper of the Two Stones though they have lain untouched for years in their goatskin pouch fastened by the collarbone of a hare with tips of silver.

Laughter had taught me little of the use of them, so even if the Fear had spoken to me through those stone lips, it would have been in a tongue I barely understood. Mine also was Laughter's scarlet mantle and the collar of jasper and topaz that had been Abraham's. Two parts of all the beasts, slaves, servants that had been Laughter's were also mine and only the third part Esau's.

If Esau cared, he gave no sign of caring. He said good-bye to me at moonrise when he was ready to set off on his long journey. He had all six of his hulking sons about him. He took me in his arms and covered me with kisses. He covered them with kisses and they me. He roared with laughter. His face was wet with tears. He gave me the silver ring he wore on his thumb. To ward off evil luck, he told me not to watch him as he went but to turn my back on him. Thus it was only my ears that knew of his going. They heard the calling of drivers and herders, the creaking of harness, the crying of beasts. What my eyes saw was only the moon and the shapes of my people's tents against the sky.

Esau has dwelled ever since in a land to the south and east of us, beyond the deep ravine of the river Zered. They say it is a red land. The rocks and hills are rust-colored. The soil is the color of raw meat. I have thought of him often there, a red man prowling the red hills, but never again have my eyes seen him. It was only the moon I saw as he left, the ravaged face of Sin, keeper of time and warden of the night.

20

THE STRIPED ROBE

BENJAMIN WAS THE SON of his mother's sorrow. Joseph was the son of her joy, the firstborn, the one she had borne after years of bitter waiting while Leah bore me son after son, naming each one for her triumph as he came; while Bilhah bore Dan and Naphtali on Rachel's knees to make it as if they were Rachel's; while plump little Zilpah bore Gad and plump little Asher on Leah's knees. Then finally Joseph.

Rachel's joy at his coming was crowned by her joy that the Fear had remembered her. "I thought he had forgotten me," she said with the child at her breast, "but he remembered me," and the light in her face as she said it became in my eyes like a garment the child was clothed in always, even when he was a child no longer but wore a silken beard on his cleft chin, had slender brown legs and arms strong enough to carry a lamb under each at the same time.

I was always giving him things. I gave him the silver ring from Esau's thumb. I gave him the ivory harp from Haran. I gave him a long robe of bleached wool woven in scarlet stripes with sleeves that reached the full length of his arms and covered his wrists with scarlet fringe.

The more I favored him, the more his brothers grumbled against him. I knew this well enough, and yet I could not stop making him gifts because he had been the Fear's richest gift to his mother and wore, like a garment, the light I had seen in her face at his birth.

In his man's body he had his mother's heart. When the time came, he taught his brother Benjamin to walk as she had charged him. Down on his haunches in front of him, he would hold his fingers out for the child to hold on to, one in each fist, and then lead him forward as he learned to place one small bare foot in front of the other trilling like a bird. When he took his fingers away and the child fell, he would pick him up again and hold him. He would say the child's name to him over and over. He would set him on his knee and catch his eye by bleating like a sheep. "You are Benjamin," he would say. "You are Benjamin, son of the south. There is only one Benjamin, and you are Benjamin," until for a while it was the child's one word for everything. He drank Benjamin out of his cup. He pointed at Benjamin perched on a branch with its beak opening and closing. Benjamin was the goat-shaped wad of rags with sticks for legs that he clutched in his arms at night. "I am Jo," Joseph would say to him, drawing his lips into a puckered O like a man blowing coals. "Seph," he would say, siffling it out, grinning like a cat, with his teeth on his lower lip, "and you are Benjamin. Benjamin my brother. B-b-b-benjamin," blubbing his lips like a man with a stammer. The child would throw his hands into the air and shrill with pleasure.

Sometimes Joseph would come and sleep at my feet in my dark tent. I would hear him breathing. I would smell the smell of him, the smell of a boy's sweat, the sweet smell of the straw we threw to the cattle for winter fodder. "Joseph," I would whisper loud enough for him to hear if he was awake but not enough to wake him. As likely as not he would answer me. "Father," he would say, and we would talk in the dark for a while. I would make him crow with laughter telling him about Laban—Laban scrambling through the fields with his bear-paws outstretched to cull the brindled goats and sheep before I found them. Laban with ropes of flowers strung around his bull neck, swinging his hips and clapping his hands over his head at the feast he gave when, unbeknownst to me, I married Leah. I told him about the tears in his mother's lashes when she saw me heave the stone from the well the day I arrived in the north with my black camel. Sometimes he brought tears to mine telling me tales of her I had never heard.

He told how she would hide from him and make him find her rolled up in a carpet or crouching with her face in her hands in the tall grain. How she and her brother Obal would sometimes try to piece back together the mother they barely remembered the way men in the Black Land make pictures out of bits of colored stone. Obal would remember his mother's brown eyes, Rachel a scarf she tied around her hair or the sound of her hands slapping dough until something like the woman herself would begin to take shape before them.

Sometimes when he woke up, he would tell me his dreams. The boy was always dreaming. A white heifer standing in a green field. He said it meant there would be a rich harvest. Seeing his face in a bronze mirror with rain falling. He said he would marry a wife who would be like a second face to him, a second self, but she would bring him sorrow as chill as the winter rains. Looking into a deep well. He laughed. He said that Leah's maid Zilpah told him a well meant a prison such as they had in Haran for men caught thieving or killing. Maybe it meant he would be closed in a prison, he said. He said he would never kill a man but he might thieve a woman. Sometimes he said he lay with women in his dreams and sported with them in such a tangle of fierce, sweet flesh that it woke him and he found himself wet from his sporting, his face flushed like a girl's with a boy's shame and puzzlement. I almost never dreamed dreams myself to tell him in return. If I have dreams, I forget them on waking.

There were two dreams he told his brothers that set him on a path through his life from which there was never to be any turning. The first I did not hear him tell myself. It was Judah who told me. Judah hated Joseph not just because I favored him but because Joseph was Reuben's friend and it was Reuben who had charged Judah with coupling with beasts.

The dream Joseph told them, Judah said, was a dream that all of the brothers were out in a field binding sheaves at harvest. The way Joseph told it, the sheaves were lying in a ring on the field with Joseph's in the center. Then, there in the center, Joseph's sheaf stood up.

"We all spat on the ground when he said it," Judah said. "He said his sheaf stood up tall as a man. And then can you guess what he said, your heart's treasure? What he said was our sheaves all bowed down to his sheaf. Issachar caught him on the side of his cheek with a handful of dung when he said it, and your darling just stood there staring at him with his great cow eyes. 'So you're to be king over us? We're to be slaves?' It was Zebulun who said that. Then Zebulun knocked him down flat, and we all had a turn pounding on him. You'll see for yourself what we did the next time you see him."

I saw for myself. There were still traces of dung in his thin beard. He was cut over one blackened eye and walked with a limp to match mine. I said, "Not all soil is for planting, Joseph. Not all dreams are for telling."

"Not all heads are for pounding," he said. When he smiled, I saw that the inside of his lip was bleeding. He said, "I think the Fear talks to a man in dreams sometimes. Some dreams, not all dreams."

He said, "I can't help what the Fear says, and I can't help telling it."

"Maybe the next time the Fear will help you get away before they black the other eye," I said.

"Maybe he will black it himself," he said, and we both laughed.

Weeks later I heard his second dream myself. We had come from watering the sheep. There was a cool gray breeze, and we had gathered around a blaze of burning brush. Benjamin was on Leah's lap playing with her beads. Joseph had wrapped himself in his striped robe for warmth and was holding his hands to the fire. I see him there still, the scarlet fringe hanging at his knobby wrists, his knees locked and his legs bowed backward. He told his dream slowly as if even then he was dreaming it.

"I saw the sun, and I saw the moon," he said, staring into the flames. "I saw eleven stars. I counted eleven of them. The stars were all bowing. The sun and the moon were bowing."

I thought: Was I the sun and moon? Was I the moon and Rachel the sun? I would have stopped his mouth with my hand if I could have reached him in time. The flames were shimmering in his eyes as he turned his hands to warm their backs.

He said, "It was to me they were bowing."

It was the first time, I think, he ever angered me. If I'd had a handful of dung myself, I would have thrown it if only for the way I saw him courting the rage of everyone who heard him, of everyone he loved or had some hope of ever loving him.

"You mean we are all to bow down to you?" I said. I could hear my voice shaking. "Every last one of us? Your mother, who is dead, and your father? My sons who are older than you and in most ways wiser?"

"I don't know what I mean," he said. He looked at me as though I was a stranger. "I don't know what the Fear means. The dreams choose me to dream them. I don't choose the dreams."

Of all his brothers there, the only one who spoke was the youngest. "Benjamin," he said, pulling at Leah's ear. "Benjamin, Benjamin." The others stood silent and cold-eyed as stars.

When spring came, it was Zebulun returning with his brothers from the farthest north of our pasturage who brought me Joseph's striped robe. He fell to his knees in my tent and held it out to me. It was his face I saw first. It was gray as stone. His eyes were lowered. His mouth was trembling. The striped robe he held in his hands was torn and ragged. It was stiff with blood. The scarlet fringe of one sleeve had been ripped away. It was as if I had been waiting my whole life for the news he brought me. I knew his words before he found a way to speak them.

Joseph had wandered off alone with his flock, Zebulun said. Some wild beast must have fallen on him while he lay asleep. Nothing but the robe was there to mark the place. The flock had scattered. He laid it at my feet and buried his face in it. His words came muffled.

He said the body of my son was gone wherever the beast had carried it to feed on it. They searched and found no sign. Zebulun knelt there then in silence with his buried face to wait for me to speak to him. I did not speak. My silence was as deep as his. Like his, my face was buried. It was in my hands I buried it.

That was the tale that Zebulun brought me. What more of it there was to tell I did not hear for many years. I was an old man when I heard it. I heard the tale, but at first I didn't believe it. I thought it was only a dream like one of Joseph's that had in its mercy chosen me to dream it. There are times I think so still.

TWO

THE DREAMING

~

21

THE NAKED BOY

I DREAMED OF A DEEP PIT, a well dug and abandoned when it was found there was no water in it. A naked boy lies at the bottom. His hands are bound behind his back. His ankles are bound. He lies curled up with his knees to his chest as if for sleep or burial. From the nape of his neck, down his lean back and buttocks to the crook of his knees the shape of him is a single curve. He has a boy's downy beard. He is a virgin. The sand is wet with spittle where his mouth touches it. He makes no sound. The only sound is the bleating of the sheep that browse above him. The pit is of no matter to them or what lies in the pit. Only the thin grass matters. They flick their fat tails as they graze. Sometimes they raise their heads to stare at nothing through the cold slits of their eyes. They drop their dung like berries.

What does the dream of a pit mean? The dream of a boy? Of the sheep to which nothing matters but nibbling and staring? What does a sheep care for the comings and goings of men, the toiling of women? What does the grass care, or the sand wet with the boy's spittle? What does the Fear care? If the Fear cares, does he come to the boy in the pit? Does he speak words of promise to the ears of the boy's heart? Does the Shield of Abraham shield him? Does he cover him with his feathers, giving him shelter under his wings? Is the rift of blue in the clouds the Fear's cold eye?

The dream is a dream of anger. So great was the anger of the ones who bound the boy's hands and ankles and tumbled him into the pit that they would have killed him instead if the oldest of them had not pleaded for his life. Thus it was a dream of mercy as well as of anger though a strange mercy since leaving him in the pit to die was only another way of killing him. The fall down the rough side of the pit might itself have killed him with the shards of rock and torn roots jutting out, but he escaped with only a bruise or two and the opening of an old cut over one eye. For days he lost the power of speech. Then together with mercy and anger, greed also came into the dream, making it as rich a stew as the heart of a dreamer.

The angry ones stood arguing and shouting at each other about what they had done because it had left them more than a little drunk and they were of different minds as to what to do next. One said better to have killed the boy outright. Another kicked sand into that one's eyes for saying it. Another said they should haul him up again and let bygones be bygones because otherwise his death would be on their heads, and if others found out, they would pay with their heads for it. While they were at it, a band of merchants came into sight down the road that winds through the hills from the north.

They had a string of rack-ribbed camels and another of asses overloaded with creaking saddle-frames and baggage. Thinking to barter a thing or two for some of the men's sheep, they drew to a halt and started haggling. To the boy in the pit they were only voices speaking a tongue akin to ours but different enough so that everything had to be said three or four times over and each time louder. A wineskin must have passed around among them too because the voices grew louder still and there was much laughter and hooting mingled with it.

Finally there was a great scrambling as one of the angry men let himself down into the pit on the end of a rope. He took the naked boy up in his arms and hauled him out again.

The boy stood there still stunned from his fall and speechless while the merchants gathered around him. They jerked his head backward by his long hair and pried his mouth open with their fingers to peer at his teeth. They pinched the flesh of his thighs and his upper arms. They inspected the soles of his feet for sores. One fat one with his hair in a knot thick with grease said he was pretty enough to use for a woman if it came to that and if there weren't any women. There was more wine, more laughter. They offered the angry men this for him, that for him, waving their hands in the air. They offered two of the half-starved camels. They offered a jar of honey and three knives with horn handles.

The men whose anger by now had cooled to greed kept shaking their heads and spitting on the ground. The boy would fetch high in the markets of Shechem, one of them said, the others groaning and rolling their eyes at the name of Shechem. The oldest, the one who had earlier pleaded for the boy's life, said they wouldn't sell him at all if he was valued so little. He said they would take him home and be done with it. He was starting to take him then and there when the fat merchant opened a cloth bag he wore around his neck and shook into his hand a palmful of silver in bits no bigger than the fingernails of a child.

The boy was worth no more than five of them, he said, but he would pay them ten because they had had wine and merriment together and his heart rejoiced in them as if they were his own brothers. The man who held the boy by his bound hands to take him away said thirty. The fat man asked the gods to have mercy on him for a fool and said he would give fifteen. The other said twenty-five with one horn-handled knife thrown in for good measure. Seventeen, the fat man said, one piece of silver for each of the boy's seventeen years. They settled finally on twenty, the fat man counting the silver bits out on his palm and weeping because he said that now his children would surely starve because of their father's insane generosity.

They unbound the boy's hands and threw him a tanned hide to cover his nakedness before leading him away down the road with a rope around his neck like one of their camels. When they were gone, one of the men who had sold him knelt at the rim of the pit and retched into it. Later they caught a lamb and slaughtered it. They let the blood of it drain onto the striped robe they had torn with their knives. Then they roasted the lamb over a fire and ate it in silence so deep they could have been dreaming.

Is it in dreams that I have seen the land where they took him? Is the land itself only a dream of land? Have I seen it with my eyes or only dreamed that my eyes saw it? It is a narrow carpet of a land, the soil so black with fruitfulness they call it the Black Land. To the east and to the west of it is the Red Land of vast dunes and towering shelves of rock and desert. The Black Land is a scarf of wet green silk flung lengthwise on the desert. It is a lotus with a slender, winding stalk. The stalk is the blue river that fans out to the sea in seven branches like a flower. Each year for a hundred days the river overflows its banks, flooding the fields and feeding them. Men look out from the doors of their mud huts on glittering sheets of water. They pole from place to place on wooden rafts. They start to plant while there are still standing pools of water because otherwise the sun will bake the soil too hard to turn. One man leans on the handles of his wooden plough to make the share bite deep while another guides the team of cows that pull it. When that is done, they turn out herds of sheep and pigs to churn the soil still further so the seed will be well puddled in. Then the men rake it. At harvest they set out at dawn, the men to cut off the heads of the tall grain, the women following to gather it in baskets.

Gods swarm like flies at their harvest and planting. They have gods with the heads of apes and bulls, jackal-headed gods, gods horned like rams. They have the great lizard god called crocodile with a dwarf's stub legs and a thrashing tail as long as a man and fangs like knives to tear a man in two. The king of their gods is the sun who sails the day in his two boats—one from dawn till noon, the other from noon to sundown—as Sin sails the night over the walls of Haran. The god's name is Ra. He is the beetle hatched from dung like life from death who rolls beads of dung as Ra rolls the sun across the sky. They carve beetles from stones no bigger than a thumb. They make them from hard-baked clay glazed blue, from amethyst and ivory. They bury beetles with the bodies of their dead to give them birth because they say their dead do not thirst and drift like shadows underneath the roots of mountains like Abraham but live again. Ra is the hawk who spreads his wings like crimson at the day's end. He is crowned with a serpent and the disc of the sun. Ra is the man also who is their king. With my own eyes I have seen the king sitting in his gold chair like any other man. He narrows his eyes. He leans forward with his slender hands on his knees and speaks to an old man. The old man has a narrow, curved beak of a nose and a bird's small eyes. His ears stand out from his head.

"How many are the days of the years of your life?" he hears the king say, who is Ra.

"Few and evil have been the days of the years of my life," the old man answers. By few he means many that seem few. There are times when his whole life seems a single day that he has been dreaming. By evil he means full of grief and waiting.

Is it for the Fear to keep his promise from the stone stair that the old man has been waiting?

Is the old man Israel?

22

THE WHITE KILT

THE DREAM OF THE BLACK LAND is a dream of
riches. It is a dream of beekeepers and magicians,
a dream of cities. It is a dream of a king's house surrounded
by gardens. Figs and pomegranates grow there, slender trees
with heavy, fringed leaves that rattle like wings when the air
stirs them, sycamores with stems the color of opal. The
house is built at the edge of the red desert at the foot of a cliff
that glitters in the sun. The walls of the rooms are painted
with wild geese flying, gazelles, serpents, oxen, gods in sky-
boats, dog-headed gods weighing the hearts of men against
feathers of judgment, gods taking fruit and meat from the
king's hands. The painted ceilings are upheld by pillars made
like stalks of blossoming lotus. Water is everywhere. Scarlet
fish swim in pools. Channels have been dug to bring water
from the blue river. There are cool, dark basins of water in
the house for bathing. The high windows are hung with reed

mats against the sun's heat. Rooms are built over rooms. Streamers wave and flap from gilded poles. The paths are paved with gravel blue as the river. The guards wear feathers in their hats. The air is fragrant with cedar and cassia.

The boy from the dream of the pit has become a man of the Black Land. A handful of years in the strong sun have darkened his skin and taught him to narrow his mother's soft eyes against its blazing. He wears a short kilt of white linen so sheer that you can see the shadow of his body through it. It is knotted below his navel. He has enameled rings around his forearms and around his neck a flat chain made of reed and gold beads with one of the dung-rolling beetles made of black obsidian hanging from it. His headcloth is of black silk ribbed to make it look like a wig of black hair and tucked behind his ears. In the manner of the land, he has darkened his brows with kohl and lengthened his eyes by drawing dark lines around them and out toward his temples.

Men with skin as black as obsidian are squatting in a circle beating drums while two naked girls are somersaulting backward, springing from the flat of their hands to the soles of their feet. The river bank is thronged with people in their kilts and skirts and long, neckless shirts, some of them in breechclouts only or thongs of hide, many of them as naked as the somersaulting girls because the people of the Black Land are without shame for nakedness, unlike our people who forbid it as tinder to lechery and wantonness. There are warriors in leather aprons with ostrich feathers on their heads. There are merchants of doves and fish, honey-sellers, old women crouching in front of baskets of figs and yellow grapes and seed cakes. Fathers hoist their children to their shoulders. Boatmen jostle women whose feet are caked black from toiling in the fields. The rich are carried in chairs by servants with feather fans and shields of cloth on poles to keep them from the sun. They are all of them pressing toward the river's bank. The bare-chested boy in his black headcloth stands on the base of a pillar of red stone many times taller than the tallest tree. The pillar tapers to a point high over the boy's head and has been cut with rows of bird-track signs and lozenges. He is shading his eyes with his hand. On one thumb he wears a silver ring.

Priests with shaved heads have carried a god out of his dark house into the sun. The god is now in a small gold house. He is swathed in linen. The house rides on a boat-shaped litter made of cedar. Some of the priests are singing. High on the western cliffs, other tall houses of gods catch the day's first light. There is a gray mist below them in the valley. The cliffs are rose. The god in his house is set on a huge gold-plated barge. Flowers and petals of flowers are thrown into the blue river, asphodel, cowslips, lotus. The music of pipes, drums, harps fills the air like incense. Incense fills the air. The barge is pulled upriver by teams of oxen straining at ropes as thick around as the arms of the men who drive them.

The king himself is on the barge with the shaved priests. He is a fat-bellied man whose navel squints like a third eye. There is a shawl around his shoulders and on his head a tall, round hat of molded leather studded with gold patens and circled by a rearing cobra. He wears a false beard of dark sheep's wool on his chin. In one hand he holds a shepherd's crook and in the other a knout. He sets the knout and crook aside and with his own hands helps the priests feed the god food and flowers. Swarms of people wade up to their waists in the water. They shout and sing. They clap their hands and call out to the god who is their king, to the fat-bellied king in the false beard who is their god, who is the sun.

The boy was sold to a friend of the king's. His name is Potiphar, and he is chief of the king's guard. He shows gaps between his teeth when he smiles and has heavy brows that meet across his nose. He has breasts that sag like a woman's and is fat-bellied like the king. He has a house outside the city almost as fine as the king's with terraced gardens where he grows all manner of fleshy lettuces, chick peas, leeks, radishes, garlic, melons, and so on. He fences in flocks of white geese and ducks which he fattens for his table with a paste of seed and worms which sometimes he thrusts down their throats with his own fat finger. He likes padding around barefoot through his gardens, here and there pulling a weed or two or watering them out of a tall jar that one of his servants pulls in a wheeled cart behind him. Sometimes he wears a loincloth knotted under his belly, and sometimes, inside and outside both, he wears nothing except for a folded kerchief on his head. Often he lies naked in a pool at the center of a pillared court with a dish of cucumbers or roasted quail at his elbow and a pot of wine and speaks out messages which his scribe scratches down for him on a roll, moistening his reed pen in a pot of thinned gum before brushing it across the red ink-cake. He bought the boy fresh out of the pit from the fat merchant with his hair in a knot and gave one hundred bits of silver for him because by then the boy had been washed clean, his bruises and cuts had healed, and he had found his tongue again.

Potiphar's wife had borne him no sons, and almost from the start he treated the boy like one. He set him to working mainly around the great house where he would be near and Potiphar could watch him. The boy would bring in flowers from the garden and water to slake them. He helped keep the hard, white gypsum floors swept clean and dust shaken out of the reed matting and carpets. He fed the caged doves and finches.

Potiphar would sprawl in his lion-footed chair and call the boy to come and sit by him while day after day he taught him to speak the tongue of the Black Land. When the boy learned well, he would smile his gap-toothed smile at him and pinch his cheek. Sometimes he would set him on his knee and run one finger down the line of his brow, nose, lips, chin, as though he was a boy carved out of stone. Sometimes he would draw the palm of one hand along the full, rippled length of the boy's spine from the nape of his neck, up underneath his thick, dark hair, down to the waist of his kilt. Once when he let his hand slip inside the kilt as far as the start of his cool buttocks, the boy leapt to his feet and stood before him with such a fierce and stricken look, his lean shepherd's cheeks gone ashen, that Potiphar never fondled him again and came to honor him. He gave him the flat chain of gold beads to hang around his neck and clothed him like a rich man's son. In time he came to put him in charge of his entire household of servants, slaves, husbandmen, beekeepers, carpet-weavers, potters, and all the others. The boy was the one who measured out to them their daily fare of bread and beer and lentil porridge. He learned to mark down the wages and labors of each with a reed pen like the scribe's. He oversaw the planting and harvesting and oil-pressing. He took his meals with Potiphar and his wife in a painted room or under the fragrant cedars. He had a servant to fan him just as there were servants to fan his masters. "Though you come from a barbarous people of wanderers and rough herdsmen and speak a harsh and uncouth tongue," Potiphar said to him, "you have grown dear to my heart and to the heart of my wife as well."

Potiphar's wife was older than her husband by a year or two and full of sorrow. She had borne him four daughters of whom only one lived to be a woman. It was a sorrow to her also that the skin of her face was wrinkled before its time like a hand kept overlong in water, and each night she bathed her face in asses' milk and slept in a mask of alum and the whites of pigeon eggs. Each morning, as soon as she awaked, she spent an hour or more at a bronze mirror rummaging through a chest of powders and oils to find the lost beauty that she mourned for like her lost daughters. She darkened her brows and upper lids with kohl to make them larger and dusted the lower lids with powdered green copper ore for brightness. With red ochre she brought the color of youth back to her lips and cheeks and with henna reddened the palms of her hands and her nails and the soles of her feet. She combed the hair of her wigs with oil of cinnamon and sweet rush. With the tip of her finger she touched herself about the neck and shoulders with scented ointments. When she was done with it all, there was a kind of beauty about her, but it was more the beauty of the wooden chests they paint with the likeness of the dead whose bandaged bodies lie inside the chests than it was the beauty of a living woman.

Not long after the boy's arrival in her husband's house, the woman fell sick. It was not a sickness of flesh. It was heartsickness. She went about the usual business of her days much as she always had. She accompanied her husband to

the marshes when he hunted water fowl. She would lie in the
stern of the light bark as a servant poled it through the reeds
with their feathery tufts swaying in the air and the swarms of
butterflies. Standing upright in the bow, Potiphar would
hurl his throwing-stick at a flicker of white wings, and when
he hit his mark, she would gather the bird out of the shallow water in her arms if it was near enough to reach and put
it in the sack for him. But if they happened on one of the
great scaled lizards with knives for teeth, she hardly seemed
to notice it. Even if it threw itself at them from the muddy
bank where it was drowsing, spraying them with the tepid
water and almost overturning them, she lay there like a
woman carved of wood. It was as if her painted eyes were
fixed on some more distant sight inside her head, and the
heart of her, which once would have made her scream out,
busy at some other work.

She went to the city, carried in her chair, to finger cloths in
the market or to see a friend or take food to a god or to her
dead daughters in their tomb at the foot of the eastern cliffs,
but all these things she did like a woman moving in a dream.
Potiphar would return from the king full of tales of how the
king had told him this or asked him that, and she would listen to him, her ochred lips parted in a smile, but it did not
seem to be his words that she was smiling at. Sometimes,
for no cause anyone could tell, her eyes would brim with
tears. Her laughter was low and throaty like a man's, and
sometimes she would lay her hand across her mouth to stifle it when Potiphar lay beside her with his sagging breasts
silvered by the moon.

In time Potiphar took note of all this. He summoned one
of the king's magicians to make her well. The old man laid

pulped olive boughs on her forehead, breasts, stomach, and thighs, beneath which he said the channels run that carry life-giving waters from the heart's chamber the way ditches carry the blue river to the outer fields. He made her swallow a paste of green dates and honey and breathe in the smoke of burning herbs till tears of kohl streaked her face like an ape's. She did not get well. She said herself that she was not sick. She said a woman has seasons like the year—the season of the flood, the season of the water's going out, the season of the harvest. She said for her it was the season of the going out, the sheets of water sinking, a parched, dry season. In time, she said, if the gods showed favor, she hoped for the harvest. They none of them understood her meaning.

Potiphar's wife was sick for love of the boy. That was her meaning. She did not tell him her love. She did not make him gifts like Potiphar. Sometimes when the three of them ate together, her hand might brush against him when she passed him a loaf or filled his cup with sweet wine. Otherwise he never felt her touch. He hardly knew the color of her black-lidded eyes because whenever they met his, she lowered them. Her words to him were mostly words she spoke to her husband meant for him. If she came upon him alone, sitting at his table with his pen and rolls or striding through the gardens with the knobbed staff of his office in his hand, her words to him were like the beetles no bigger than a thumb which they say are filled with all the power of the sun. Her words to him were small words, words about the coming rain or a cat's new litter or one of her maids' wages, but they came hushed and heavy with the power of her love and sickness. There was a garden of lilies and juniper on the raised part of the roof, and sometimes at dusk the boy would catch a glimpse of her waiting there on the chance of seeing him come back from his work. She would be holding her fan to her face. He would see only her eyes.

The boy was kind to her with a boy's clumsy kindness. Not knowing what she wanted of him, if she wanted anything, he gave her only whatever he happened to have at any given time to give. If a bird flew overhead which he had never seen before, he might ask her the name of it in her tongue. Sometimes he told her the names of things in his. He told her the names of his father and brothers. He told her once about his blue-eyed sister who had brought sorrow down on all their heads although she herself was as innocent as a dove. She would listen to him with her lowered eyes. Perhaps she would smile and nod her head from side to side. Sometimes silence was the gift he gave her. Seeing that, like the magician's herbs, often his words seemed to fill her eyes with tears even when there was no sorrow in them, he would speak no words at all but just wave his hand to her if he found her wandering through the gardens or put his palms together and bow his head if they passed each other in a painted room. If he saw her coming, sometimes he would take another way to spare her the troubling sight of him. It happened rarely, but if ever by chance their eyes did meet, he was quicker than she to lower his.

Once their eyes met when they were sitting at the table where they ate. Potiphar had risen in such a hurry for some meeting he had with the king's guard that he had overturned a bowl of juniper berries stewed in radish oil, spattering their purple all over the white cloth. The woman and the boy both raised their eyes at once and looked at each other over the spreading stain. The boy looked down before the woman did, the color rising to his cheeks almost as purple as the cloth. It was the first time he ever heard her speak his name. She spoke it as a question.

"Joseph?" she said. It sounded on her lips like a name he had never heard. "Joseph?" Her face was stiff with alum.

The second time he heard her speak his name came not long afterward. The magician told Potiphar that for three days his wife must drink wine spiced with cumin. Two cups of it she must drink on rising, two cups at noon, and then one cup each hour until nightfall when she must drink two cups more at the moon's rising. On the second night of it when the moon was newly risen, Potiphar told the boy to take the wine to her.

He found her lying on her bed. It was sloped down toward the foot and carved at the foot and at the head with the gilded feet and heads of falcons. Never before had the boy seen the woman looking as she did then. The wine from the day before had so befuddled her that she had done nothing to her face that morning. Her eyes were her own unpainted eyes, her mouth her own pale mouth. Her brow was webbed with lines, her cheeks and upper lip seamed. Her hair, without the heavy, plaited wig that the wife of a friend of the king wears, hung thin and streaked with gray about her shoulders. Her breasts were bare and could have been her daughter's breasts they looked so much younger than her face. And yet the boy saw a beauty in her face that was new to him. It was not the beauty of the faces of the dead they paint on chests. It was a kind of blurred beauty with years of sorrowing to soften it, a harrowed, harvest beauty like fields under a cloudy sky with the mist rising.

The boy knelt to set the wine down at her side and started to fill the cup. She laid her hand on his arm and spoke his name the second time he ever heard her speak it.

"Joseph," she said.

This time it was like the answer to a question. Her face was close enough for him to smell the wine and cumin on her breath. Her breath was warm. She took his hand and set it on her breast as the magician had set his olive boughs. The boy felt his flesh stiffen like an olive bough. All in that moment, he understood the cause of her sickness and felt a sweet sickness of his own filling him. She ran her hand down the curve of his neck and onto his brown chest and ribs. He was wearing a kilt of pleated linen, and like Potiphar before her she slipped her hand underneath the knot, setting the flat of her hand on his warm belly. When she took him in her hand, he went as dumb as he had when they had thrown him in the pit. He had never lain with a woman. His mouth was at her breast where she had drawn him down beside her.

He thought of the mouth of Potiphar at her breast with its gapped teeth. He thought of the kindness of Potiphar. He thought of his brother who had lain with one of his father's women old enough to be his mother. He thought of his own mother and of the woman's hand mothering him where they lay tangled together on the sloped and falcon-headed bed. He thought of it as a dream that he was dreaming. He thought of dreams as the Fear's words if the Fear speaks words in the Black Land. With her hand she was drawing him into her. With her mouth she was breathing his name again and again into his mouth. He found he could speak.

"I can't," he said into her mouth. He spoke it in his own tongue, not in hers. He raised himself on his elbows to say it again into her eyes. He said it in her tongue so she could see it and hear it. He said, "Can't."

They were throwing him into the pit. She was drawing him with her hand into the pit. He leapt up off the bed. His rump was silvered by the moon. She held his kilt outstretched in a silver hand. She cried out to him. He cried out to her. He fled her, falcon-faced, like a bird with silver wings.

23

THE DREAMS OF THREE

S HE SAID THAT THE BOY had tried to take her. She did
not want to say it, but there was nothing else that she
could think to say instead. Dizzy in the head from the magician's wine, she could not have found words to say anything else even if she had thought of it.

Potiphar had come running when he heard their cries.
He had seen the boy's nakedness with his own eyes. He had
seen his wife sprawled on her bed stuffing the boy's kilt into
her mouth to muffle her sobs. Perhaps he guessed the truth
of what had happened, but it was a truth that he could not
bring himself to utter. Better to lose the boy than to lose the
wife. Better to have the boy cast into the king's prison than to
have the wife cast into the blue river and held under with
poles. There was a moonlit moment when all three of them
were weeping at the same time. Covering his nakedness as
best he could with his trembling hands, the boy was weeping
out his shame and innocence. The woman was weeping not

just for the boy who had fled her but for the beauty that had fled her and the dead daughters who had fled her. She wept for the dry, parched season that she knew would be hers until the end of her days. Potiphar was weeping for the loss of a son, for the loss of his honor, and weeping also at the sight of his wife's seamed and tear-streaked face because he knew that his eyes would never behold her again without mistrust and horror. The painted rooms echoed with their noisy grief. Sin hid his pitted face in a web of clouds. The stag-hunting hounds with their pointed ears and curling tails howled in their kennel.

The next morning the boy was taken in ropes to the city. The wife lay all day in her bed with her face buried in the kilt. When the magician came to her with poultices, she kicked them out of his hands with one henna-soled foot. She refused all food. She refused all drink. Potiphar went off into the marshes with two servants and missed every bird he hurled his stick at. He watched one of the great lizards tear a hind to pieces. Behind their hands, the servants smiled at each other and rolled their eyes.

The prison was a warren of underground chambers behind the king's kitchens. In the season of the flood, water seeped up through the mud floor. Such food as there was was let down through the ceiling on a chain. The little water for drinking was stale and bitter. The boy was given one of the drier chambers where there was light enough through an iron grille to see the faces of the two men who were with him. One of them was a towering bony man with a stammer. The man spent most of his time sitting hunched up against the damp wall with his head resting on his knees. He never spoke of why he had been imprisoned. When the boy asked him, he only shook his head on his knees without raising it. He was butler to the king and in charge of the endless cellars where the white, red, and black wines grow sweet and strong in jars. He was in charge of the king's larder as well and the king's table, and nothing was set before the king without passing first through his hands. With those same hands he himself served the king, touching his forehead to the floor at the king's golden sandals and holding the tray up over his head like a priest feeding a god. He spoke very little partly because of the unsightly stammer which made his jaw shake and his eyelids flutter and partly because the shame of finding himself where he was seemed to have left him almost speechless.

The other man, who was a dwarf and chief over the king's bakers, rarely stopped speaking. His forehead bulged like a melon, and as he stumped back and forth, and then back and forth again, across the floor on his bandy legs, his buttocks bounced like a pair of melons even larger and more bulging. He wore a leather cap on the back of his big head and spoke mostly about women. Women flocked to him like flies to honey, he said, because a dwarf's member is believed to be mightier than other men's, and when he raised his apron to show them, the boy saw that it was so. He brought color to the boy's cheeks also by telling him all the things that he had done with women and that he had persuaded women to do to him. With a stick he scratched pictures on the floor of some of the things that the women had done to him. He laughed over his pictures sometimes until tears rolled down his cheeks and his chin was wet with spittle.

He spoke also about the craft of baking. He spoke of how the wheat and barley and emmer were ground fine as the finest powder between heavy stones and of how the dough was mixed by pouring in measures of milk and water and working it with a copper ladle taller than he was. He told about how sometimes, for sport, he himself helped with the kneading of the dough although such work as that was beneath his high station and was usually left to underlings. He said the dough was placed in a wooden tub as large as one of the king's barges and three or four of them would climb into it together and knead it with their feet. They used long poles so that they could jump up higher and come down harder, and he went laughing and jumping about in the striped light that came in through the grille to show the boy how they did it.

The ovens they used for baking were beehive-shaped with flames leaping out of their tops, he said, like a bird's flaming feathers. As to the loaves they baked, he said that they were made in as many shapes as he and the other bakers could think of. Some of them were coiled like snails, some were cows lying down, or beetles, or birds with folded wings. For jest he shaped some like a man's member or a woman lying on her back with her thighs spread apart and a red berry between them. For feeding to the gods he made god-shaped loaves and loaves with the faces of the gods' beasts or glazed brown or dark red to look like the kind of meat that the gods find pleasing.

It was when he went on to speak about all the different sorts of cakes he made—honey cakes, cakes with figs and dates ground into them, cakes spiced with cinnamon and fennel—that he told the boy the evil thing he was charged with. It was said that he had tried to poison the king with a honey cake into whose dough he had mixed nightshade and cockles. An enemy of the dwarf's had whispered the charge into the king's ear, and when the king fed the cake to one of his hounds, the hound howled and flattened himself under the table, retching. Even that tale caused the dwarf mirth as he flattened himself on the mud floor to show them how the hound had retched, but then his face suddenly grew grim.

Only that night he had dreamed a troubling dream about the cakes, he said, and even the butler raised his face from his knees to hear him tell it. The baker said he had dreamed that he was kneeling before the king with three baskets on his head and that the cakes had been lying in the uppermost basket. Birds were pecking at them, and just as the king was about to reach for one, he withdrew his hand. The birds had evil in their eyes, the dwarf said, and then for once he stopped speaking. Then for once the butler spoke.

He also had dreamed a dream of three, he stammered, his eyelids fluttering. He said that the likeness of their dreams seemed a strange thing although it seemed less strange that his dream too was about the king. First he had seen a vine that had three branches on it. Then before his eyes the branches budded and shot forth blossoms, and then the blossoms ripened into fat purple grapes. Then he found himself standing at the king's side holding a bunch of the purple grapes. Slowly he squeezed the sweet juice of them into a cup, some of it running down his wrist as he did it, and placed the cup in the king's hand. The king smiled and took it.

The boy believed that he heard the voice of the Fear in the two dreams of three, and tears wet his lashes. The butler's dream of the cup, he said, was a dream of good fortune, but the baker's dream of the pecking birds was a dream of sorrow.

He reached out his hand and laid it for a moment on the baker's leather cap. The baker shrugged his shoulders and went off and stood underneath the grille looking up at the sky.

Three days later there was a great feast to honor the day of the king's birth. Even the two men and the boy in the underground chamber were pressed into attendance. Potiphar was there although his wife was not with him. He wore the ostrich plumes of victory in his tall hat and, slung around under his fat belly, the heavy apron of the guards with scales of gilded leather. If he saw the boy among the crowds who were there, he gave no sign of it. The boy saw him, but he also gave no sign. There were pipes and drumming and naked girls in thongs standing on each other's shoulders and still other naked girls standing on their shoulders and all of them dancing. There were naked boys with painted eyes tumbling and throwing each other about. There were cages of singing birds and three golden lions on a single leash batting at the air with their thick paws and snarling. Such mounds of every kind of fruit and meat and loaves and cakes were heaped up on the enormous table that the knob on top of the king's towering hat of stiff white linen could barely be seen over it.

The king received many rich gifts in painted chests and woven baskets of sweet grass which were piled up between two of the huge, round pillars, and after he had received them, it came time for him to give gifts. Potiphar as chief of the guard received a gold chain to wear around his neck. The master of the king's horse received another like it as did the master of the scribes and the keeper of the king's bees. Many of the priests and magicians who were there received smaller chains and so did the steward of the king's bed chamber and his armorer.

Then to everyone's surprise it came the turn of the butler. The king summoned him to kneel before him, and the
tall, bony man stumbled forward pale with terror. The king
narrowed his eyes at him for a moment and then reached
out and took him by the ears and raised his head to look at
him. The king's cup was at his elbow and he nodded at it to
show the butler that he was to take it. The butler took it and
held it out to the king, and the king received it into his hand
as a sign that the butler had been restored to his favor.

It was the baker's turn next. Like the butler before him,
the little man stumped forward to kneel at the king's chair,
nodding and smiling at people he knew as he passed them,
and again, as with the butler, the king took him by the ears to
raise the great melon of his brow. The king narrowed his eyes
at him and then bared his teeth and spat into the dwarf's
face. At the king's command, two black men in silver collars
carried him away between them, holding him high off the
floor under his armpits with his feet kicking. To the astonished cries and laughter of the swarm of goggle-eyed guests,
the blacks then lifted the dwarf up in their arms and hung
him by his neck from one of the high gilded rafters where his
bandy legs flailed in the air for a long time as though he was
kneading it and the leather cap fell off the back of his head
into a bowl of brined cucumbers.

Weeks went by before the boy could wipe the sight of his
friend's death from his eyes, but they were weeks of good
omen. Perhaps Potiphar or even Potiphar's wife spoke into
the ear of the prison-master, or perhaps it was the boy's
manly beauty and bearing that by themselves gained him the
prison-master's favor. In any case, the boy was moved into
another chamber above the ground and in time was placed

in charge of the other prisoners so that nothing was done to them without his knowledge and he found ways of easing the lot especially of the ones who continued to live underground like ants and spiders. He saw to it that the water they were given was sweet and clear. He made it possible for their women to visit them from time to time with extra food for them in their baskets. He had the covers over the grilles drawn back with chains so that they would have light enough below to see each other's faces. There was a male child born to one of the women in the prison, and the boy learned the name that the woman had given the child, and sometimes she would hold him up to the grille and the boy would kneel with his face close to it and say the child's name to him over and over again so that in time the child would surely learn it.

Two years went by, and then the king, like the butler and the dwarf before him, began finding that his sleep too was being troubled by dreams the way the surface of the blue river is sometimes stirred by a traveling wind. They were dreams not of threes but of sevens, and two of them he told at dusk one evening to his butler. The butler was cutting him off a haunch of roasted venison when the king stayed him with his hand and spoke. His first dream, he said, was a dream of cows. Seven of them came clambering up out of the river, fat and glistening with the water that ran down their sleek flanks and puddled the reed grass around them. Then seven more cows rose up out of the river after them except that these were as gaunt and rack-ribbed as the others had been fat. To the horror of the dreaming king, the gaunt ones then took the fat ones in their whiskered, sideways-chomping jaws and tore them apart and devoured them. It woke the king up, and he lay awake long enough under the dark hangings of his bed to try to drive the unpleasant sight from his heart's peace before falling asleep again and dreaming the second of the two dreams.

This one was a dream about seven plump ears of grain growing from one stalk. These ears were followed by a second stalk of seven which were thin and blighted by the sickness-bearing wind that blows from the east. Then just as with the cows, one stalk of seven opened its bristled green mouths to devour the other seven, only this time it was the plump ones that devoured the ones that were blighted. Again the king was awakened by his dream although he did not go to sleep again because by then the boat of Ra had started its voyage across the sky, and already the rose-colored light had found the wings of the flying geese with which the ceiling of the king's room was painted.

At first the butler was so honored by the king's telling him his dreams that he stood there speechless with the blade of his knife trembling in the air above the haunch of venison. But when the king narrowed his eyes at him, he found his tongue again and began to flutter his lids and speak. In the beginning his voice scarcely rose above a whisper, but it grew bolder and stronger as he continued.

There was a boy in the prison, he said, who was wise beyond his years in the reading of dreams. He did not tell the king how the boy had read his own dream about the cup and the dwarf's dream about the pecking birds because he was afraid that the king might somehow find it a cause for anger, but he made up several other people's dreams which he said the boy had read with great wisdom, and the king listened to all that he said with unusual care.

The butler was to fetch the boy out of the prison, the king said, and set him before him. If he was not back with the boy before the god's ship had disappeared behind the western cliffs, then he would with his own hands remove both of the butler's ears with the knife which by now the butler had laid down on the table.

It was in this way that the boy and the king looked into each other's eyes for the first time, and the meaning that the boy found in the king's two dreams and told him changed the whole course of the Black Land's life from that day forward and the whole course of the king's life as well, and of the boy's life and of the life of their peoples.

24
THE DREAMS OF SEVEN

THE BOY BOWED BEFORE the king, not raising his eyes till the king spoke, but he did not touch his forehead to the floor at the king's feet as is the custom because if he was to speak to him, he needed to look not at his feet but at his eyes. The king was without his wig and lamb's wool beard. He was clothed as simply as any man in white linen. His thin hair lay gray and flat on his skull. Rush lamps had been lit against the coming night. From the high terrace, beyond the lotus pillars which held the roof, the sky was between light and dark though nearer dark. There were stars. Over the western cliffs there was a feathering of crimson clouds. The king told the boy his two dreams much as he had told them to the butler, and looking into his eyes, the boy listened. When the king finished speaking, he motioned the butler to leave them alone together and with his own hands filled his cup with wine. Raising the cup to his lips, he narrowed his eyes at the boy over the rim of it and waited to hear what the boy would say.

"Your dreams are from the Fear," the boy said. "The dream has been spoken to you twice, but it is one dream. Twice is sometimes the Fear's way of speaking."

"The Fear?" the king said. He smiled a thin smile and wet the end of one finger in his wine.

"It is the name my people use for God," the boy said.

"I fear nothing," the king said. "If I find something that is to be feared, I destroy it."

"The king does not fear the gods?" the boy said.

"I do not fear them, I feed them," the king said. "Tell me the meaning of my two dreams that are one if you are as wise as they say. If you are not as wise as they say, you may count yourself lucky if all I do with you is send you back to prison where you came from."

He touched his finger to the white cloth making a row of seven dark stains on it.

"They are both dreams of seven," the boy said. "Twice seven cows, twice seven ears of grain."

"They are dreams of great rejoicing in the Black Land," the boy went on, "and also dreams of great darkness."

The king's smile faded on his lips.

"I see that you are a clever one," he said. "If there is great rejoicing, you will be proved right, and if there is great darkness you will also be proved right. I have no patience with such cleverness. Leave me before I have them put out both of your clever eyes."

"The rejoicing will be first," the boy said. "That is the seven fat cows and the seven full ears. There will be seven years of plenty in the Black Land. They will be followed by seven years of dark famine. That is the meaning of the lean cows and the ears that have been blighted."

The lamplight flickered in the boy's face. His bare chest was a cleft shield of brightness and shadow.

"You are not a boy as my butler told me," the king said. "You are a man. How many years of your life have you lived?"

"Thirty years," the boy said.

"What is your name?"

"I am Joseph," the boy said.

"I will not remember your name," the king said, "but I will remember my dreams and the way you have read them. Perhaps I will have you brought to me again."

"The king must hear with his ears the words that the Fear has spoken to him," Joseph said.

"Must?" the king said.

The lion feet of his chair rasped harshly on the stone floor as he pushed back from the table. The panels of the chair were painted with black and gold lions. He leaned back in the chair with his hands folded across his fat belly. The rest of him was lean. He had lean arms and a sinewy, lean neck. He cocked his head slightly to the side looking at Joseph.

"The king must make himself ready for what the Fear will bring to pass as surely as he brings night to follow day," Joseph said.

"You are not without courage even if you are altogether without manners," the king said. "What is there about your god that makes you call him the Fear and fear him?"

"It is his promises that I fear, and I fear his favor," the boy said. "I am afraid of the dreams he sends."

"Sit where I can see you," the king said. "I do not speak to men I cannot see."

There was a bench made like a two-headed jackal at the far side of the table, and Joseph sat on the jackal's long back between the two heads. He rested his hands, palms down, on the white cloth in front of him. On his thumb was the silver ring that his father had given him and that Esau had given his father.

"Tell me in your wisdom what I must I do to make ready," the king said, looking at the dark, young hands on the white cloth.

"In the time of plenty you must garner," the boy said. "Name men you trust to watch over the harvest. Let them take a fifth part of all that is harvested and set the king's seal upon it. Let them store it in the great granaries of the king's cities. When the seven years of famine come, there will be food then for the king's people, and the Black Land will not starve."

The servants who counseled the king came clattering up the broad torchlit stairs to the terrace when the king summoned them. They were seven old men. One of them was a blind priest of Ra whose name was Potiphera and who for years had lived in the city of On. He was led by the hand of his daughter Asenath, a thin woman of Joseph's age with a pinched face and a heavy tasseled wig that came down to her shoulders. All of the old men were more grandly clothed than the king. About their necks they wore the gold chains that the king had given them, and they leaned on the bird-headed staffs of their high office as they stood in a row awaiting the king's pleasure.

"Tell them my dreams and the meaning you have found in them and the counsel you have given me," the king said, and Joseph stood there like the old men's grandson and told them.

You could read their thoughts in their eyes as they listened. The young man with his strange manner of speaking their tongue was too young to be wise. He was too wise to make so much of dreams, even of a king's dreams. Dreams were the playthings of magicians and women and of priests acting as priests rather than as counselors. The king was too old to be swayed by a handsome young man though there had been handsome young men and beautiful young women before him who had won a month or two of the king's favor. The king had no particular taste for the beauty either of men or of women, but he had a taste for youth. The old men well understood such a taste even if they did not approve it. That too you could see in their eyes as they listened to the young man's scheme of garnering a fifth part of the harvest for seven years in the king's granaries against the fear of famine.

Maybe there would be a famine. Maybe there would not be a famine. It was of no great matter to the old men. They had granaries of their own. They would not starve. If famine waited seven years to come as the young man counted it, the chances were that they would have long since passed through the dark gates of the shadow-eater, the eye of flame, the breaker of bones, and been led by the hand of the god Osiris himself, son of Seb, into the Everlasting Land of which Osiris was king. They found peace in knowing that for all time their bandaged bodies would be fed, famine or no famine, by the shaved priests they hired so that their everlasting bodies could draw strength from the food left at their tombs as a man draws strength from the air he breathes. Let the king have his fifth part and his granaries if that was what the king desired. If, as they could see with their eyes, he had already given the young man his heart, let him heed the young man's reading of his old man dreams.

"Say you yea or nay to what you have heard?" the king asked them, and to a man they said yea when he moved down the line of them jerking each one forward by the gold chain around his neck and baring his teeth at him as he had done when he spat in the face of the dwarf.

Within days the king set the young man over all his house with its terraces and vast pillared halls and the houses of the gods and the fragrant gardens and said that it was for the young man himself to see that what he had proposed was carried out. He gave him a new name to replace the one that he said he would not remember and called him Zaphenath-Paneah, which means in the tongue of the Black Land, The God Speaks and He Lives, though which god is meant the name does not say. He gave him a gold chain of eagles wing to wing to wear around his neck and took from his own finger the ring with the king's seal upon it and with his own hand placed it on the young man's finger. When the king drove through the streets in his high-prowed chariot of two wheels holding the reins of a blue stallion named Strength and a roan gelding named Trumpet, the young man drove the chariot immediately behind him and only then, behind the young man, the other lords with enameled bracelets on their arms and false beards on their chins.

For seven years as the dreams had foretold the harvest was plenteous, and the tall mud hives in the courts of the granaries, with one door at the top for putting the grain in and another at the bottom for taking it out, were filled to overflowing. Sometimes Joseph and the king would walk among the hives, sending the mice scuttling that scavenged about the bottom doors. Often the king would have one hand on his winged staff and the other on Joseph's shoulder. His golden sandals would be dusty with chaff. Beggar cats with their long tails in the air would come and rub themselves against the embroidered skirts of his mantle when he paused. Sometimes Joseph and the king spoke together of death, Joseph because it was so far away and he was so little certain of what it contained, and the king because it was so near and because there was nothing it contained that was any less familiar to him than the furniture of his bed chamber with the wild geese painted on the ceiling which caught the first light of dawn and the shallow bowls of powdered herbs to sweeten the air.

If there was anything about death that the king did not understand, he would go for its meaning to his priests who had endless rolls that told every twist and turning of the way that leads from one world to the next. On the walls of the gods' houses and of the cliff tombs there were pictures he could see with his own eyes of all the gods and wonders that a man could expect to find as he traveled it. There were pictures of how men and women were weighed in the Hall of Maat until, if the god who is shaped and headed like a lean, black hound found them guiltless of the forty-two evils that lurk in the heart and if the ibis-headed god at his side set their guiltlessness down on his rolls, they were allowed to pass on into blessedness. He knew from the lips of the priests that he, as the king, would proceed there directly in the boat of Ra, his breath wafted across the sky like a bright wind until it found a new and golden body to breathe it.

He had long since caused his tomb to be built on the western side of the blue river where the boat of the sun finds its

nightly harbor, and sometimes he took Joseph with him to
see it. It was built of blocks of stone as big as houses and faced
with glittering white limestone that made it rise up out of
the rocky red land like a cloud. Its four soaring walls sloped
upward to a single point as high as the flight of birds, and
beneath it was a deep shaft that led to a chamber of rose-colored granite where his waxed and bandaged body would lie
like a child in the rose-colored womb of its mother surrounded by treasure and the mounds of food and jars of life-
restoring wine that the priests would bring to it daily for as
long as there were priests and the world endured.

"Your god will doubtless care for you in death as gener-
ously," he said to Joseph as they stood in the darkness lit only
by the guttering torches of the servants, "because you are the
friend of the king and have been given the king's ring with his
seal upon it and great power over all of the Black Land."

Joseph thought of his mother's spent body buried, unban-
daged, on the road they had been traveling with only a pillar
no taller than a tall man to mark it and of the body of his
grandfather Isaac lying under stones near the bodies of Abraham, Isaac's father, and Sarah, his mother, where Joseph's
father and Esau had placed it with no treasure of any kind to
bring him comfort and only the two ash cakes for food which
Esau had placed under his two arms. His father had told him
that he heard it said that the dead move like shadows. They
dwell, thirsting for light, deeper than the feet of mountains in
a land where no light falls. Did the Fear remember them
there, Joseph wondered. Did the Fear have a silver boat for
sailing them to blessedness, a golden boat like Ra?

"My god is a god of those who are alive," Joseph said to
the king.

The chamber where they stood smelled of the cool stone and the burning pitch of the servants' torches.

"He makes us no promises about death," Joseph said. "He makes us promises about life. I do not know what he promises to the dead if he promises them anything."

"The priests know," the king said. "Only command them, and they will tell you. They will show you their rolls and pictures."

"He speaks to us sometimes in dreams that are like torches to light our way through the dark," Joseph said. "He gives us daughters and sons so that our seed may live after us and the promises he has made us may be kept to the world's luck and blessing."

"You have no daughters and no sons either," the king said.

He was leaning against the stone chest, taller than his head, where his body would lie when the time came. Its lid was carved with his likeness and stood propped against it. The king ran his finger over the likeness of his staring stone eyes and nose.

"I will give you a wife. I will give you Asenath," he said. "She is daughter to the priest Potiphera, who is one of my counselors. I will give her as a gift to you, and I will give you to be as a son to her father because he is an old man and has served me well."

It was the only time after the night he had lain with his mouth at her breast that Joseph again saw the wife of Potiphar. Potiphar brought her to the wedding feast in an enormous wig threaded with silver, and from her throat to her breasts she was hung with shining blue beads. Her eyes looked only straight ahead. If something moved in front of her, her eyes did not follow it, and Joseph believed that even if he was to go stand in front of her himself, her eyes would not see him. She stood against the wall under one of the high gilded rafters where the dwarf had kneaded the air with his feet. Potiphar was close at her side with his eyes under their single brow always upon her as though ready to seize her if she started to flee or to fall. Joseph believed that Potiphar would have had no trouble seeing him if he had chosen to see him, but as far as he was able to tell, Potiphar never looked his way.

Asenath was thin as a bird and all but breastless. She made Joseph a good wife. She treated him as though he was blind like her father. She would lead him by the wrist through doorways. She would guide the cup to his lips when she gave him wine. When people were shown into his presence at a time when he was sitting at his rolls with his pen to his lips or when the men came with their reports from the granaries, she would always speak their names in his ear as though his eyes could not see them. When she lay with him in his bed at night, she gave herself to him the way she would give food to an old man with great care and patience so as not to over-heat his blood or choke him.

Before the years of plenty came to an end and the years of famine started, she bore him two sons. To the first of them he gave the name Manasseh, which means Making to Forget. He said that by giving him a son, the Fear made him forget all the griefs of his youth. First among those griefs was the death of his mother, and then the pit where his brothers had thrown him, and the night of his shame when Potiphar's wife had sti-fled her mouth with his kilt, and the death of the dwarf who had been his friend. It was true that now and then for as long as a day and a night at a time when he was busiest at his work he was able to forget them, but more often, especially in the night, not even the gift of his first son could stop him from remembering. And sometimes in the night he thought that the remembering was better than the forgetting because to forget the griefs was to forget also the gifts born out of the griefs like the life of his brother Benjamin born out of his mother's death, and his own rise to great power born out of the pit where his brothers had cast him. The Fear had two hands, he thought, one of them a hand that takes away and the other a hand that gives as a father gives to a child he has brought to sorrow.

The second son that Asenath bore him he named Ephraim which means To be Fruitful and the way he explained that name was by saying that the Fear had made him fruitful in the land of his exile. It was a name with something of gladness in it like the name Manasseh, but the Black Land of his exile had become in many ways more home to him, in his heart, than the land of the desert and the hills and the black tents and the season-following herds which more and more came to seem to him like a friend he had abandoned, and so there was grief as well in the name of Ephraim.

To the two small boys, however, their names were of no matter. They didn't even know what their names were let alone the hidden sadness of their meaning, and they brought both noise and laughter into the house that the king had given Joseph with peacocks trailing their tails from the lower branches of the trees and a stone-flagged court where he could sit in the cool of dusk and look out at the river. There was never a mother who took more pains with her children's care than Asenath, but even her blind father could see that it was Joseph who was the child she held dearest.

When the years of famine finally came, Joseph was able to sell grain in abundance from the king's vast stores so that there was no one in all the Black Land who starved. But there was famine in many other lands as well and men who came from those lands to buy still more from the king's granaries. Joseph heard that even in the land of the black tents there was starving.

25
THE TEN MEN

THE TEN MEN WERE brought in to Joseph together.
They bowed to the ground before him. He was
clothed in the chain of gold eagles and wore the king's seal
on his hand. A lamb's wool beard was on his chin and his
eyes painted out to the side as long as almonds. Believing
he could not understand their tongue, the men talked with
their hands and eyes. Their eyes were dull with hunger. Their
hands were calloused and broken-nailed and empty. They
pointed to their mouths. They pointed to the panniers of
snail-shaped loaves on a table. Joseph called a servant to him
who spoke several tongues besides his own and spoke to the
ten men through him, pretending he needed the man as well
to tell him what the men were saying. They were of various
heights and shapes—a fat one with a soiled cloak that hung
about his shins, a tall one who never raised his eyes from the

floor—and Joseph saw at once who they were. He had named his first son Making to Forget, but he had not forgotten.

There was a moment when he almost pulled the beard from his chin and threw his arms about them. There was a moment when he thought that the oldest of them, Reuben, saw who he was beneath the beard and painted eyes. Reuben had his eyes on Joseph's face with such a searching look that Joseph thought he was searching back through many years for the face it resembled, but soon it was plain that he was searching only for grain to buy. One of them had a leather purse of silver bits slung from his shoulder, and Joseph wondered if among them were the selfsame twenty that the merchant with the knotted hair had paid them for the naked boy in the pit. He remembered the pit and the naked boy. He remembered how the boy's mouth had leaked spittle into the sand.

The servant told him what the men were saying. They were saying, the servant said, that they were starving. They were saying they were twelve brothers, one of them dead and the youngest left with the old man who was their father. They had come a long journey. Joseph thought of the long years of the old man's grieving for the dead son. He thought of the youngest who had had no one to teach him to know his name and to walk as a man walks.

"You are secret men. You are spies," he said in the tongue of the Black Land.

He had learned from the king how to narrow his eyes as the king had narrowed his when he spat in the dwarf's face. The servant repeated the words in the men's tongue. The oldest looked the way the dwarf had looked with spittle in his face. He bowed his head before Joseph, and Joseph remembered the dream of the eleven sheaves bowing to the one sheaf, and of the eleven stars and the sun and the moon, all of them bowing.

He said, "You have come to see the weakness of the Black Land so you can work your evil upon us. You are secret men, but I am the king's eyes, and I have read your secret."

The servant repeated Joseph's words. Issachar, the one who had thrown the handful of dung when Joseph told them his dreams, took his shirt in his two hands and ripped it down to his navel. His chest was matted with black hair. He fell to his knees at Joseph's feet. His voice was cracked like a boy's voice changing to the voice of a man though he was a man and the father of half-grown men. He said, "As the Fear is my witness, we are men of truth. Our people are starving. The words we have spoken are words of truth."

He had his hands on Joseph's gold sandals, and Joseph withdrew them roughly, kicking the hands away and stepping backward.

"Show me your truth then," he said through the servant. "I will send you back with grain for your silver, and one of you will stay here in a chamber under the ground that I have good cause to know about."

His eyes traveled their faces where they stood on the stone flags with the blue river behind them and the peacocks trailing their tails from the trees. He stopped at one with the narrow face of a weasel. It was Simeon, who had knelt on Shechem's legs when he gelded him. Joseph pointed at him the finger that wore the king's seal.

"That one," he said. "That one will stay under the earth like a spider until you return. You will bring me your youngest brother, and then I will know if it's truth you're telling me or if you're spies and secret men as I think. Only on the day when I see the twelfth brother with my own eyes will this man be taken up out of the pit."

Tears filled Joseph's eyes which made it like seeing his brothers through a clear gem. They wobbled and swelled as he gazed at them, and the sun struck sparks from their faces into his eyes like fire. Asenath came to him, and he turned aside to her so they would not see that he was weeping. She dabbed at his eyes with her kerchief.

"There are ten of them," she said into his ear. "They have hunger in their faces."

"Bind him with ropes," Joseph said to his servants, pointing at Simeon. "Take their silver and give them their grain. Send them away. Their people are starving."

We were starving. I was an old man starving among women who starved and the dull-eyed starving children. Bilhah paced in her tent like a tall ghost. One morning I found Zilpah crawling on her knees among the goats, her teeth tearing at the stubble. Leah had long since died, and I had buried her in the cave next to Laughter. Dinah, her daughter, helped me place the stones on her. Dinah's was the only one of our faces untouched by hunger. Maybe the secret of her blue eyes was food enough. Shechem was the only man who ever lay with her. She never spoke his name or the names of Simeon and Levi, who had slain him. When they moved before her speaking her name, her eyes, like the eyes of Potiphar's wife, did not move to follow them. Except for Benjamin, who was too young, my sons had all taken wives by then and had sons of their own and daughters. Sometimes I could not remember their names or their faces either. When children are starving, their faces are all one face, and even if you remember their names, they are not apt to answer to them.

Save for Benjamin, I had sent all my sons to give silver for grain in the Black Land where merchants told that they had it in great plenty. Benjamin alone I had kept with me who was near the age of Joseph when he was torn by the wild beast. Once, when he was first able to walk, I thought Benjamin was mocking my way of limping. He was coming by the well with his goat-shaped wad of rags in his hand. One hip was dipping something like mine though not so deep, and I thought he was doing it to dishonor me. I struck him across the face with my hand though his face was hardly as big as my hand, and he crumbled there like old Deborah at the pillar. I found he was not mocking me at all. It was some sinew that had been twisted at his hard birth or that the Fear himself had twisted to remind me of the Jabbok. I never found a way to forget how I had struck Rachel's child or to forgive it. From that day forward, I always kept him close to me and favored him as I had favored Joseph before him who had slept with me in my tent at night and brought me comfort. It was why I did not send Benjamin to the Black Land with his brothers although he was all but grown by then and swift and sharp-eyed as a wolf in spite of his limping.

Then the nine came back again and tried to take him from me. They told me of the great lord in the golden chain who had bound Simeon in ropes. If they did not bring him Benjamin, he would keep Simeon in a pit forever. My father was right about an old man's tears. Like his urine, they come when they come. He cannot master them.

I said to them, "Joseph is gone. Simeon is gone. Now you take Benjamin from me."

I wept before them like Laughter the time in his tent when he first told me how Abraham had tried to kill him. I could feel the dribble of it running out of my nose. My gums were bared. My chin was shaking.

Reuben said, "Kill my own two sons if I fail to bring Benjamin back to you again. Kill Hanoch and Pallu," and I wept also at that, at the shame of a father saying he would kill his own two sons and the shame of a son hating his father as Reuben hated me for the day I had struck him for milking himself into the dark at Laban's. My tears were for all the sadness there ever was between sons and fathers, fathers and sons.

I let them take Benjamin from me in the end. I did it for Simeon's sake. I had almost been the death of Simeon when I bound him to the tree with Levi at the time of Shechem, and my heart went out to him, the same heart that losing Benjamin almost broke in two.

"Take a little balm of mastic along with you as a gift," I said. "Take what little honey is left in the jar. Take gum and myrrh and pistachio nuts. Take almonds." I was an old woman of a man bartering for mercy from the lord of the Black Land. "Take double the silver you took before and come back with more grain. What we have won't last. Come back with the son who was bought by his mother's death. Come back with Benjamin."

The dream I have told of the Black Land is a dream of riches, of beekeepers and magicians, a dream of cities. It became then also a dream of tears and trickery, of the tears that Joseph shed like the ones that Asenath dabbed from his eyes with her kerchief, and the trickery he worked on his brothers. I think he worked it less because he was punishing them for how they had used him than because like the god in the shape of a black hound he was weighing them, probing their hearts for the forty-two evils that dwell there so that perhaps in the end the pain of the probing would cleanse them. When they brought home the first grain, for instance, they found he had placed in their sacks the silver they had paid for it so he could charge them with thieving. He did this because they had hardened his heart against them. Yet then when they came back to him the second time with Benjamin, he said it was the Fear who must have placed the silver in their sacks, and said it because they were also dear to the very heart they had hardened. There was the trick as well of the silver cup that came later. To piece back together all the trickery and tears of the dream is like piecing together a jar that has been shattered in the tomb of a king by robbers. I have only a handful of the dream's shards for telling and less than a cupful of the tears.

"Is your father well? Is he alive, the old man your father?" Joseph said as the brothers bowed before him when they came back the second time with their sack of almonds and pistachio nuts and the small jar of honey to trade for his mercy. His servant put his words to them in their own tongue.

"Your servant our father is alive. He is well," they told him through the servant although if their eyes had been sharp they would have read in Joseph's face that he understood their meaning before the servant had even begun to speak.

Joseph saw Benjamin then. It was the first time he had seen him since the days when he had bleated like a sheep to catch his eye and said, "There is only one Benjamin, and you are Benjamin." The boy had hung back behind the others for fear of the man who sat in his gilded chair like a god, but when he saw the joy that came into the man's face at hearing that I was alive, he limped forward on his twisted leg, and with his own eyes Joseph saw him. He saw the boy's face, and in it he saw as well some shadow of his mother's face, some way she had of looking through her lashes. He rose from his chair.

"May you look upon the face of light," he said to the boy. "Tell me your name."

"I am Benjamin," the boy said.

"There is only one Benjamin," Joseph said, "and you are Benjamin."

The brothers drew aside to let him pass through them, his sleeves fluttering like bird wings at the speed of his going. There was a small chamber off the pillared hall. In it there were ten white doves in a cage and a pool of water set into the floor with flowers floating. Joseph crouched on the floor by the pool. He buried his head in his arms. The sounds from him startled the doves. They skittered from side to side on their red feet and opened their wings. He parted the flowers and cupped water into his palms to bathe his face before he went back to the pillared hall.

Another shard of the dream is a silver cup. It was a cup the priests used for divining the will of the gods by inspecting the lees. It was shaped like the flower of a lotus and as wide across as a man's hand. It was also the lotus shape of Joseph's love for his brother Benjamin whom he could not find it in his heart to part with although Benjamin never dreamed that he was brother to a great lord who held the power of life and death over all of them. When the men were preparing to return again to their father, bringing Benjamin back to him, Joseph had Asenath secretly place the cup in the grain-sack that Benjamin carried. Then when they had been gone for only part of a day, he sent men on swift horses after them telling them to search their baggage. When they found the cup in Benjamin's, they accused him of thieving and brought him and his brothers back again to Joseph. Joseph said the boy must pay for his theft by remaining in the Black Land for the rest of his days as Joseph's slave, and the others must return to their father without him.

It was a dream of a silver cup and also a dream of madness. All this time Joseph had been speaking in signs to his brothers who did not know him for their brother, and it was driving him mad. He had been speaking to them in the language of dreams where the things you can see with the eyes of your dreaming stand for the things that are hidden, like the seven lean cows standing for the seven years of famine. He had been speaking to them in a tongue they did not understand and pretending that he did not understand theirs. Again and again he had paused on the threshold of telling them the truth, but always some madness in him stopped him. He was the hound-headed god weighing their hearts and searching them. It was his own heart as well that he was weighing and searching, sifting through his love and his anger till one or the other came uppermost. He stood there in the cobbled yard where the king's horses were stabled pointing his finger at Benjamin and charging him with theft while all the time he knew that the boy was innocent. The boy was in tears. The silver cup was trembling in Joseph's hands. The truth was already in Joseph's eyes although he could not bring his mouth to speak it. It was all but choking him.

It was his brother Judah's tears that finally unchoked him. They were tears for the old man who was his father, and they ran down Judah's cheeks and into his beard as he knelt before Joseph among the droppings of the horses on the cobbles.

"When our father finds that this boy is not with us," Judah said, "the old man will die. How can I go back and say he will never see this boy again? Give me the words I can tell him."

Joseph looked at his brothers' raggedness, their clumsy faces, the broken nails of their hands that hung helpless at their sides. They were tongue-tied herders and planters, the followers of spring and winter. They were wanderers over the hills, the desert, the stubbled pastures, whose path had led them to a land rich and treacherous beyond their wildest dreaming. They were the seed of Abraham, the bearers of luck and blessing. Their luck lay scattered about their bare feet in steaming mounds like the dung of the horses. Where was their blessing?

"Let the boy go home. I'll stay," Judah said from his knees. He took the fringed gold hem of Joseph's skirt in his hands. "I'll be your slave. Take me in place of Benjamin. The old man will die if we come back without him."

"You said the old man is well?" Joseph said. "He is alive?"

For the first time Joseph spoke to them in their own tongue, and Judah was too afraid to answer him. He could only nod his head. He took a handful of the dung and bit into it. Perhaps it was to show the bitterness of the death the old man would die if he lost his heart's last treasure. Perhaps it was to show the bitterness of slavery. The dung was on his teeth when he opened his mouth to spit it out.

Joseph waved his hand to send away the riders who had brought his brothers back. Then he threw back his head and cried out to his brothers.

"I AM JOSEPH!" he cried.

It echoed even as far as the king's high terrace where the stammering butler heard it. The horses whinnied in their stalls. A flock of sparrows rose and scattered in the sky.

26

GOSHEN

O N MY JOURNEY to the Black Land, the Fear spoke
to me. He spoke in the night. It was at Beersheba,
where, years before, my father and Abimelech had slaughtered a white ox and sworn peace together in the matter of
the wells. Abraham's tamarisk grows there, shading with its
gray-green wings the altar Laughter built. The Fear spoke
to me by the name that Laughter gave me—not Israel.

"Jacob," he said. "Jacob." He spoke the name they had
called me as a child as if it was a child he spoke to.

I said, "Here I am," and there I was, an old man on his
long, last journey. The king of the Black Land had sent for all
of us, my sons and their wives, my children's children, our
flocks and herds. They all lay asleep under the stars. He had
sent carts drawn by oxen for our baggage.

"Do not be afraid to go down to the Black Land," the Fear
said. "I will be with you there. I will make of you a great
people there. I will bring you out again."

I could hear the oxen feeding. I could hear the tamarisk stirring in the dark.

He said, "Joseph's hand shall close your eyes."

I had thought it was a dream when my sons returned to tell me that Joseph was alive. I thought so still. It was no dream that I had eyes to close, but it was a dream that he had living hands to close them.

It was a dream when my eyes finally beheld him. I beheld him in the grazing pastures of the Black Land which they call Goshen. He came out from the city to meet me there as I was coming southward. It is a green land that lies where the river spreads like a flower in seven branches to the sea. I saw him coming toward me through the grass. Joseph. I saw his hands. He wore the king's ring on his finger. All that my lips could speak at first was unshaped air. He did not speak. His hands were on my arms.

I said, "Now let me die, since my eyes have seen your face."

They were Rachel's eyes I saw in his face. They were Rachel's eyes I saw them with. We took each other in our arms. There were white birds in the grass. There were cattle grazing.

I cannot speak of the city when I saw it first because I did not see it. I saw the dream of a city and of a blue river. I saw the king's house as a dream the king had dreamed. Not even the king's voice waked me. He was in his lion chair and crowned with a serpent and the disc of the sun. Joseph was by him. The king leaned forward with his hands on his gold knees.

"How many are the days of the years of your life?" the king said.

"Few," I said, "and evil."

By few I meant many that seemed few because they had
fled like a single day. By evil I meant evil because they were
so few, evil because the last of them was drawing close.

The king spoke next to Joseph.

He said, "The Black Land is before you. Settle your father
and your brothers in the best and greenest of it. Settle them
in Goshen where your men can graze my flocks along with
theirs."

Then I gave the Fear's blessing to the king who knew no
fear. I did not touch him with my hands because the life in
a king can bring death if you touch him. I only raised my
hands before him. There was a stirring among his leather-
aproned guards, but the king stayed them with his hand. The
Fear's name stirred the air about the king as I spoke it, and
he narrowed his eyes against it the way a man narrows his
eyes against the wind. I never saw his face again except in
dreams. Perhaps he saw my face in his as well. Who can tell
what a king sees in his dreams?

Going on seventeen years of days I have dwelled in
Goshen. Joseph has often come to me here. He has told me
much of what befell him in the Black Land. At first he did
not tell about the pit, but Reuben had already told me some
of it, and Joseph added more when I pressed him. For days
afterward I could not bear to look upon my other sons as if
the evil they had worked would strike me blind. But then I
looked on them again. Perhaps their evil was only a dream of
evil which they had waked from. They had done much
dreaming since, and so had I. And it was through their evil
that the Fear had worked the saving of us all.

Joseph told me about the wife of Potiphar. He told me
about the butler and his friend the dwarf, about their two

dreams of three and how he had eased the lot of prisoners ever since by uncovering the grilles to give them light. He told me about the king's dreams of seven cows and of seven ears of grain and how he had read their meaning. He told me about the king's gods and how they would sail him to an everlasting land at death and even take poor folk there too if their hearts weighed right.

One day Joseph took me on a journey to see the king's tomb where it rises like a glittering cloud out of the red land, and it was there that I made him swear an oath to me. We were standing in the deep chamber of rose-colored granite, just the two of us alone, and I made him rest his torch on the stone lip of the king's great chest. I made him set his hand between my thighs, where he himself had sprung from, the way I once made Esau also set his there.

I said, "Swear on my seed that you will not bury my body in the Black Land when that day comes. Carry my body home. Bury it with the bodies of my fathers."

I might have said to bury it with the body of his mother, but I could not bring myself to speak into that place of death the name that held her life in it. Nor does it matter much where bodies lie if there are only bodies left and their lives forgotten as a man forgets his dreams.

He took me also to the house the king had given him. I saw the peacocks in his trees. I saw Asenath. Her father had died by then, and she rejoiced to have another old man not yet as blind as her father had been but blind enough by then to need her hand to take him by the sleeve when he climbed stairs or walked through rooms he did not know. She set her sons before me and made them show me how already they had learned to use reed pens and ink-blocks like the scribes.

They were tall boys by then, Manasseh with a pinched face like Asenath's and Ephraim with the same cleft chin that Joseph had and Joseph's mother before him.

One day I gave the boys my blessing. I had set my right hand on the head of Ephraim to give it, my left hand on Manasseh's, when Joseph took both my hands in his.

"You have them wrong," he said. "Manasseh is the older boy. Place your right hand on Manasseh's head. Like this. Your left hand is for Ephraim because he is the younger."

He took my hands and switched them, but then I switched them back again. I could see I had displeased him, but I did it anyway. Perhaps I did it because, by minutes, I had been the younger son myself.

Perhaps because Ephraim's chin was cleft like my beloved's.

I said, "They will both grow up to father peoples for the Fear." The boys poked each other in the sides and fluttered their eyes at the thought of fathering. "But Ephraim's people will be the greater of the two and so my right hand is for him." Perhaps one day it will prove so. Who knows?

It was at Goshen that I blessed Joseph and his eleven brothers. I brought all of them together beneath a grove of willows near the river. My eyes had grown so dim by then that I was glad to have Asenath at my side to speak their names into my ear as each one came and kneeled by me.

Reuben, my firstborn, was the first to come; then Simeon and Levi, Shechem's bane; then Judah, who had offered to be a slave in place of Benjamin; then Zebulun, who had brought me the striped robe torn and bloodied; then dung-throwing Issachar; Dan red-headed like his mother, Bilhah; and bony Gad; fat Asher; Naphtali, the most beautiful of the lot, who looked like my beloved's brother Obal. Then Joseph. I told him he was like a fruitful bough by a spring, like a tree with branches running over the wall and peacocks in them. Then finally Benjamin. I said he was swift as a wolf, no matter that he limped like me.

I had some word for each, and each word had both blessing and some judgment in it, and something too—who knows?—of what I dreamed might one day come to each. I have seen them often since and will see them again if my eyes don't lose the power of seeing first as Laughter's did, but I think it will not now be many months before the coming of the dark where no man sees.

I have heard the way they bandage the bodies of their dead in the Black Land. It is the priests who do it. First they pulp the brain and draw it through the nostrils with a hook in such a way to leave no mark upon the face. Then they open up the stomach and take out the bowels, dividing them into four jars and each jar put in the care of a different god or wife of a god. The heart they wrap in linen by itself and set it back inside the chest, then pack in sawdust and sweet spices after it. They anoint the body then with wax or pitch and let it lie for as long as ten times seven days to dry and settle, and only then the bandaging. Each finger, each toe, the penis if it is a man, is swathed apart from every other part and then all swathed together and swathed again with pauses in between for prayers and placing charms and beetles of ivory or stone among the different layers. Before the work is finally done, there may be as many as sixteen linen swathings if it is the body of a king. Then they set the body in a wooden box painted with the living likeness of the dead, and the box is set in a stone chest and the chest set in a tomb where ever afterward the priests will bring it food and drink and call the gods to favor it.

I suppose they will do something of the kind with me since I am father to the king's friend who wears the king's seal on his finger. Joseph will be true to the oath he swore on my seed even though I displeased him when it was to Ephraim that I gave my right hand instead of to his brother. He will set me on a cart and take me to the desert and the gray hills where once we pitched our tents. Doubtless he will place me in the cave where Abraham and Sarah lie near Rebekah and Leah, and where Laughter lies under the stones that Esau and I with our own hands heaped over him. Even to this day I have tears in me to shed for Laughter's sorrow and for how I always got the right hand and Esau always got the left yet how Esau always covered me with kisses even so.

When the time comes, Joseph will bury me not as Jacob, but as Israel because Israel is the name that the Fear himself gave me the night he blessed and crippled me. He who has Wrestled with God and with Men and has Prevailed is the name's meaning, the Fear said.

The Fear himself well knows how I wrestled with him, and with my father, and with Laban, and my sons. And with myself. Only the Fear knows—the Fear of Isaac, Abraham's shield, the wrestler in the dark, light's face—if I will prevail someday in death. If my beloved will or even the king. If any of us will.

As Joseph said of the Fear to the king in the granite chamber, "He makes us promises about life. I do not know what he promises to the dead if he promises anything."

As Joseph said, "He speaks to us sometimes in dreams that are like torches to light our way through the dark. He gives us daughters and sons so our seed may live after us and the promises he has made us may be kept to the world's luck and blessing." Perhaps that is enough.

The night in Beersheba when he said that he would be with me in the Black Land, he promised that he would bring me out again. Who knows the full meaning of his words? Who knows from how far he will bring me and to what place even farther still?

Is his promise only a dream?

Is it in our dreaming that we glimpse the fullness of his promise?